C000319935

NOT IN OUR HANDS

NOT IN OUR HANDS
Charlotte Gringras

Tollington

By the same author

The Purple Rose

First published in 2015 by Tollington Press, Machynlleth, Wales
www.tollingtonpress.co.uk

Copyright © Charlotte Gringras 2014
Charlotte Gringras asserts the moral right
to be identified as the author of this work.

All rights reserved. No part of this book may be reproduced or
transmitted, in any form or by any means, without permission.

A catalogue record for this book is available from the British Library.

ISBN 978-1-909347-06-9

Cover design by jenksdesign@yahoo.co.uk
Typeset by Helen Sandler

Printed and bound in Wales by Y Lolfa, Talybont, Ceredigion,
on FSC-certified paper

Che sarà, sarà

– What will be, will be

This is the Italian spelling of a saying which appeared in two songs: one Italian, written by Fontana and Migliacci; and one American, written by Livingston and Evans, first sung by Doris Day in 1956. The original saying, in wide usage, seems to stem from a sixteenth-century heraldic motto. It is also sung at football matches, with the words: 'Che sarà, sarà, we're going to Wemberley!'

PROLOGUE

Sitting on his hospital bed, eager to leave the place, Jake opened his iPad and searched for the sports report on the *Times* website. He found it, all too easily, and knew most of what it would say.

'Italian player and three British students injured after…' Jake quickly closed the iPad again – he couldn't face reading the piece after all. He lay back on the bed and closed his eyes, unable to believe that his life here in Italy had changed so much, in a few short weeks. He could remember that first day, which seemed to belong to another world.

ONE

In that other world, it's only seven o'clock on Jake's first ever morning in Italy. He swings his legs out of bed and swears as his feet land on the cold floor, his toes curling up in response. The sharp morning light woke him a short while earlier, as it pierced the slatted shutters. Now, through a gap, he makes out silhouetted trees against the misty sky.

He goes to the window, opens the shutters fully and peers out, smiling as he does so. Through an archway opposite, he takes in more of the fresco-like view of the Umbrian countryside, where everything is shrouded in low cloud. Could it be a heat haze? Judging by the temperature of the stone floor, it's hard to imagine. He recognises picture-postcard cypress trees in the distance, as they feature in so many paintings and guide books. Their tips poke through the mist like spring shoots through soil.

Jake surveys the street below and sees morning life beginning. It is only 7.30am but there are already women out there, carrying shopping baskets and trotting energetically up steps towards other alleyways which, he imagines, lead to an early morning market. He hears the occasional "Giorno!' as they pass neighbours.

'Awesome! Living in Todi for six months. And they call it studying?' he thinks.

The street is so narrow that, if he wanted, he could see into the rooms opposite. He sees people who must be other students, not locals, because they're on their little balconies, looking around in the way only visitors do. He quickly moves further back into his room, realising they have a good view of his underpants.

He looks in the cracked mirror over the small sink in his room, ruffles his dreadlocked hair with his fingers and shakes it into suitable disarray, knowing the shower steam will do the rest. He wonders how his fair, freckled skin will cope with six months of Italian sun. He fishes out his sponge bag and towel, then peeps out of the door to check that the coast is clear to the bathroom.

Jake manages a shower of sorts, spraying water all over the tiled floor through the inadequate, stained plastic curtain. He puts wads of hard, useless toilet paper under his feet, in an effort to dry the puddles, but promptly skids onto his backside with a thud.

'Ow!'

Someone knocks on the door. 'What *are* you up to?' says a voice. 'Open up. Can I join in?'

'I, er, I slipped. On the wet tiles,' Jake replies, struggling to stand up to open the door a little.

'They all say that.' The voice comes from the smiling face of a guy who leans nonchalantly against the door jamb. 'Hi. I'm Tom.' He is fair haired, over six foot tall, with well-developed chest and shoulder muscles that show under his bath towel, worn toga-like, as he makes to shake hands. Jake offers a wet hand, which Tom declines.

'I'm Jake.'

'So, Jake, when you're ready, come for P.C.? Which is your room?'

'Number 13, across the corridor,' Jake replies. 'P.C. – meaning?'

'Brekkie – Italiano, you know. See you in ten,' Tom says, as he takes his place in the bathroom.

'Abbreviations as well?' Jake thinks. He is brought up sharply to remember why he's here – to perfect his fluency in the second of his three foreign languages.

He puts on a shabby, sleeveless T-shirt, shorts and flip-flops, and ties an overshirt round his waist. The T-shirt, out of which he has ripped the sleeves, sports a faded, abstract pattern, designed ages ago by his uncle, Ernie. Since his death, the shirt has become Jake's comfort blanket. He shakes off the pang of homesickness and struggles to sort out his things – the little chest of drawers looks nice but holds nothing. Then Tom calls at the door.

'Come on,' he shouts from outside.

'Won't be a mo,' Jake says.

'See you down there, OK?'

Jake thinks Tom could have waited, but says, 'OK.'

When he's ready, Jake locks up and leaves his room. As he jumps off the last two steps of the spiral, stone staircase, the smell of fresh coffee increases in intensity.

'Mm, smells good,' he says, to no one in particular.

'Ha. Try tasting it,' says a guy next to him. 'You'll soon want tea.'

'There's only coffee for breakfast, here, isn't there?'

'Exactly. That's the problem.' The stranger seems very much in the know.

By the dining room, the mêlée of students causes a major blockage; crowds of young people try to make themselves heard, jostling for a place in the queue.

'Prima Collazione' reads the large notice, with an arrow pointing the way to breakfast and – presumably – a dining room. The hostel isn't solely for British students, so it's a polyglot; the Tower of Babel had nothing on this. Jake feels nervous, yet he shouldn't be. He's a third-year student, after all, but not used to being away from home.

He goes in to the steamy, airless dining room and cannot see Tom anywhere. *Hm, why did I think he'd save me a place?* He grabs a tray, picks up a cappuccino and one of the hard rolls and butter, and gradually makes his way along the queue. He'll have to sit with strangers if he can't find Tom, whom he should be able to see, because he's so tall. Suddenly, there's a shriek from behind.

'Oh my God, I'd know that T-shirt a mile off!'

Jake doesn't realise the comment is for him; he looks through the crowd behind him but, seeing no one he knows, continues along the queue. A girl with a shaven head, black lipstick, piercings in just about every visible orifice and, he observes, wearing nothing under *her* T-shirt, peers into his face while putting her arm round his shoulders. 'Come stà, càro?' she says. 'Gotta practise the lingo y'know.'

Jake thinks her a bit forward, but she carries on.

'Aren't I clever, recognising you, after all this time? And with those dreadlocks,' she says, grinning. It's the smile that does it. Trish – his childhood friend. He hasn't seen her for… how many years? Must be about ten.

'Hey? When – I mean, are you here?' Jake asks.

'Looks like it! You?'

'Same thing.' They both laugh and Jake tries to give her a continental peck on each cheek while holding on to his tray. His unshaven chin gets scratched by one of her nose-rings and he rubs it better with a hunched shoulder as he speaks.

'Come with me. I've spotted a guy I know – there.' He feels a fraud implying he really knows anyone, least of all Tom.

Trish pops another roll on his tray, takes a paper cup of water from the end of the counter and follows him. Jake heads for Tom's table but it's full and Tom makes no attempt to fit them in. *Nice guy.* However, Trish sees two free chairs at a nearby table and slides them over. Jake suspects that the look on Tom's face is one of amazement, that he, Jake, has already met someone – and a girl, at that. What with her piercings and his dreadlocks, Tom must have them sussed as a couple of weirdos with an immediate mutual attraction. Trish introduces herself with her usual confidence, while Jake watches the way Tom eyes her. He can't tell exactly what it means.

'Squeeze those chairs in here,' says Tom, eventually. 'Have you two just met – instant passion at the breakfast bar?'

'Not exactly, we –' Jake starts to explain but Tom carries on.

'There're more romantic places, like in a piazza, under a sunshade.'

Jake doesn't find him quite as charming now, as when they were upstairs.

'Hey, listen, we were friends as kids. This is a crazy coincidence,' Trish says.

'I moved to London, y'see, when I was twelve,' Jake explains.

'When was it? About 2005?' Trish adds.

'Ten years ago. Bloody hell,' Jake says.

'So little Jakey's twenty-two?' Trish says.

Jake blushes. *I wish I didn't do that.*

'We promised to write – kids do,' Trish says.

'We did write, a bit. Too much going on. And little Trish is twenty-two as well, ha!' Jake says, while Tom looks from Trish to Jake and back in a decidedly bored manner.

'I did wonder... what *was* going on?' Trish asks.

'And with you?'

Tom breaks in. 'Listen, you two. You've got to catch up. I'll leave you to...' He gets up. Jake pulls him back down.

'Sorry, Tom, don't. It can wait.'

The three of them carry on trying to chew the unchewable and drink the undrinkable. Tom tells them why the bread is so awful. In that area, bread is traditionally made without salt. Centuries ago it was to avoid paying an ancient salt tax, and today it's still the case, apparently. Weird one, Jake thinks, but he's here to learn: not only language but culture, too. They discuss their plans for their six-month stay here and Tom becomes a little more open.

'Which uni are you at, when you're at home?' Tom shouts, over the din.

'London, University College. You?'

'Bristol. What're you studying, apart from Italian?'

'I'm doing a combo,' says Jake, 'French and Italian with Japanese – a bit mad.'

'Sounds it.'

They each have ideas for jobs. Trish wants something to do with old buildings or archaeology, or maybe restoration work; Tom wants work in hotels. They all wish their universities had given them more help to set up these placements.

'It's hard, knowing where to start,' Jake comments, wondering why Trish still isn't really making eye contact with him.

'I fancy working in the countryside, in an *agriturismo*,' Tom says. 'They're guesthouses on farms, but they're all a bit far away.'

'Sounds cool,' Jake says, noticing that Tom is still looking intently at Trish. 'I want to teach English.' He is trying to deflect attention from Tom's fascination with her.

'Oh grim, Jake, teaching English? YOLO. Be adventurous!' Trish says. Jake thinks she's showing off, using text speak like that.

'Hey? I fancy teaching, OK?'

'Keep your hair on.' She covers her mouth with her hand, affecting a snigger. 'And there's a lot to keep on.' At that, Tom joins in the joke and starts laughing, too.

Jake is embarrassed and furious. Jokes about hairstyles, piercings and so on are taboo in his student circles. Trish's manner shocks him but he realises that, when he and Trish were friends, they were different people. They were only twelve when they last saw each other – kids, really. And his life has changed totally since then. Maybe hers has, too. Trish stops laughing and puts her hand on his arm.

'Sorry, mate.'

'Hm. Anyway, *you* shave your hair off.'

Tom sits there looking amused and condescending. 'You may have known each other for yonks but you're scrapping like kids,' he says.

He's right, but was 2005 such a world away? Perhaps people who lose touch as youngsters can't shift their friendship easily into an adult one. Jake changes the subject.

'So, Tom, where d'you live when you're not at uni?' he asks.

'I alternate: Dad's in Dorset, Mum's in Cardiff.'

'I'm also an "alternative" person,' Jake says, making quote marks in the air with his fingers. 'I can alternate, but we all live in London.' *Why did I say that? I never go to Dad's.*

'I go to uni at home, too – Manchester,' says Trish.

'Manchester? Why not get away from the rain?' asks Tom.

'It's a great place, lots going on and the tram runs door to door – we live in Chorlton now,' she explains to Jake.

'And it's OK in London too,' he says. 'It's so vast, there's loads to do. Plus, my kid sister would miss me if I'd gone away – before now, I mean.'

'Not many guys care about kid sisters,' Tom says.

'She's twelve years younger. I'm a kind of extra parent.'

Jake knows that, maybe, it is he who needs Flo. She is his cuddly teddy bear who loved him unconditionally when everything spiralled out of control when his parents split up, soon after they moved to London. Those were an awful couple of years, after he lost touch with Trish. How could he tell her everything? He should have written or emailed but that time passed like a wisp of steam.

They all start to move away from their breakfast table but Trish turns, tugs on Jake's T-shirt and says, 'Hey there, Jake. Sorry.'

Jake shrugs her off. 'Why?'

'You know, laughing at you. Really mean. Sorry.'

'Apology accepted.'

'You seem miles away,' Trish says.

They tell Tom they'll see him later, and she pulls Jake away from the table and out of the hostel.

'Mm. It's so long since we last saw each other,' Jake says.

'Loads of time to catch up now, though.'

'Actually, *you* stopped writing, not me,' Jake says.

'Really?'

'Yep.'

'I had lotsa shit going on, too.'

What does she mean? They amble along the street.

'How do you walk, in those, on these cobbles?' he asks, pointing to her giant boots.

'Martens are great!' she says. They laugh. Their reconnection is instinctive now; they chat like brother and sister.

'Come and see my room,' Trish says. 'I'm not in the hostel but I can still have my meals there.' She turns into an even narrower alleyway and goes up an external wrought-iron staircase. 'This is a real garret,' she comments as she gestures to Jake to go through the heavy, wooden door of a building which is itself timber-clad with beams.

'It's quaint,' Jake replies. 'Looks very old.' He looks up at the internal beams and its sloping ceiling, then peers out of the little dormer window to see the view she gets from this height. It is even better than the one from his room. He notices that the mist has lifted, so what he saw earlier must have been a heat haze. 'I'd be happy painting up here.'

'An artist in a garret?' she asks, patting the bed. Wondering if that means something, he sits. But Trish pulls over a box, pushes some clothes off it, and sits on that.

'I don't know if I should sit on this, it's so old,' she says. 'So – about painting?'

'I love dabbling. Runs in the family. D'you remember Mum's mural for Flo?'

'Vaguely... oh yeah, I do.' Trish frowns, then smiles in recognition.

'Well, it's her business, now, painting murals.'

'Nice. Look, why don't we start, er, looking for jobs? Exploring?' Trish asks, smiling excitedly.

Jake isn't sure about the 'we', or her suggestion that they'd do that together – surely he should make new friends? She opens a drawer, takes out piles of guide books and glossy travel brochures, spreading them out over the bed. Most slip onto the floor. Jake picks them up.

'You've got unpacked and sorted quickly, haven't you?' he says, looking around her room. 'My stuff's mostly still in bags. There's nowhere to put anything – and it's not like we're just on a fortnight's holiday.'

'My little box holds a lot,' Trish says, patting it with both hands. 'But it looks a bit precious for clothes, so I put books in it.' She lifts the lid to show Jake, stroking the inside lovingly. 'There's some kind of carving on it but I can't make out any words.'

As she closes the box lid and sits on it, Jake tidies the leaflets into a pile and stops to look more closely at one of them.

'What's this?' He picks up one showing an old building with a carved Star of David on the lintel.

Trish grins. 'The synagogue in Pitigliano – one of the ancient Tuscan Jewish communities – we're just on the boundary of Umbria and Tuscany,' she says.

'Thanks, Miss, as if I didn't know,' Jake says.

'OK... and, we're between Pitigliano and Perugia. Look.' She points out Todi, their base, on a map, and drags her finger from it to Perugia, then from it to Pitigliano.

'Yeah right. And?'

'You know me and Jewish history. It's a place where Jews had to hide.'

'Oh, not that again,' Jake says.

'Aren't you interested?'

'No way,' Jake replies.

'Oh.' Trish looks crestfallen. When they were at school, they researched an old envelope together, sent by Jake's Romanian grandmother. Even then, Trish was more fascinated than he was.

'Why bother, you not being Jewish or anything?' Jake mumbles.

'Nothing to do with it!' Trish replies. 'And why don't you bother, *being* Jewish and everything?'

'Cos being Jewish is a hassle,' Jake grumps. 'Nothing but trouble.' Still, Jake is glad that Trish still finds it interesting – it means she hasn't changed.

'Remember when you thought you might be Jewish?' Jake asks, trying to be more cheerful.

'Only cos I was adopted, so I researched my background. Then my so-called Dad left –'

'Think I knew. Are you in touch?'

'No.' Trish sighs. 'Long story. Tell you later.'

Jake had always admired Trish's acceptance of her life and her self-deprecating humour. She was there when he was trying to sort out his own identity, the year before his Bar Mitzvah. They became kindred souls – too young for romance but very close. And here she is, he thinks, investigating the history of a little Italian town. Jake can't imagine anything less gripping. Trish suggests that he go back to finish unpacking and that they might meet up later.

'Yeah, good thinking,' Jake says, knowing he ought to, yet wondering how to separate his new Italian life from Trish's. 'Listen, I must start looking for jobs and stuff. I...'

'It's OK. We aren't joined at the hip any more,' Trish says. 'We were, back then, weren't we? Were we a bit weird?'

'Maybe,' Jake replies. 'Anyway, I'm off. See you later.' As he makes to leave, he instinctively gives her a peck on both cheeks and finds it strangely fascinating to touch her shaved head with his ear. For her part, in that moment, Trish manages to run her fingers through his dreadlocks.

'Ciao. See you around. We can't avoid each other for long, in a small place like Todi,' she says, smiling and winking.

Jake still finds her smile engaging. He looks down. 'That box looks like an antique,' he says. 'Why not research that, while you're at it?'

She bends down and rubs her hand over the gnarled wood. 'Probably will,' she says.

'I'll get an Italian SIM for my iPhone and leave you the new number on the hostel notice board,' Jake says. He has seen that overcrowded cork board by the dining room, where layers of Post-it notes compete with drawing-pinned and Blu-Tacked scraps of paper. 'Seeya at 9 – Jenny x' and similar messages.

He goes back to the hostel and his room, knocking on Tom's bedroom door on the way. Perhaps he shouldn't have left him so abruptly. Or was it Tom who was off-putting? There is no answer. He wonders whether to leave a note under his door – not yet having his mobile number to text him – but then thinks, 'No. Why should I? He knows where I am.'

As he crosses to his room, there is a ping from his mobile with a text message from Flo. 'MISS U ALREADY.' He simply sends an 'x' in reply. Flo is quite dependent on him and, much as he likes it, Jake feels his time abroad will be good for her.

He continues to unpack and put things away but it's not easy to fit in six months' stuff. He is a bit of a stickler for tidiness, which his peers find weird. He lays his books one on top of the other, spines facing outwards, on the floor in a corner. He uses the one little bookshelf for his bits and pieces, including a bi-fold leather frame holding a photo of him with Flo as a baby and another of him with both his parents. It's ages since they last had a family photo taken. He puts out another photo: his grandparents, Joe and Malkah, with Uncle Ernie – all three, now dead.

He stands his sketching pens and paint brushes in a mug on the desk – yet the sheet of plywood on a trestle is hardly a desk. He wonders if it's safe to put his iPad out but isn't sure, so stashes it in his big satchel with anything else he cares about. He remembers seeing lockers downstairs and some sign about the way to buy a key card. 'Must look into that,' he thinks, when there's a banging on the door. It's Tom with a couple of hangers-on. They all barge in and snoop around the room.

'Hi, I'm just sorting my stuff.' Jake begins.

Tom grins. 'Leave it till later,' he says. 'Let's find some fun.' This a change of tone since the cafeteria. He puts his arm round Jake and tries to steers him, with the others, to the door.

Jake does not want to seem too eager. 'Give me a mo, OK?' he says.

'Oh, bet you're meeting that little punk of yours?' Tom says.

'No. And she's not a punk –' Jake stops, knowing protests won't work with a guy like Tom. 'I'll follow you.'

Tom, crestfallen, backs out of the room, as do his followers. Once they have all left, Jake locks things away and picks up his bag of precious possessions, then goes after them, down the stairs.

On the ground floor, in the usual crowd, he sees Tom giving high-fives to at least half a dozen people. Jake is in awe of someone who's met so many people so soon, even with a two-day head start. Although he doesn't enjoy being bossed around, he follows the group out of the building, feeling ridiculous as he doesn't know any of them. He makes small talk until, eventually, they reach a small piazza with the usual café tables and chairs around it.

Tom, leader of the pack, quickly sorts out a table, so Jake can finally take a look at the people around him. Cute girl with striped hair and thick-rimmed sun-specs and a nerdy guy. Cute girl is the first to introduce herself.

'I'm Suzanna, I'm with Tom,' she says, quashing any ideas Jake has of wanting to get to know her.

He answers, 'And I'm –'

'I know. You're Jake. Tom's told me about you,' she interrupts. Jake wonders what, exactly, she was told. She then introduces Sanjeev. Jake doesn't get why Tom seemed so interested in Trish, if he has a girlfriend. *Hm. One of those guys.*

'D'you all know each other from home?' Jake asks.

'I know Tom, but Sanjeev is across my corridor,' Suzanna replies. 'We crashed into each other, hauling stuff to our rooms. I'm from Bristol. And you?'

'I'm a Mancunian,' replies Jake, 'but the family moved to London ten years ago. Never call myself a Londoner.'

Jake starts to feel more at ease. Tom smiles a lot, has a full face with notably light grey eyes; his fair hair is wavy and bushes out a bit. He looks very fit and is wearing a sleeveless vest usually worn for running – shiny and purple, with matching short shorts.

Sanjeev leans in, over the little round café table and, in a Scottish accent that Jake always finds appealing, says, 'Hi. Call me Jeeves.' He grins. 'From Glasgow.'

Jake smiles. 'Hi. Jeeves has a posh, English-gentleman ring to it.'

'You mean it's like an English butler,' Tom comments.

'Whatever,' says Jeeves. 'I was born and bred in Newton Mairns. D'you go running a lot?' he asks Tom.

'Run? Why? Oh, this,' he says, pulling at his running shirt. 'I do run but it's just the first thing I put my hands on.'

'Running's not my thing. You?' he asks Jake.

He likes Sanjeev's manner – not in the least nerdy, after all. 'Not mine, either, I like *watching* sport,' he replies. He decides not to mention sketching yet, not sure how it would be received.

'Which sport?' This from Suzanna, who until now hasn't seemed to be listening, as she caresses Tom's hair, arm, hand and any other part of Tom that is unclothed.

Sanjeev – Jeeves – meanwhile, listens with a constant smile, his dark eyes concentrating on whoever is speaking, while habitually stroking back his shock of thick, black hair. Jake sees that his hair, unlike his own, does exactly as Jeeves wants, and he's dressed so smartly, in a well-fitting, short-sleeved white shirt and navy, tailored shorts.

'Footie,' Jake answers.

'Oh God, not that,' Suzanna says, faking boredom and pretending to yawn. Jake feels himself riled by her. Typical southerner, he thinks. Suzanna is good to look at, if not so good to listen to, though he can't see her eyes behind her giant sunglasses. She constantly fiddles with her long, multi-coloured hair, twisting it behind her, draping it over her shoulders, flicking it back and forth, or sucking the ends of it provocatively.

Jake reckons she is provoking Tom, but also that she enjoys being the centre of attention, as the only girl in the group. Her tight T-shirt with two sequined strawberries on the front, and jangling bracelets on both wrists, are definitely not signs of a shrinking violet.

'Yeah. I love football. Mancunians have it in their blood,' Jake says. 'Soccer's good there, too, y'know.'

'So, which is it, City or United?' asks Jeeves, now rejoining their conversation after ordering the drinks.

'It *was* United – now I'm in London, it's Tottenham,' Jake replies, ignored by everyone. Jeeves struggles to the table, carrying four bottles; he's stuck the straws behind one of his ears.

'Here,' he says, as he leans over for them to take the drinks. When a waiter comes over, briefly asking if everything is OK – without really wanting an answer – Jeeves manages to reply in impressive Italian. That's followed a few minutes later by the waiter bringing a plate of biscotti, which they soon empty.

'So, Jeeves, how come your Italian's so good?' Tom asks, still entwined round Suzanna, whose back he is stroking with a finger, inside her T-shirt.

'From uni. Where else?'

'Course, but I can't speak like you,' Suzanna replies. 'I'm hoping it'll come, while I'm here, just like that,' she says, clicking her fingers in the air. With that, an officious looking waitress comes over to ask what she wants. Between them, they mumble an apology, trying to explain. Suzanna can't control her laughter. She masks it with a hand which holds a bunch of her hair.

'It usually takes more than a click of your fingers to attract an Italian waiter,' she whispers, giggling.

'Sh,' Jeeves says, embarrassed by her. The waitress seems to gather what's going on and turns her back on them with a loud 'tut' and a flounce. Just then, Jeeves waves in the other direction.

'Hey, come over,' he says to a girl who is passing the table. She is wearing a headscarf.

'This is Zainab. Zainab – Jake, Jake – Zainab,' Jeeves says. 'And this is Tom and that's Suzanna.' Those two say a surprisingly quiet 'Hi.' Jake stands and offers his hand but not his cheek; he isn't sure whether Muslim girls do air-kissing.

'Everyone calls me Zany,' she says, as she pointedly but politely keeps her right hand to herself.

Jake puts his neglected right hand in his shorts pocket, realising she does not even shake hands and says, 'And I'm Jake for Jacob – or JT – Jake Taylor.' He drags a chair over for her from the next table and she takes it, grinning at everyone. Jake thinks Zainab has a beautiful face – slim with high cheek bones. Unable to see her hair, which he assumes to be thick, black and shiny, he's drawn more to her features. Her eyes are dark, almond-shaped, framed by long, curly lashes and thick, shaped eyebrows, and he can't take his own eyes off them. They're quite heavily made up, penetrating and expressive. And there's her smile and her immaculate teeth. As she smiles, her nose wrinkles, a light furrow forms on her brow. She is petite, so she looks up at him, which he enjoys; his eye is taken by the thin row of sparkly beads on her silky, cream-coloured hijab.

'Thanks, Jake,' she says, eyelids lowered. The dynamic of the group suddenly changes when she joins them. They all make small talk but Suzanna goes quiet. Would she be put off by any other girl joining them, or is it because that other girl looks different? Jake is not fazed – he's intrigued. But the group soon breaks up and they go their separate ways.

TWO

Jake still doesn't feel confident when meeting new people but, with all the moves he's made, he shouldn't have a problem. After moving to London there was a new school, new youth group, new everything; and his parents divorced, so there were two homes to go between. Later, there was the challenge of fresh people at uni, but he chose to study in London to avoid another move, so for two years he has felt fairly settled.

And now this. He's always known that studying languages meant going abroad but thought he'd be fine. However, those old feelings of insecurity have crept back in, on meeting those guys today. Some of them seem like toffs but then, he judges people too quickly and really, Jeeves and Zany are fine. Especially Zany. *God she's pretty.*

He decides to go exploring, on his own. At least he'll acquaint himself with the place, if not the people – maybe he shouldn't have left Zainab behind but he will see her again. Meanwhile, that matter of finding a job is starting to loom large. He organises his room a bit, using some discarded boxes as makeshift storage. He plans to cover them with fabric or fancy paper; Jake is known for using his creative streak, like his mum. *Maybe I should have studied art, after all.*

He ruffles his hair and, ignoring yet another message from Flo, puts his iPhone in his pocket and iPad safely in his man-bag. He worries about Flo, though he shouldn't. This is his opportunity to ease the symbiotic relationship they have developed. So despite his mum's email asking him to reply to Flo's messages, Jake heads out. *For the next few hours, I'm ignoring anything from home.*

He leaves the hostel and purposefully makes off up a steep alleyway. Most of Todi's ancient buildings cling precariously to a hillside, which makes the town picturesque, even if everywhere is a climb away. Although the alley is steep, the steps are wide and provide resting space occasionally. What shocks him is that cars are allowed in the narrowest of streets and he is nearly knocked over by a big car clambering down the stepped alley. It is driven by a woman using her mobile phone with one hand; he presses himself against a wall to avoid being hit – the car driver doesn't notice him. *Better not swear at her, I'm a visitor.*

The street winds round to the right and then, quite unexpectedly, there's an open space. Across it, unseen until he actually reaches the square – Piazza del Popolo – is a beautiful, small *duomo*. Ceramic pictures adorn the front and, over the door arch, a carved name: Santa Maria Annunziata. He wonders how many Santa Maria cathedrals there are in Italy. On another side of the piazza is a grand-looking building, which he discovers is the Palazzo del Popolo – now, the Town Hall. Something else to explore. He walks up to a wall alongside the cathedral where there is a stunning view, but the sky is now threateningly dark, after that sunny beginning. He is drawn into the cathedral. It's cool and, at midday, welcoming for that.

''Giorno,' he nods to the lady sitting by a desk at the entrance. He notices a dish with change in it and drops in a coin.

'Grazie,' she says, smiling, 's'accommodi,' and gestures to him to go further inside. This he does and, when his eyes are used to the dim light, he sees quite a few people kneeling, praying or sitting. He sits on an empty pew at the back and looks around. Initially it doesn't seem an impressively beautiful church, but when he turns round he sees some exquisite frescoes and a small stained-glass window. He breathes in the atmosphere and gets up to look around; Italian church architecture interests him from a design perspective.

Jake walks round the outer walls, picking up leaflets on various shelves, which he tries to read and understand. He hopes to translate them properly later. He does gather that the site of the cathedral is ancient but was rebuilt in the twelfth century, after a fire. *Old enough even then*, he thinks.

He comes to a narrow door and a worn stone spiral staircase, which leads up into the *campanile*. He decides it's too hot to be climbing up bell towers, then he notices another little doorway with stairs, leading down. They are open to the public, so he goes down into a cold cellar. There are scratched shapes and letters on the dank walls. He can only make out some of them: an E, a B, maybe a C, and some other kind of script. A monk comes down the stairs and nods a greeting to him, followed by a long, unintelligible sentence.

'Scusi,' Jake begins. 'Inglese. Parla lentamente per favore.' He speaks slowly himself to make clear his request.

The monk smiles benevolently. 'Ah... studente?'

'Si,' says Jake, thinking this won't be the most exciting of conversations, as he's still far from comfortable in Italian.

The monk gestures to the wall. 'Ebraici – ecco!' he says, pulling him nearer to it. Jake has no idea why this monk is trying to chat to him, so he nods to confirm that he's heard, and starts to move off. The monk is having none of it. He beckons and turns to a hollow in another wall and points, grinning, to some more roughly carved shapes. Jake just about recognises a Star of David in the old stonework and it dawns on him that 'Ebraici' means 'Hebrew' – or 'Jewish'. 'I knew that,' he thinks. 'The monk's pronunciation confused me.'

'Ah, si! Molto interessante,' he says, having no idea why it should be there or why the monk has chosen him to look at it. 'Could just be a carved star,' he thinks. 'May mean nothing.' Then he realises that his own gold star on a chain has partly worked its way out from under his T-shirt. 'Clever guy, this monk. Knows a Jewish boy when he sees one. He won't collar this one so easily,' he thinks, recalling all he has ever learnt about the early popes through to Mussolini.

'Grazie. A domani,' he says and shakes the monk's hand vigorously, not really planning to come back. He points to his watch and rushes back up the stairs – the view from the top of the *campanile* can wait. He wants to avoid any further encounters with monks.

He emerges from the building, squinting at the bright midday sun, and breathes deeply to inhale the warmth. If he isn't going to the top of the church tower, he'll at least walk uphill, to see where that takes him. He strides up the shallow-stepped alleyway as briskly as the heat allows.

Jake lets the lanes take him different ways uphill. As he reaches what he reckons is the top of the hill on which the town stands, an uninterrupted mass of blue greets him, framed by old brick walls on two sides, terracotta roof tiles above and below him, fields as far as he can see.

They're surprisingly green, hardly scorched at all; it has been a wet summer for this part of Umbria. He spots vines on the slopes and, between them, olive trees, so he takes his first photo. It probably shows Tuscany, beyond the fields. He will send it to his mum and Flo when he gets back to his room and Wi-Fi; his resolution to resist answering emails and texts is fading fast. He plans to come back to this spot again, with his sketch pad and paints.

On the way down, going a different route, he takes in some shops. They are mostly closed for siesta, so he looks at the posters affixed to the buildings. He tries to read some, hoping that at least one will advertise an interesting job. Some hope. In fact, the first poster he can understand is about a football match: Todi v Perugia. In a photo of them at play, he sees that Todi wear red and white, like Man U. *'Martedì'* – yes, it's next Tuesday. 'I must go,' he thinks, wondering how to get hold of a ticket.

He somehow finds his way back to the square where that café was. He's thirsty again – and hungry – so heads towards the hostel. From the corner of yet another tiny alleyway, he hears English, spoken with a girly lilt and accompanied by giggling. He squints to make out silhouetted people in the half light, then takes a step or two towards the voices.

'I don't believe it; I can always find him,' he hears. 'Jake, it's me, Trish.' He approaches her and the other girl – Zainab. Today, he notices that her headscarf has silver thread running through it.

'Hi,' he says, aware that he's blushing.

'This is Zainab –' Trish says.

'I know. Hi, Zany. We've met,' Jake tells Trish.

'Hi,' Zany replies, also blushing.

'So, what are you two up to? Can you answer that in Italian?' he asks, trying too hard to impress.

'Looking for jobs, càro,' Trish says, giving him a friendly punch.

'Benissimo,' he responds. 'And that's the limit of my vocabulary. Let's find something to eat, eh?'

'We're going to the hostel; the snacks are cheaper. Coming?'

He nods and walks along with them, hoping his fascination with Zainab shows – but not too much. They chat as they walk. Zany has a delightful turn of phrase and they quickly find a mutual interest in art and in books. He tries to include Trish in the conversation but she doesn't seem concerned; rather, she seems to encourage their chatter, which surprises him.

Back at the hostel they pick up some stale filled rolls and more stewed coffee. Trish and he swap mobile numbers, emails and Facebook connections.

'D'you want mine?' asks Zainab, coyly – or perhaps, not so coyly. *Can Muslim girls be this forward?*

'Sure, of course,' he replies.

Trish winks as they beep their numbers to each other; the two girls met only this morning, yet seem like old friends.

'I don't use Facebook much,' Zany adds.

'So, where d'you come from?' Jake asks her.

'Well, not from Pakistan.'

'What? Course not. I mean which town? Manchester, Birmingham...?' He's bemused.

'Only kidding. People often don't get it,' Zainab says. 'I live in Leeds and go to uni there – still a protected species, y'know.' She giggles at this.

'No worries, I get it,' Jake says.

'You're pretty unusual.'

'That's what my parents say.' Jake hopes he's not being too forward. 'I like that,' he says, pointing to her hijab. 'All floaty and mysterious.'

'I'm really not mysterious. I'm quite ordinary except for living at home.'

'But I live at home too,' Jake says.

'Does that cramp your style?'

'Hardly,' Jake smiles. He surprises himself, flirting like this, especially as he knows that Zany is not likely to be his 'type' – or he, hers. Still, who cares? He's in sunny Italy, free, a puppy unleashed in a field. After silently flicking through the leaflets on the table, Trish interrupts. Jake has forgotten she is there.

'Don't know about you two, but when you've finished, I need to get sorted and start vaguely looking for some meaningful occupation.'

'We *are* meaningfully occupied, making new friends,' says Jake. 'You're right, though. All I've spotted so far is a poster for a local football match. Is that local culture?'

'You won't learn much *repeatable* Italian from football. Aren't Italian crowds a bit ugly?' Zainab asks.

'British ones aren't so perfect,' says Jake.

'Mm, but...'

Jake goes on. 'Well, I know there are gangs. The worst are called "Stremi".'

'Meaning?'

'Short for Estremi: Extreme. I'm trying to buy tickets on the internet – and I'll need Italian for that,' he says, smiling. Mainly at Zainab.

'Watch it, Jake,' says Trish. He thinks she is warning him off Zany. However, she says, 'Their football crowds are pretty nasty.'

'I'll cope. I'm a big boy, now, Trish, no worries.' He punches her gently on her arm. 'So, I'll see you both around, then, eh? Text or whatever? There's an intro social tomorrow evening, Sunday – free drinks and a disco. At the hostel. Coming?'

Trish says she'll be there. Zany shrugs her shoulders. 'Not sure.'

'It's not all alcohol,' Jake reassures her.

'Still not sure.' Zany blushes. 'Whatever, maybe. See you around.'

They leave in opposite directions and he turns round surreptitiously, to catch another look at Zany, as she and Trish walk off together, laughing. Even though her dark, long summer dress over loose trousers more or less hides her shape, he is completely captivated by her. It doesn't bother him that he hasn't seen her hair, her arms or her legs; the sight of her ankles makes his imagination work overtime.

This is ridiculous. No Muslim girl would get involved with him or any guy, let alone a Jewish one. Jake is usually known to be well in control but he doesn't feel it. Luckily, just then, he bumps into Tom and Suzanna, hunched over each other and looking at the notice board, which diverts him.

'Hi, you two. Anything interesting on there? I thought everyone would use Facebook, not notice boards.'

'This is still the place for job hunting. Locals know students want jobs and they all come and put up notices here.'

'Found anything?' Jake doesn't know whether he really cares, but has to say something.

'Maybe, yah: look! There's one notice with a little list, translated into English for us – how cute. Not bad spelling.' She points to it: '"Need help in Locale Caffé. Good pay." Hm. I bet. Lowest of the low. Usually have to rely on tips,' she comments.

'Here's another,' Tom chips in. '"Help pleeze with English. Evenings." Is that all about language?' he sniggers.

Jake wonders whether these two are wise or simply sceptical. 'We can check up on the people, though,' he ventures.

'Sure y'can,' Suzanna replies, flicking her hair back so that it almost hits him in the eye. 'But how?'

The conversation winds down at this point, because Jake has no more idea how to check out adverts than they do.

'Listen you guys, I'm going to check some websites,' he says, turning towards the stairs to his room.

'Seeya soonest,' Tom and Suzanna say, sickeningly in unison. Jake feels the insincerity of Suzanna's wish to see him soon, even though the proximity of Tom's room will make it inevitable.

He flops onto his bed with relief and not a little despair. Jake has looked forward to this trip but he feels he doesn't make friends easily and wonders if he'll cope with it all. Making friends is one matter; falling for a girl, quite another. He has had a few girlfriends along the way – with or without romance, he's always found girls easy to talk to. He wonders if that's a bit odd but till he met Trish he'd never had such a close friend, someone who thought like him. That never happened again, after he moved to London.

As usual, he's rushing it. Two days is hardly long enough to judge people. He lies back on his bed, puts in his earphones and turns on his music. Taking in the amazing view as he lies there, he realises how lucky he is. And if he can make a killing with Zany... *I must be mad.*

There's a text ping on his phone. 'WHEN CAN WE SKYPE? FLO :)'

Jake realises he's forgotten to get the hostel's Wi-Fi code, so he runs full pelt down the spiral stairs and along to the office. He finds the code number on the wall, by the opening at reception, laminated and stuck fast. He copies it into his iPhone and goes back to his room.

As he breathes out at the thought of a few peaceful minutes, a hand grabs his shoulder; it's Tom's. 'Hey, what's doing?'

'Not much, why?'

'Thought we could go on a job-hunt and see who we meet on the way.'

'Tried that earlier. Not found much.' Jake really wants to be left alone.

'Jobs or people? Hey, you're only going to live in Italy once. Make the most of it. Come on.'

'Er... give me five minutes, OK?' Jake softens. On second thoughts, it would be wrong to rebuff Tom, who thinks he can come and wait in Jake's room – and is in there before Jake can stop him.

'Oh, I, er –'

'Calling your girlfriend?' he asks, as he sees Jake's open iPad.

'No. My sister.'

'Mind if I stay? It's only your sister,' Tom smiles.

Jake doesn't know what to say. 'Well, OK, if Flo doesn't mind.'

'Fuck off – what's to mind?'

He starts to skype and soon, Flo appears on the iPad screen. Looking at her like this, he realises how cute she is, with her freckled face. They've both inherited their mum's complexion – Flo has a mass of curly auburn hair and a grin that makes dimples form in her full, if not chubby, cheeks.

'Hi, Jakey!' she says, waving her hand from side to side. 'Look who's saying "Hi"!' She holds up a tiny kitten and grabs its paw to make it wave.

'Where d'you find that?' Jake says.

'It isn't a *that*, she's Milky. She is sooo cute. Dad bought her for me when you went away and I was, like, "That's sick, Dad." and he was, like, "Use proper language, Flo."'

'Don't blame him,' Jake says.

'Jakey, you're getting old. Anyway, I called her after Grandma Malkah and also cos she drinks so much milk – good name? Look.'

'I'm looking,' says Jake, as this tiny kitten's face takes up the whole screen. 'So I've been replaced by a cat? Mm. Can't think that Grandma would want a cat called after her but... I've got someone at this end, too, who wants to say hello.'

Tom leans over, in front of Jake. 'Hi, Flo. I'm Tom.'

'Hello. Do you share a room?' she asks.

'No, I just popped by and we're off out in a mo, looking for jobs.'

'I'll send a photo of Todi for you and Mum to look at,' Jake says, and he does so from his mobile.

'Bet you're off looking for girls,' replies Flo.

'No, they look for us!' Tom jokes.

'Y'look nice,' Flo says. 'And I don't always like Jake's friends.'

'I think that's a compliment,' Tom replies. He has an easy, friendly manner, talking to Flo as though she's an adult. Jake warms to that.

'So listen, Flo,' Jake continues, 'like, now I've got the connection, we can skype whenever I'm in the hostel, OK?'

Flo hides behind Milky's head and does a ventriloquist act, pretending the cat is speaking. She squeaks: 'Bye bye, then. Miaow.'

'Say hi to Mum,' Jake replies.

'Will do. And to Dad,' Flo says pointedly. 'He's coming round this evening to see Milky.'

'Hi to Dad, then,' Jake adds grudgingly. 'Seeya, Milky.'

'Bye, and bye, Tom.'

'Cheers.'

'She's cute,' Tom says.

'Flo or Milky?' Jake teases.

'Milky. But Flo's funny,' Tom replies.

'Never noticed that. She's got charm, I know – at least, when she wants something. She twists Dad round one little finger and Mum round the other.'

'So your parents are separated, as well? Stuff happens,' Tom says.

'Mm. I try to be the voice of reason,' Jake replies.

'Get away from that – and get out there,' Tom says.

They chat for a moment more whilst downloading a map of the town to their phones. 'It's easy to find your way around, it's so small,' Jake says.

'Yeah – but it helps to know where we're going, first, don't y'think?'

Tom unfolds a couple of pieces of paper with addresses or email addresses on them. Jake taps his phone where he's stored all the football information. They start walking and Jake leads them towards the duomo, trying to remember where he saw the football poster. It was in the window of a kind of newsagent shop but he can't remember the name of the street.

'Let's go to the tourist office,' says Tom. 'We may need to go to Perugia in the end, but let's see.'

'Yeah and I may have to, to buy football tickets. And the tourist office will give us bus routes, too.'

Tom strides ahead of him, his longer legs showing up Jake's non-athletic gait. Jake pats his fabric satchel, constantly checking the safety of his iPad and his other pad: the one for sketching. He wonders about using the iPad more, like Hockney. This trip could be the time to try.

'What're you thinking?' Tom says. 'You're quiet, aren't you?'

'Hm. Dunno. I was wondering when to start sketching.' He blushes. He is always embarrassed to talk about drawing if he isn't among arty types.

'Arty *and* a linguist? I'm impressed,' Tom replies.

'Don't be. My languages aren't that brilliant.'

'What does the newsagent's look like? There's an *edicola*, look, that kiosk over there,' Tom says.

Jake shakes his head. 'It wasn't a news kiosk, it was a shop with all sorts of stuff inside, newspapers near the door and leaflets stuck to windows. Hey, am I taking up too much time? Isn't Suzanna waiting for you?'

'So, she'll wait a bit longer. She is a mate but... a bit too clingy. We really should have gone to separate places, this year.'

'I thought you were an item.'

'We were – are. For now.'

That makes it clear enough. Tom strides on while Jake looks round corners.

'I think I've spotted it,' Tom shouts.

'That's the one,' Jake replies. They step up their pace and stop to read all the notices in the window. Jake notes down the information about football tickets and they go inside. He tries to be especially charming, aware that many students must use this shop as he is doing. 'Per favore, signore,' he begins, continuing in his best Italian, smiling at the man behind the counter, who barely acknowledges him. 'Questo,' he says, showing the man the advert with jobs on it.

Tom steps in, asking where they could find the places mentioned.

'Momento,' the surly man says, as he goes into the back of the shop. He gestures to a young girl about their age.

'Permesso?' she says and takes the notices from them. 'I can 'elp you?' Speaking faltering English, she draws a little map, adding some crosses, naming a few of them. She has obviously done this before, Jake thinks.

'Perugia, quà,' she says, pointing to a bus stop across the street. He nods; Tom also understands and gestures to his watch. The girl answers by ushering them out, so there must be a bus coming.

'Grazie. Grazie molto,' they say and rush across the road. The bus arrives almost immediately and, after a quick glance at the timetable on the shelter, they see they're lucky to catch this hourly bus service.

'Better make sure of the times coming back. Maybe they stop for siesta and don't start again,' Tom says.

Jake loves the view from the bus window; whenever it stops, he makes square frames with his fingers, thinking that each scene could make a painting. Tom simply taps away at his iPhone, apparently oblivious to the splendour of the Umbrian countryside and Tuscany in the distance. Uncle Ernie taught Jake not to be embarrassed about his interest in art; he remembers their conversation:

'Don't take any notice of the macko guys who sneer at art,' Ernie told him.

'Ma*ch*o,' Jake said. 'It's not like "me*c*kanical".' Jake always corrected Ernie's English – he arrived in the UK as a teenager.

'Bit of a dreamer, aren't you?' Tom asks, shaking Jake up.

Jake thinks: *He's a macko type!* He says, 'Not really, I just love this scenery, it's unreal.'

'See, you *are* a dreamer,' replies Tom.

'Maybe. It's just... I love colour and shape – seeing what I could paint. An uncle of mine encouraged me,' Jake says, feeling embarrassed.

'Cool.' Tom is unfazed by Jake's admission. 'Why didn't you study art instead of languages?'

'Couldn't make up my mind. But I can draw and paint anywhere; I might do something postgrad.'

'Mm. Hey, this must be the bus station – everyone's getting off.'

Jake is warming to Tom, who is far more *sympathique* than he first thought. They follow signs for the university, without looking at the addresses on their sheet of paper.

'Look, another tourist office. Lucky us.'

'Well, it would be near the main bus station,' Jake says, spotting that tickets for local football matches are on sale there. Tom grudgingly agrees to go to a match with him so they buy two tickets. The girl in the office tells them more about the places with crosses on a map.

Tom asks about jobs in agriturismo, miming digging and dusting. The girl brings out brochures for some agriturismo guesthouses but, according to the map, Tom sees only a few are within reach, so he takes hotel brochures as well.

'I think my best bet, for finding people to teach, is through the uni,' Jake says. 'People must know there are foreign students around in the summer.' Before they leave, they scour all the notices pinned on the board and see a couple of job adverts that look useful. Tom reads one out to Jake.

'Someone here wants to learn English – *quickly*, it says. "Must speak English before autumn. You teach English, I teach you Italian."'

It sounds good but Jake wonders, if it's a quid pro quo, whether he'd be paid enough. He takes down the mobile number and the email; Tom does the same for the agriturismo place and a couple of hotels.

They continue their walk towards the university, passing the duomo and the palazzo. They then sit in a café that advertises free Wi-Fi and start making contacts. They order cold drinks, though Jake thinks he can't keep doing all this café-sitting, at least until he's earning some money. They're both sending texts and emails to the advertised contacts, when Tom clears his throat as though he's making a big announcement.

'All this café-sitting is great but pricey.'

'My thoughts exactly,' Jake replies.

'We'll have to come to some kind of deal like one lemonade between two, or only one café a day, or –'

'Sharing a chair?'

'Yeah right. I –'

'Only kidding,' Jake replies, smiling. 'But I agree.'

'Let's have a quick look round Perugia, before the bus leaves us here for the night,' Tom says, as he starts to collect his things.

They walk around with no plan in mind but find the main university area. Swarms of young people are milling around, sitting on steps, leaning on walls, standing smoking under mossy, mediaeval arches. With Perugia's established 'University for Foreigners', there are more students than would usually be found in the summer months. It seems to Jake that they are unaware of the uniqueness of their surroundings, as they drop cigarette stubs and chewing gum, which settle in the crevices of ancient cobbles.

'That must be the main building; there's some kind of notice board outside, let's look.' Tom points to it. Jake senses the familiar feel of all universities; the casual camaraderie, the indolent appearance of people with seemingly nothing to do.

They both collect some emails, phone numbers and addresses, copying what they can and photographing others with their mobiles. On seeing a kiosk for the foreign students, they each buy a student's season ticket that gives concessions at various places of interest.

'Look at it later – the bus leaves in ten minutes,' warns Jake, ever cautious. They run from there to the bus stop and reach it, exhausted and hot.

As they bend over to get their breath back, a voice behind them says, 'Hey. Nobody rushes, over here. And the last bus is always late. It loses at least ten minutes over the course of the day. Then it waits for ages, here, cos the driver knows students always arrive late.' It's Sanjeev.

'Hi Jeeves, thanks. Good to know,' Jake says, greeting him with a pat on his arm.

'Frightfully sorry, old chap. In future I'll be your guide, to provide all the local info. OK?' Jeeves grins, enjoying hamming it up as their butler and amused at Tom and Jake's exhaustion. Jeeves looks cool in every sense and unflustered, even in the afternoon heat. When he hears about Jake's football tickets, he's envious.

'Wish I'd seen you before,' he says, as they all get on the bus, which has crawled sluggishly to their stop, as though it, too, was puffed from running.

'Listen. You can go to the match instead of me,' Tom offers. 'D'you mind, Jake?'

'No, as long as I don't go on my own, it's OK. You know it won't be top league stuff.'

'Maybe interesting, though,' Jeeves says.

They travel back to their hostel sleepily, the bus trundling up and down the steep alleys, bumping over the cobbles.

THREE

Exhausted but pleased to be on his own, Jake decides to call his mum, who has been busy lately with her mural-painting business. Years ago, he helped her with an early mural she designed for baby Flora. He loved painting with his mum and life seemed good to him then.

And now Trish is here again, in Italy. They were far too young, back then – or too immature – to have a romantic attachment. But if he had not moved, who knows? Might it have grown into one?

He skypes his mum. 'Guess who's here?' he asks her.

'No idea,' she replies.

'Trish.'

'You mean *the* Trish? In the same town? Coincidences... D'you remember what Great-grandma Freidl said? "Things that change your life are rarely of your making."'

'Well, not sure that Trish will change my life, exactly, but –'

'Is she gorgeous now?'

Jake knew his mum was fishing for more. 'She's got a great smile.'

'Always had.'

'And lots of piercings and a shaved head,' Jake says.

'Makes up for your dreadlocks, then.' His mum smiles.

'That's what she said.' Jake scowls. 'She's still fun. It's weird how things happen, though.'

'Send her my love, OK. Met anyone else interesting?'

'Yep. Some really different types. Italy's madly expensive though. We're trying not to sit drinking too many cappuccinos.'

'Any news about jobs?'

'Not yet. Still looking.'

'OK, I'll leave you to get on. But can I show you the design for my latest mural? It's here.' Jake's mum holds up a painting of an underwater scene.

'Great. Take photos of it as you go along, to put on your website.'

'Will do – I've upped my iPhone for one that takes moving piccies.' She holds up its screen for him to see her website: *www. nickibespokemurals.co.uk.*

'Sick! I'm off now, OK?'

His mum blows a kiss. 'Love you. But "sick" for "great"? It'll never work for me.'

'Tough. Love you too,' Jake says. 'And kiss Flo for me.'

'Will do. And Dad?'

'Say "hi" to him.' His reticence regarding his dad hangs in the air like a cobweb, as they switch off Skype. Jake has wrestled with his conscience about their relationship but feels that his dad should be the one doing the wrestling. Even so, he decides to email him, later. Or maybe the next day.

He splashes his face in the sink in his room, cleans his teeth and lies on his bed to listen to music. It's great using earphones, listening to the music he's downloaded from iTunes. This way no one knows how old-fashioned his taste is; he can relax with it.

He wakes to find he slept the night away in his clothes. Shocked and ashamed that his first day tired him so much, he rushes to the shower before the masses get up. Sunday still has a soporific effect on him, even though most days are like Sundays. In Italy, however, everything is closed – except for churches.

Outside, various church bells are ringing and, through his window, he sees people obviously in their Sunday best.

He intends to contact some of the people advertising for

English teachers but is easily sidetracked into looking at websites about local football. Just then, a new little email envelope shows on his screen. It's a reply to his email about teaching English in time for autumn. It's in Italian but he can understand written Italian; the spoken word is harder.

The email simply gives the name of the person and a phone number. The thought of phoning someone in Italian is even more daunting than speaking directly, but he has no choice. He knows only to ask for 'Gianni'. The voice on the phone says something about football. Jake thinks he's got the phone number mixed up with the one for the tickets.

'Do you speak English?' he asks, disgusted at himself for his cowardice.

'Leetel,' says a female voice, laughing.

Jake reverts to Italian, explains that he wants to speak to Gianni and checks he has the correct phone number.

'Gianni, he football,' says the voice. 'No, Gianni gioca,' she says, giggling again.

'Gioca... plays. He's a *footballer*?' Jake gulps in disbelief, whispering 'Yeah!' and flexing a triumphant fist. He asks his full name. 'Come si chiàma – Gianni...?'

'Gianni Trevesi,' replies the girl on the phone.

'Oh. Grazie molto,' he says.

He nearly rings off but the girl says, 'Écco Gianni. 'E spik you.' There's a fumbling as the phone is passed to Jake's potential pupil.

'Come si chiàma?' the man's voice says.

'Jake. Jake Taylor.'

'Bene, Jekke. I Gianni. Where you live in Inghilterra?'

''Giorno, Gianni. London, now,' Jake replies and pre-empts the next question. 'I used to watch Manchester United.' He hears an intake of breath.

'Manchester United. Magnifico. No good now? Giggs good, no?'

'Si. He helps the manager. Now, I watch Tottenham.'

'I must speak Eenglish. You 'elp me? I live in England soon.'

'Oh,' says Jake. 'Where? Why?'

'I football –'

Jake interrupts: 'No, you are a football*er*.'

'Si si, footballeur,' Gianni says. 'I play in Vegan in Settembre.'

Hey? Is he a vegetarian or something? What's he on about? Oh!

'Wigan? Do you mean Wigan?'

'Si si, Weegan. You teach me?' Gianni asks.

'Sure I will,' Jake replies. They arrange to meet at a café nearby; the place Gianni suggests is the one Jake had a coffee in with his new mates. They will meet the next day, Monday, at noon.

'Grazie, ciao,' Jake says. He rings off, bounding round the room, whispering loudly, 'Yeah,' and punching the air like a mad thing. He cannot believe it – an Italian footballer on transfer to Wigan? He runs out of his room and nearly knocks Suzanna over.

'Things looking up, then, Jake, my boy?' she asks, purposely patronising, trying to tousle his hair. 'Didn't know you could be so animated.'

Jake ignores this jibe and tells her he's busy replying to job adverts before the social. He's determined not to share his news with her – or anyone – until it's confirmed. 'See you later,' he says, and ducks back into his room.

'Be like that,' Suzanna shouts after him.

I will be 'like that', till everything's sorted. The idea of teaching a footballer is overwhelming, not least because he'll have no problem getting hold of football tickets and maybe, just maybe, he could see a big league match. He's so excited that, almost without thinking, he emails his dad.

Football and Dad are inseparable, even if they themselves have been separated. Jake came late to the football passion of Mancunian kids, since he was ten when his dad first bought two season tickets. That meant they only went regularly to Old Trafford for a couple of years before moving away. They went back to matches occasionally afterwards, though, and visited the remaining Manchester family. Eventually, his dad gave up the Manchester United seats and bought some for Tottenham. It was a kind of 'bonding thing', he said. *Which was hardly a good idea, just before he left for another woman.*

That was ages ago. Currently, they communicate, but not like they used to. Yet Jake still wants to tell his dad the news. He emails and his dad replies immediately.

'Hey, Jake, why not skype?'

Jake isn't yet up to speaking face to face and explains that he's rushing to a social. 'But I will do, after meeting Gianni.'

'Promise?'

'Sure, promise. Cheers Dad xx,' Jake writes. Strange. It feels quite natural to put kisses after the message.

Jake knows he won't manage to keep his job secret all evening. Before he goes down, he organises his room a bit more, using the end of the curtain rods as coat hooks – *who needs curtains and shutters?* – and putting his jeans in folded piles. He plans to get more boxes to hold the leftover clothes, and will spray-paint them in bright, graffiti designs. With six months in a place, he wants to put his stamp on his room. There's a knock on the door.

'Who is it?' Jake shouts.

'Me, Tom. Who else?'

'Hang on, nearly ready,' Jake replies, while changing his underpants; as he zips up a pair of cut-off jeans, he opens the door. Tom is standing in the doorway exuding his usual confidence, wearing the kind of clothes Jake would never think of wearing. A cream, lightweight jacket, its sleeves pushed up above his elbows and, apparently, nothing underneath except for a wide, jazzy tie round his bare neck. He wears tight, cropped jeans, which are bright green; his sockless feet are contained in red sneakers. Seeing Jake's glance, he pulls open his jacket, to reveal a tight, low-necked black vest.

'No worries, I'm not quite naked. But it's bloody hot, don't you think?'

'The outfit or the weather?' Receiving no reply, Jake fishes out a jazzy sleeveless top. As he checks his appearance in the mirror, he looks again at Tom, who is looking through Jake's books. His fair, curly hair is now shaved up the back and one side; the other is gelled and, while still curly, it flops purposefully over his right eyebrow. He looks up, revealing again his green eyes and full smile of perfect teeth.

'And...' he says, 'what's out of place?'

'Nothing at all,' Jake replies, honestly. 'That's just it.'

'Hey?'

'You look so... so... cool. I never know what looks right, clothes-wise,' Jake says.

'Oh, come on, who gives a shit?' Tom ushers Jake out of his room.

They trot down the spiral stairs and make for the social, in a room off the dining room. The band is set up in the dining room and the room dividers between the two are folded back. The walls are decorated with all the flags of the world, with a big Italian one in the centre. A banner runs across the wall welcoming everyone: 'Benvenuto in Todi, Italia.' The bar is set up where food is usually served, light bulbs are dim and multicoloured, and hostel staff are dressed in red, green and white outfits.

'Nice feel to it,' Tom says. A fair crowd has already gathered and as soon as they each have a drink, Jake loses sight of Tom. He doesn't mind – he likes the guy but is happy to make his own way. He leans on the wall and searches the room; he spots Zany in a small group of girls and goes over to her.

'Buona sera, signorina,' Jake says and bends over, as though to take her hand to kiss it.

Zany gives a start, pulls her hand in but grins openly at him.
'How's it going, then?' she asks, as she sips her water.

'Good – really good. You?'

'Fine. Bit by bit, you know. Oh, this is Aisha,' she says,
introducing her friend.

Aisha is French and speaks good English. She is the only
other girl in the room apart from Zany wearing a hijab; Jake
decides not to try kissing anyone else's cheek or hand – not
even air kissing.

At that moment, he spots Trish. At least, from behind he
thinks it's her shaved head. He excuses himself from Zany –
'Back in a mo' – and pushes his way through the crowd. As he
gets near, he sees she's with a group: some chic, some shabby
chic and most with piercings. They seem to know each other
well, considering the short time they've all been there.

'Hi Trish,' he says, giving her a hug.

'Hey, Jake, meet my mates.' She introduces him around. He
takes in one name, Xanthe, mainly because she is so pretty.
'How're things?' Trish asks.

'Really good: come and sit at a table while there's still one
left,' he suggests.

'Mm, well... I came with these guys from my building. I
do want to chat, catch up, y'know. I'll skype you to meet up.
OK?' With that, she gives Jake a peck on the cheek, flashes her
winning smile and returns to earnest conversation with her
friends.

So it goes. Jake wanders nonchalantly back, stopping on the
way to say 'Hi' to Jeeves, Suzanna and some others. He notices
Suzanna is not wrapped round anyone, wonders why, and then
goes to where Zany is sitting with her friends. By this time the
music is in full flow, provided by different groups of student
musicians. He fancies going on the floor and nods towards
the dancing, then back at Zany. She shakes her head shyly but
stands up next to him. Her perfume is inviting.

'Couldn't you dance, without touching?' Jake asks. 'There isn't much of it.'

'Mm...' Zany hesitates. 'But we might – that's the thing,' she says. 'Sorry, but why not sit and chat, though?' She pats a space on the window ledge where she is perched.

They chat for a while, then Jake is restless and makes for the dance floor alone; he often meets girls by simply jigging around on the edge. He spots Trish again. She has her arm round someone, who is leaning on her shoulder. As they turn round, he realises that Trish has her arm round a girl, one of those she came with.

Hm... So far, one of the girls he fancies is – in appearance at least – a practising Muslim, and the other might be... gay? *Not doing too well!* No, surely he'd know if Trish were gay.

He chats to some other guys he's seen around and, just as he's thinking about going back to his room, Trish taps him on the shoulder.

'Come on, let's go chat,' she says.

'It's OK. I'm going up. You stay with your mates,' Jake says.

'Oh. Be like that.'

'See you around.' Jake knows he's being rude but he is confused. Seeing Trish scowling, he changes his mind. 'Sorry, why not come up?'

'Now you know I'm safe, d'you mean?' she says.

'Safe?' Jake replies, missing her inference, with his back to her. 'No, just to get away from the crowd. Grab a drink to take up.' They go up the stairs.

'So, how's it going, so far?' she asks.

'Good. You?'

'Fine.' They are both avoiding sensitive topics, even though they know each other better than most.

'You want to ask me, don't you?' Trish says.

'Well...?'

'When I first knew I fancied girls?' Trish says, nudging his

– 47 –

shoulder with hers, as they sit at the end of his bed. 'Don't know exactly. I never quite got it when girls said there were boys they fancied. When I was about sixteen, I went to a book launch. The crowd were all lesbian cos the author was – I didn't know that beforehand. That was *the* day when everything made sense.'

'Did it make you happy?'

'Very. Awesome,' Trish replies.

'Funny. I never thought –'

'You wouldn't, would you?'

'I thought you were flirting with Tom – or that he was flirting with you,' Jake says. 'At breakfast, y'know.'

'Oh. Well, I can still smile at people.'

'Yeah,' Jake says. 'So you're OK?'

'Yep. I've got really good boy friends with no hassle and I've got girl friends and... others. Reckon I've got more friends of all kinds than most heteros.'

'What about here?'

'It's OK. But can I change the subject? I've found out lots about those lost Jewish communities. While I was looking for work in building restoration, I've –'

Jake cuts her off. 'Trish, I'm not into Jewish shit any more, I told you.'

'Well, I –'

'I'm just not, OK?'

'It's not OK. Explain yourself. I told you about my... my stuff.'

Jake recognises Trish at her most persuasive.

'What's happened to you?' she asks.

'Hm. Well. After all the fuss and faff over Dad's conversion to Judaism so he could marry Mum...'

'Before they married, y'mean?'

'Yeah – well there was more heavy stuff before my Bar Mitzvah.'

'Why?' Trish asks.

'Oh, about the different synagogues and… it was bonkers.'

'But you did have a Bar Mitzvah.'

'Oh, I had that, yeah, parents put on a show, you know.'

'They seemed great parents to me,' Trish says.

'Till Dad upped and left Mum, for a non-Jewish slag.' Jake blushes.

'Slag?'

'OK, woman, then.'

'Hm. Would you use 'slag' for a Jewish woman?'

Jake looks hang-dog. 'Dunno, sorry. But I mean, how could he? After going on about what mattered in our lives. Being Jewish is just a pain.'

'What about your little sister? How's she?' Trish asks.

'She'll blow with the wind – or wherever she gets more presents. But she's a great kid.'

'So… what's with Jewish history?'

'There's so much else. That's so narrow – it's always about persecution.'

'OK, what interests you? Apart from that cute Muslim girl,' she says, winking.

'Sketching actually,' Jake replies, ignoring her comment, 'and football.'

'And football's not narrow?'

'Aha, but my job is teaching English to a footballer. He's going to the UK on transfer. It'll help my Italian.'

'That does sound good.'

'And I might get free match tickets.'

'Mm… what about those hooligans?'

'Oh, those. It's just a big fuss.'

'There's lots in the media about it.' Trish looks worried. 'Careful.'

'You sound like my mum. Listen. I went exploring Todi and saw something – some carvings – in the vault of the local church. Afterwards, the monk asked if I was Jewish.'

'Why would he do that?'

'Cos the carvings were in Hebrew.'

'But you didn't tell me?' Trish is bouncing around on the bed.

'Hold on, I haven't had time! What with... everything.'

'And now you find I'm not available,' Trish says, running her hands through Jake's locks affectionately.

'No big deal. This way we stay friends. Suits me.' He shows her where he saw the carvings, in his guide book, before they go back downstairs.

They soon lose each other in the crowd and he joins Sanjeev. After a couple more dances with no one, he goes upstairs.

Jake has a quick shower, checks his emails and Facebook messages, then lies on the bed, hoping to keep cool with the night air wafting through the open window – the nearest thing there is to air conditioning.

So. Trish doesn't fancy boys, then. How things can change. Many of Jake's friends of either gender are gay – it's not an issue. But he feels confused. It's weird when someone you knew intimately proves to be someone about whom you really know nothing.

FOUR

Trish was once like part of Jake's family, especially over the time when his mum was pregnant with Flo. Jake remembers that lovely summer when Trish would often breeze in, ready to chat to her – and to everyone. She slotted in to his family and he enjoyed the research they did together into his family history and her own origins. He was still an only child then and Trish was always good company.

Jake feels let down in some way by his ignorance of her sexuality, but snaps himself out of this melancholy. *What am I doing? There's a new life out there, you idiot.* He pictures his first meeting with Gianni, his first official Italian class, and plays music from iTunes to help him go to sleep. His first Sunday in Umbria has been good. Why should his friendship with Trish change anything?

As Monday morning dawns, Jake has to rush – which is good, after much indolence; the Mediterranean climate and way of life seeps into everything. His meeting with his pupil is at eleven. He grabs breakfast in the cafeteria, having learnt already that you dunk the bread quickly into the coffee; the two together are almost palatable. He waves briskly to a couple of familiar faces and sets off to look for a bench and somewhere to sketch. Time passes quickly and at 10.40 he packs up, wipes the pastel crayon off his hands and goes to meet his pupil.

This is a new experience and he doesn't feel prepared. Starting a job isn't like making casual friends. What's more, it strikes him that he doesn't know what the footballer looks like. Fortunately, there is only one guy there, waiting. It's hard to see, as the sun has not yet moved round to shine on the outdoor tables. Perhaps he's inside? *No, that must be him.* Thick neck, broad shoulders, suntanned, well dressed, with a certain sportsman's confidence. Not that he would be as well paid as a British player – Wigan must be a step up for him.

'Gianni Travesi?' Jake asks, offering his hand. The young man stands up and nearly breaks Jake's fingers as he shakes it.

''Giorno! Come stà? 'Ow are you? You Jecce?'

'Yes, right first time,' Jake says, sitting down opposite him, under the parasol, as the sun is on its way. He weighs up this handsome young man, biceps tensing as he leans on his elbows, rocking the rickety table. Gianni mimes drinking and points to his glass. 'Limonata,' he explains. 'You want?'

'Si. Per favore,' Jake answers. He isn't sure which language to speak, but between them and with their two languages, they manage to sort out Gianni's requirements for learning English. The hourly rate Gianni offers to pay will help enormously. All the time, Jake is working out how to plan the lessons. He knows that it will help his Italian too, but that doesn't need a formal agreement. Initially they agree to hold lessons at another café, further away from Jake's hostel, which Gianni points out on a local map.

'Is good. I know café,' he says, standing up as they finish their drinks.

'Grazie molto,' Jake says, as Gianni pays for his lemonade. 'À domani.'

'Till tomorrow,' Gianni replies.

This could be fun, Jake thinks, walking off in the direction of his class. He eventually finds the ancient building which houses some classrooms – not like the lecture theatres he knows. There are far too many tables in the room, which has only two spinning fans and no air conditioning.

Many students have already gathered, so he climbs over desks and people to the only space he can see. He trips over a massive rucksack on the floor and promptly draws more attention to himself than he wants.

'Fall in, Jake!' says a girl's voice, from behind. It's Zany. He turns and waves, mouthing, 'I'll see *you* later,' frowning but smiling at her. Gradually, he takes in the setting and atmosphere of this, his first class in Italy, in Italian. *Oh my God, it's all happening.*

The tutor waltzes in, ten minutes late, offering profuse apologies. She is young and gorgeous and, at first, Jake finds it hard to concentrate on anything except her slinky T-shirt and tight jeans, or the long, curly hair that she keeps flicking over her head. Eventually, she scrapes it back into one of those stretchy things he's seen Flo using.

The class goes by in a whirl, with scrawled words on the blackboard in illegible, continental handwriting that make it difficult. *What? No PowerPoint? Not even a whiteboard? WTF?* He tries and fails to take notes, instead concentrating on understanding at least some of what she says. He's relieved when it's over and, as he walks out, Zany catches up with him.

'Jake! Wait.'

'Hi, Zany.'

'What d'you think? How're we going to learn anything from that kind of session?'

'Dunno. But blackboards and chalk, for f... for goodness' sake.' He is not sure if she disapproves of swearing. 'Pretty antiquated. Still, I suppose we'll learn by osmosis.'

'You love using odd words don't you?'

'What? Oh – osmosis? I mean we'll absorb Italian cos we're immersed in it.'

'I knew what you meant. But if we always talk to other Brits, we won't.'

'Mm.' Jake knows she's right, but he really wants to get to

know Zany – what makes her tick. He looks sideways at her, noticing that her loose trousers are in a floaty fabric that moves as she walks, just about revealing the outline of her legs and then, the tiniest ankles and sandals with jewels on them. His gaze moves upwards to her face; her profile reminds him of many Jewish girls he's known, with a prominent but straight nose, though her skin is ever so slightly darker.

'Listen. I've got my sketching stuff with me. I want to capture some scenes round here. Come with me for a while?' he ventures.

She looks at her watch. 'I've got no more than an hour. Then I'm off to my parents'.'

'Hey?'

'Oh. I didn't tell you.'

'You're flying home?'

'Course not, silly,' she says, giggling. 'My parents have rented a friend's house for us all, for a few months, to keep an eye on me. It's only a bus ride away.'

'So you *are* protected,' Jake says.

'Mm...' Zany replies. 'My grandparents are looking after the business – and they live in our house in Leeds. Soon, my dad'll go back and my grandparents will come out here. Swapping over, y'know.'

'Aha. D'you mind?'

'What?'

'Being spied on,' Jake replies.

'No choice,' she says, shrugging her shoulders. 'It was that or I couldn't have studied languages at all.'

'Brill. D'you always see them during the day?'

'No, but it's Mum's birthday.'

'Fair enough,' Jake says, as he starts to climb up to the vantage point he saw on his first day. 'Did I tell you about my job?'

'Here, d'you mean?' Zany asks, smiling. 'No one else has got one yet.'

Jake tells her about the footballer as they make their way up the steep, cobbled alleyway.

'Here, look,' he says, as they reach the brow of the hill and a gap in the tall, ancient buildings with a spectacular view over Umbrian countryside.

'Awesome, or what?'

'Is it cos of the sun, d'you think?' she says.

Jake doesn't answer. All he's thinking about is how he'd love to put his arm around her and have her rest her head on his shoulder, to share the moment. It's hard to resist. Instead, he pulls an old, spare T-shirt from his bag, rolls it up and puts it on a boulder, gesturing for her to sit down, which he does too, on a boulder next to hers. Then he takes out his sketch pad and some pastels.

'Have you any spare stuff?' Zany asks. 'I actually love sketching, but I didn't bring my things with me.'

'Cool. Here, dip into the bag. I'll tear some pages out of my pad and you can have the clipboard.' He fishes for it in his bag, not knowing that Zany also has her hand in it, feeling for pastels and charcoal. He can't bring himself to remove his hand abruptly, just for the sake of propriety; nor does he want to draw away from the feel of her skin. He strokes her fingers with his but needs more; he doesn't dare look at her, because that touch tells him everything. She does take her hand away but he's sure she stroked his palm more than necessary, en route. When he looks up, she is blushing and looking down.

'OK,' he says, to break the ice. 'How to do justice to that view, eh?'

'You tell me,' she replies.

'Mm. I'm not a teacher, but maybe do an all-over background with the side of the pastel first. It'd be much better on coloured paper, really.'

Zany uses a pale blue pastel across what would be the sky and, at the horizon, changes to an ochre.

'That works,' Jake says. 'It's a good base for the bright soil and corn and tree trunks.'

'You can't see the trunks of cypress trees,' Zany observes.

They both laugh and look at each other. Jake is almost in physical pain, having to resist the urge even to hold hands. How will he cope with this? Keep away from her? Her smile is mesmerising.

They carry on sketching. Jake notices that she can draw and can't believe his luck. This luck could turn rapidly into misfortune – and there lies the quandary. They decide to finish for the time being and it is automatic for him to help her up from the rock. He takes her hand gently but, as she tries to get up, holding on to her drawing and also trying to hitch up the loose fabric of her trouser legs a little, she starts to lose her balance. How can he not catch her? She leans against him and he feels her slender frame in his arms, but she draws away as soon as she is steady on her feet.

'Oh, I shouldn't have, sorry. I... I couldn't let you fall, could I?' he says.

'Don't worry, of course not.'

And that's all that is said about the incident. They make their way down together, in an embarrassing silence. Before they part, Jake asks if she'd like to go sketching again some time.

'D'you think it's wise?' Zany replies.

'Not wise but nice.' Jake's feeling daring.

'Nice things are rarely wise.'

'We could challenge that,' Jake replies, thinking it's Zany who is wise.

'OK, we can try.' With that, Zany quickly goes off the other way, turning once to wave, just as Jake turns to look at her walking away. Could a wave be sexy just because it reveals a bit more of her arm? He knows it is all he has.

FIVE

What a find! Gianni Travesi: Italian footballer. Jake spends the rest of the afternoon preparing for his first lesson, using football, loosely, as a basis. He downloads images of various Italian football strips, including some English ones – with Wigan amongst them. That way, he will teach the colours. He then finds statistics of football pitches, sizes, numbers of seats and so on, to introduce numbers. Jake chuckles to himself, because his own knowledge of Italian numbers is weak, so he should also come out of this quite well.

Then he sets up a couple of scenes to encourage conversation. He looks through the photos on his phone and transfers images onto the presentation he has set up, for Gianni to describe the scenes in whatever English he knows. The same scenes can be used again later, with additions like adjectives and adverbs. He makes a list of those, that he can drag to the appropriate place on the pictures, to combine reading and speaking. Jake is pleased with himself and everything is downloaded ready for the lesson.

He feels upbeat, not only about this preparation but thinking of Zany – but on that level, he should be feeling downbeat, knowing how dangerous the relationship could be. Taking his mind off it, he texts Trish's mobile, now that she's got an Italian SIM card. 'BUSY THIS EVE? JT.'

Strange, that. Haven't used 'JT' since Trish and I were kids. While he waits for Trish's reply, he skypes his mum and Flo. His mum picks up, looking harassed. That's the downside of Skype, you are seen and heard.

'Hi Mum. You OK?'

'I'm OK, sorry I look a mess, but I never know when you're calling. I'd have brushed my hair, at least,' she says. 'So… what's new?'

'You'd be chuffed. I've prepared my first English lesson.'

'Great, Jake. But look.' She holds up her hands; the palms and fingertips are purple. 'Planning out a mural.'

'D'you enjoy painting more than teaching?'

'Not sure. I loved teaching,' his mum says, 'but it's great to change track.'

'Is it good money?'

'If I'm busy.'

'And does Dad still keep you and Flo?'

'None of your business.'

'It is,' Jake insists. 'I'm an adult, Mum.'

'Well, he makes sure Flo has a roof over her head, and funds her education. It's fine.'

'Aha.'

'Hey, stop checking up on Dad.'

Jake says nothing.

'Oh, Flo's here. I must wash my hands. Ciao.' With that, she leaves the screen.

Jake realises he may never understand how easily his mum has forgiven his dad.

'What was all that?' Flo asks.

'Telling Mum about my teaching. Can we chat another time? Or I'll email you?'

'Mental.' She blows him a kiss as usual and waves Milky's paw.

He closes his iPad, feeling guilty now for quizzing his mum like that. He keeps meaning to say something nice about Dad. He still needs to sort out his head about family shit but his parents' split had to be Dad's fault. Mum was pregnant the year before – what could *she* have done wrong? How his parents could fall out, make it up, then fall out again, he didn't know. That year had its good points, though, like spending a lot of time with Mum – and with Trish, who really was his best friend that year. Yet at twelve, nearly thirteen, the idea of moving to London had seemed a fun prospect. That was beforehand.

A text ping shakes him. Trish says she'll meet him in the downstairs cafeteria – not very private, but he replies, 'C U.'

As Jake strolls into the cafeteria, Trish is waving some papers around to attract his attention. He waves but picks up a snack first, taking a pasta dish with a tomato salad and looking hard at the sad tomatoes, which really should be better, here. He fills a paper cup with water, pays and joins Trish.

The papers she's waving are guides to old buildings and also information about a job in restoration and conservation work, which she's applied for.

'I doubt there's much money in it, but if it's enough for the basics I'll have a such a good time – and I'll have to use Italian.'

'Good,' Jake says. He picks up one of her leaflets. 'That's the church I went into, and it's the one with the cellar.'

'I know – that's what I wanted to tell you. But first, have you met your footballer?'

'Yeah. And I've planned my first lesson on the iPad. Dead chuffed.'

Trish pats him on the back. 'Well done, you.'

'So, tell me? Have you found the remains of Moses, yet?'

She nudges him forcefully. 'Cheeky! But it is fascinating. Really. Don't look so sceptical, you're disgusting. I went to one church that also had cellars – crypts like the one you went to – where they're excavating stuff. Bit like a dig. They know that Jews used to hide down there, or at least, they hid their artefacts.'

'When?'

'1569.'

'Why?'

'Cos that's when they were banned from living near the Papal States.'

'Here we go again,' Jake says.

'What?'

'Whatever we discover, Jews are victims. Why not... oh, I don't know...'

'Heroes?' Trish ventures.

'I suppose. At least, something positive?' Jake sighs.

'It *is* positive,' Trish replies. 'Isn't it positive that they kept up their practices against the odds? That is... *heroic*.'

'It's always about persecution.'

'But it's history – maybe undiscovered history. It's cool.'

'So, what's there?'

'Markings on the wall, a Magen David or two. And you know I showed you Pitigliano?'

'In the brochures?'

'Yeah. Well the old Jewish area there is called Piccola Gerusalemme. Amazing or what?'

Jake tries to draw breath to say something but fails. He knows Trish at her most enthusiastic. Unstoppable.

'And there's even a synagogue. Will you come with me?'

'Don't go to shul any more,' Jake moans. 'I'm totally off all that.'

'We're not going to pray, cuckoo. We might discover something epic.'

'Like what?' Jake asks. No one has called him 'cuckoo' since he was last with Trish – terms of endearment haven't changed.

Just then, Suzanna and crew spot them and rush over, joined a moment later by a couple of Trish's friends whom Jake met the other night. Brief introductions are made as they all drag chairs over to sit in a huddle around them. They grab the pamphlets on the table and peruse them with varying levels of interest. Tom wants to know what they are for.

'It's going to be my job, while I'm here,' Trish replies, collecting the pamphlets up again.

'What is? Are you an archaeologist?'

'No, but Jewish communities were once hidden around here. In the Middle Ages. I'm looking for more –'

'More what, exactly?' Tom asks, genuinely interested.

'Evidence – ancient artefacts, things – not sure exactly what.'

'Are you both *Jewish*, then?' Suzanna asks, looking at Jake and Trish as though they're from outer space.

'She's not, I am,' Jake replies. There's a moment's hush.

'I've always been into Jewish history,' Trish adds.

'She's more interested than me,' Jake says, then tries to change the subject. 'Anyone found a job yet?' There is a universal shaking of heads. 'Cos I have,' he adds.

'Lucky… you,' Suzanna says. Jake wonders if her pause was to avoid saying another word, rhyming with 'you'. Surely not?

'What?' This, from Jeeves.

'Teaching English to… a guy.'

'You look really chuffed. Is there more to it?'

'Yeah, I'm teaching a footballer.'

'A footballer? Wow.'

'Yeah. He's going on temporary transfer to Wigan next season.'

'Bet you're in for free match tickets,' Jeeves says.

'No idea. When I can ask him in good Italian, I might suggest that instead of payment,' Jake replies.

One of Trish's friends moves in closer and, putting her arm round her shoulder, gives her a quick hug as she stretches to pick up one of the brochures. Trish returns the hug as she flicks through it.

'I'm more into culture than football,' says her friend. Showing the brochure around, she goes on. 'Look, there's a little Jewish Museum in Pitigliano. Is there more to find?'

'There may be,' Trish replies. 'Oh, this is Xanthe, by the way, everyone.' They all acknowledge her.

Jake takes the brochure again, looking at it more carefully. He scans over the pages, seeing that there are some interesting relics in Pitigliano – an old Jewish bakery, and an ancient menorah.

'Maybe I will go with you one day, OK?' he says to Trish.

'Me too,' says Xanthe.

'I'm more into meeting this footballer,' comments Jeeves.

'Me *too*!' says Suzanna, winking. 'Is he dishy?'

'I wouldn't know,' Jake replies.

'We'll suss him out for you, won't we, Trish?' Xanthe says, giggling.

Suzanna blushes; no one knows what to say.

'Actually we're good judges of fit guys, aren't we, Trish?' says Xanthe. 'Even if we don't actually fancy them.'

'For now, I've got my "fit guy",' Suzanna says, nuzzling Tom. 'But I'll let you know if things change.' She, Xanthe and Trish smile.

Jake is pleased that comfortable relationships are forming. Gradually, people move off, with hugs and kisses, and he goes to his room to make sure everything is organised for his lesson and to look over his recent sketches.

Jake feels calmer, now he's making friends. As he goes into the sanctuary of his room, Zany re-enters his thoughts. Something like panic hits him, together with passion; he lies on his bed and thinks of her. He gets out of bed and goes through a short group of exercises to use his energy. Bed is exactly the wrong place in which to put her out of his mind, since parts of his body are out of his control.

SIX

Jake's new life really is beginning – he's about to give his first lesson. That *and* a football match the day after. At last, his apprehension is mixed with excitement. He dashes through the lunch routine, waving to Tom, Jeeves and Suzanna across the room, eating his roll as he leaves the hall and taking his coffee with him in a paper cup.

As he approaches the café Gianni recommended, he sees him waving. Jake runs over and they shake hands. Gianni has ordered him a cappuccino with a really fresh roll and croissant. When Jake offers to pay for it, Gianni refuses; Jake pours the contents of his paper cup into a plant holder.

'Per favore,' Gianni says, gesturing to Jake to eat and drink. It's a good start to the hour. The two-way exchange of language works well, although Jake remains in charge of the session. Gianni seems a nice enough guy and honourable, ready to pay Jake in cash, there and then, as they finish. Jake has a notebook for recording lessons and payments, and they agree to extend each lesson to an hour and a quarter, making extra time for speaking Italian.

'A martedì? Prossima settimana?' Gianni asks.

'Yes, next Tuesday,' Jake says, confirming it in his iPhone diary. They shake hands and he sets off, satisfied by giving his first ever lesson – and by earning his first euros in Italy.

He sends a text to Jeeves. 'FOOTIE 2MORROW. MEET AT 1700 HRS?' Jeeves's 'OK' comes back immediately.

All's right with the world. Then he spots Zany.

He feels unreal – his heart does that thing in books – it skips a beat. It's never done that before. But with the beauty of the place, the sunshine and everything else, he is living some kind of a dream. Zany is with another girl; he thinks it's Aisha, whom he met the other day.

'Hey. How goes it?' Zany asks, smiling. Jake sees her dimples and crinkly eyes and melts inside. *OMG, I'm like someone in a Mills & Boon.*

'Brill. Really benissimo!' he replies, and he tells the two girls about his first lesson with Gianni.

'Great,' Zany says and, to her friend, she adds, 'And this guy can draw, too.'

'Really?' Aisha says. 'I'm impressed. Where did you find him?'

Zany, blushing, says nothing but nudges her friend.

'And I wouldn't mind meeting your Italian footballer,' Aisha says. 'Bet he's a dish.'

'Wouldn't know. He's like most footballers, muscly, fit – athletic, y'know – all that. But I'm keeping it professional for now. Later on, I'll find a time to introduce him.'

'OK,' Aisha says.

'Are you off somewhere?' Jake asks.

'Yep. Literature course.'

'Literature? Italian literature? Didn't know about that.'

'It's an option,' Zany replies. 'That and Italian history.'

'Mm,' Jake mutters. 'I'd love to do Italian *art* history.'

'I think you can. Look...' Zany fishes in her bag and gives him a little brochure. 'These are the extra courses. Haven't you seen them?'

'No. Must've been asleep.'

'They're all in a stand in the hostel. Have mine.'

'Thanks,' Jake says, smiling at Zany and taking longer than necessary to let go of the hand which passes him the flyer. He sees that there is indeed an art history option.

*

The next morning, Wednesday, Jake manages to keep his mind off Zany by preparing for his first foray into Italian football. The match starts at 7pm. At least it will be a little cooler then. He is glad they are allowing plenty of time to get there on those lethargic Italian buses.

He can't help but browse online about the hostile football gangs. He needs to find out whether what he has heard is true: whether they are really fascist. Since he's going with Sanjeev, whose skin is markedly darker than his, it will be hard to be invisible. He looks at various websites and the perception of the Stremi depends on who writes the sites. They themselves hate being called fascists, but from his British perspective, Jake thinks they are – displaying the swastika on their banners can't be for nothing.

The government, the powers that be, don't accept accusations of racism made by players like Balotelli. However, he finds an article from a British newspaper about the new man heading up Italian football – and he seems worse than ever. Jake decides not to read any more but to wait and see for himself. *Looks like they're the new Mafiosi...*

He still has part of the day to kill, which unsettles him because he currently kills any spare time by dreaming of Zany. So he decides to take some sketching things – no paints, simply charcoal, to be different and quicker. However, he notices a new email icon.

Breaking the golden rule to neglect emails till he has time for them, he peeps at the sender – Flo. And there's a photo attached, of her with Milky and another girl.

'This is me and Milky with my new best friend, Susan. Skype me when you can, hey, bro?'

Jake emails, 'In about an hour, OK?' and goes out.

He walks up a different alley and peeps round undiscovered corners to see where a new scene might capture his imagination.

He decides to concentrate on buildings and roof tops, although the way in which mediaeval buildings huddle and cuddle each other makes the perspective difficult.

He settles down on a rolled-up sweater at the top of a steep but wide-stepped passage, where old stone washing-troughs sit on each flat area. They are still used, as evidenced by the washing-lines and pegs stretched above them, but he is glad no one is there. He takes out a few pieces of charcoal and his putty rubber and begins.

A text arrives. 'WHERE R U RIGHT NOW? TRYING TO MAKE CONTACT. JEEVES.' Jake isn't exactly sure where he is but tries a brief description of the way he came. He carries on drawing, more in the mood than last time. A few minutes later, two hands appear from behind him and silently cover his eyes. Then one takes his sketch pad to look at his efforts. Jeeves has brought Zany. *I can't escape.*

'Hey – give that back!' Jake says.

'I love this,' she says, 'it really gets the feel of the place.'

'It's great. Really,' Jeeves says, looking over at the sketch. 'I found Zany coming out of a lecture.'

'Cool,' Jake says, now up on his feet, so near to Zany that he can smell her perfume. 'And?' He senses they have a reason for coming, yet how can Jeeves know about his feelings for her?

'And... Zany is worried...' Jeeves begins.

'About what?'

'About us both going to football,' Jeeves replies.

Zany looks embarrassed. 'There's trouble at Italian football matches,' she says.

'I know. We'll be careful,' Jake says.

'But how can you *be careful*?' she asks. 'I mean, Jeeves is...'

'Dark skinned? You can say it, you know,' Jeeves says.

'S'pose so. And you... with your Star of David round your neck. Jake, they're *fascists*.'

She looks really concerned and Jake is touched. He makes to

put his hands on her shoulders to comfort her but stops himself.

'They deny they're fascist,' he says, 'but thanks for mentioning it.'

'Then why're you going?' she asks.

'Yes, why are we?' says Jeeves. 'Cos we like football... I know, I know. But we don't need hassle, do we?'

'We've got the tickets now,' says Jake. 'I'll quiz Gianni about it when I see him next, OK?'

'OK,' Zany says, smiling again, showing her sparkle, which excites Jake as much ever. 'Can I sit and watch you sketch?'

'I'm leaving soon,' Jake says. 'It's already dusk and light fades quickly here.'

Jeeves must have recognised something between Zany and Jake, because he says, 'I'm off now. You OK to get back alone, Zany?'

'I'm fine,' she says.

'I'll see her back,' Jake says, knowingly taking another risk.

'Seeya later, with football battle gear on, OK?' Jeeves says to Jake. They wave him off.

'Where are you going next?' Jakes asks.

'Meeting some girls at their lodgings,' she replies.

'So, I'll walk with you,' he says.

'Y'don't have to,' she says.

'I know. But can I?'

'Sure,' she replies. On the way, they chat comfortably about their favourite artists – they both like the Impressionists – and the books they're reading.

'D'you read on a Kindle? I hate them,' Jake says.

'I prefer book-books, but for this trip I'm using a Kindle,' Zany says. 'So I could bring lots.'

'Who's your favourite author?' Jake asks.

'God, I couldn't say. I've just finished the Booker winner... not sure I'd have voted for it.' They chat so easily, they almost don't notice how late it's getting. Walking together on narrow, crowded pavements – where there are any – they are nearer each other. An awkwardness returns; tension grips them, as their arms might have done in a normal situation. This is not normal. Their hands touch as they walk but neither takes hold of the other. Jake looks at her sideways and, once or twice, he finds her looking at him. They are playing a game in which there are no rules.

Their embarrassment is diverted as they both notice the sky darkening and it starts to rain. Heavily.

'Hey! It's summer, in Italy,' Jake says.

'But it rains in Umbria,' Zany says as she pulls her hijab further round her face.

'That fabric won't keep you dry,' Jake comments, and they laugh.

The rocky downhill path is now wet and slippery. They nudge against each other accidentally and he takes her hand to stop her falling. He can't avoid it. It feels so fragile… and it dawns on him that, perhaps, no other guy has ever held it like this. He strokes her fingers with his thumb, then opens and re-clasps his hand, to intertwine his fingers between hers. She doesn't resist at first, as they walk on quietly, not looking at each other. Eventually she loosens her fingers slowly and takes her hand away.

'That's it.' Zany breaks their silence as she points to a building.

'Oh,' Jake says, thinking she was going to declare something about hand-holding.

'We didn't chat much, did we?' Jake comments.

'Suppose we didn't have to. Next time? Bye.' She moves off.

'Seeya,' Jake says. *Next time? Wonder when that will be.*

'Text me when you're safely back from the match, OK?'

'Will do.' Jake is pleased she cares. Very pleased.

SEVEN

There is just under an hour before Jake goes to plan the football outing with Jeeves, so there's time to call his dad. They have begun to speak more civilly to each other over the past year but Jake can't remember the last time he initiated a conversation – Skype or otherwise – with him. Dad and football just go together, so he contacts him instinctively. He fails to reach him via Skype, so he sends off a quick email.

'Off to my first Italian football match. Going with a guy who's tall enough to protect me from marauding gangs. Will try you after the match or tomorrow morning, OK? Jake.'

At that moment his dad's Skype number rings through. He hopes his dad will understand if he has to rush off.

'Hi, Dad.' *How can I just say 'hi' when I haven't called him for ages?*

'Hey, Jake – good to see you. Tanned already. Seems good out there. What's with this football?' There are no scathing references as to how long it is since they last spoke – *nice one*.

'Looking good y'self. I've got tickets for a local match. I'm going with a mate, Jeeves.'

'You've employed a butler?'

'It's his nickname; he's called Sanjeev.'

'Are you a good combination for an Italian football match, with those racist thugs around?'

'Who knows? Listen, I've started teaching.'

'So tell.'

'I'm teaching a footballer. It's good pay.'

'Proud of you. Any new friends... girls – or boys?' his dad asks.

'Yeah, but look, don't be mad – I've got to dash – can't be late and the buses are so slow. Bit cray to call in such a hurry, soz.'

'Cray?'

'Crazy... new speak, y'know.'

'Oh. No worries, Jake. Text me when you're back safely, OK?'

'Mm. They all say that,' Jake replies.

'Meaning?'

'Oh, nothing. I will, speak soon.'

'Sure, Jake. Good to see you.'

'You too,' Jake says – and means it. It felt natural, chatting to his dad again, and it leaves him feeling good.

He goes to meet Jeeves and spots him across the square. It's dusk already, so much earlier than at home. They dive into a seat at the nearest café.

'Cold drink?' Jeeves says.

'I'll get it,' Jake replies, and does so. Just then, his mobile pings.

'U SAFE & BACK?' It's not from his dad but from Zany. How cute. But ahead of time. *She probably thinks I won't see this till after the match.* He sits down opposite Jeeves.

'Jake, I – I'm sorry, mate, but this is bonkers.'

'What?'

'Going to a football match.'

'God, bit late now,' Jake says.

'But why look for trouble – and in a foreign country?'

'We've got the tickets now.'

'That's not the issue,' Jeeves says. 'It's so risky.'

'Hm. But I do want to see a match somehow.'

'I know – so wait and ask your footballer guy. Then he'd be with us.'

'Mm, I guess.'

'Agreed?'

'OK,' Jake says. 'Shame. Too late to put the tickets on eBay.'

They high five to cement their decision.

'FINE. DIDN'T GO – LONG STORY CU X,' he replies to Zany, hoping the little 'x' is all right. There's also a message from his dad, reminding him to text on his return.

'Sorry Jeeves, anxious Dad, that's all.'

'No worries. My dad hardly knows I'm in Italy, let alone at a football match.'

'Oh. Why? Is something wrong?' Jake asks, wondering whether his own family know too much. He doesn't tell Jeeves that one of the messages was from Zany.

'No. Nothing. It's just the way he is. He reckons I'm a man now and his responsibility is over. He was never a student; he worked from the age of 16, so he expects me to be mature enough to look after myself.'

'Fair enough,' Jake replies, wondering what best to say next. 'Maybe my parents intrude too much. But they *are* genuinely interested in stuff.'

'That's fair enough, too. Dad does care about me – and Mum. It's just their way.'

'Have you ever been a victim of racism?' Jake asks.

'Only veiled hints – but they're bad enough.'

'Yeah, they're fucking disgusting. Let's get back, OK?'

They leave the cafe a bit more solemn than when they set out, but closer friends. They hug each other as they part.

'A presto,' Jake says.

'See you soon,' replies Jeeves.

Back in his room, Jake lies on his bed, arms under his head, his usual thinking position. He wonders how childish Jeeves thinks him for keeping in touch so closely with home. But all families are different, so, as he promised, he skypes his dad.

'Jake, hi. Are you there yet?'

'Well… We got sensible,' Jake replies, being purposely evasive.

'Come on, what d'you mean?'

'We didn't go.'

'What?'

'Jeeves pointed out how mad it was.'

'He wasn't the only one,' his dad smiled.

'We'll go when Gianni can take us. Safer that way. *If* Gianni invites me.'

'OK. So, how're things? Y'know, it's been a while.'

'No worries. We're speaking now.'

His dad looks up and smiles but Jake thinks he's about to cry.

'You OK, Dad?'

'Absolutely. It's just… I've missed you.'

'Same here,' Jake says. He has never imagined saying that. 'I've gotta go soon, though.'

'Course. Made any other friends, apart from Jeeves?'

'A few, yes. Did you hear that Trish is here? Mad coincidence, that one.'

'Mum mentioned it.'

'We still get on well.'

'Good. Send her my best. Look, you go off and enjoy yourself. Just skype when you can, OK?'

'Will do. Cheers.'

After that, Jake doesn't contact anyone else. He feels drained from calling his dad, even though he is glad he did. He is ashamed about his previous behaviour towards him. But that is over.

So, what to do about Zany's message? That's the big one. Was she simply caring or was she trying to say, 'Get in touch'? He decides to leave the ball in her court for a little longer.

He takes out his notes from the Italian class and also tries to translate fully a piece from a football website, checking any new words in his online dictionary. At least he is making some kind of effort.

Then he carries on doing up his room – he's quite pleased with it. He also tries to complete an earlier charcoal drawing of silhouetted cypress trees, drawn in the late afternoon. He rummages in his art bag but can't find any hair lacquer – he usually uses his mum's to seal the charcoal. He smiles to himself, knowing that neither Trish nor Zany would have any to lend him. Maybe he'll ask Suzanna.

EIGHT

As the days in Todi go on, a routine takes shape. Jake teaches Gianni, Gianni teaches him; he sketches, paints and attends a few lectures. He has to pay for some of them, so he only goes once he can afford it. He catches up with either Tom, Suzanna or Jeeves as he nips in and out of the shower, or rushes through the dining room.

He's still not sure whether to contact Zany directly, afraid to appear pushy. Anyway, he expects to bump into her. He looks on the board – there's nothing from her there. Zany obviously doesn't want to be too forward either, but silence is getting them nowhere. He texts her.

'RU OK? WHERE'VE U BEEN? WHEN 2 MEET? :) J X'

That is sure to work.

And she phones him back, instead of texting. It's good to hear her voice. She says she's been doing lots of babysitting work and meant to call, but does want to see him.

'Tell you what,' she says, 'let's go out somewhere? There are some galleries in Perugia I'd love to see.'

'Good idea,' Jake replies. 'You mean the main art gallery?'

'No, two others I fancy. One shows the history of fabric weaving, the other shows stained glass and they restore old stained glass there. They're kind of working museums.'

'Cool. I've got a student ticket,' Jake says. 'Makes it cheaper.'

'Yeah, my parents bought me one when we got here.'

'Right then.' Jake can't believe he is chatting away to Zany so easily, or that they have so much in common.

'Listen to the name of the fabric one: Museo Laboratorio di Tessitura,' she says, rolling her r's emphatically. 'It's not that different from the English – but lovely to say.' She is giggling. 'Maybe Trish will come?'

'Bet she'd love it. Brill idea,' Jake says.

'Tomorrow?' Zany suggests.

'No can do – sorry. Trish and I are going to Pitigliano.'

'Aha. Well, just let me know, OK?'

'Will do. Good to speak.'

'Yeah. A presto, Jake.'

'Ciao.' Jake feels good, speaking to Zany. However, he is beginning to wonder where Trish has disappeared to... when he spots a note on the board from her. *What the fuck? Why not text?*

'Jake! Must meet. Out of reach of Wi-Fi most of day. See you next Wed eve, here?' Our fourth week here, amazing, Jake realises, as he looks at his iPhone calendar. He says 'YES' by text, telling her to come to his place instead. With the little hand-drawn smiley faces on her note, Trish seems to be on the cusp of some exciting discovery. Typical. Years back, in their other life, she was always upbeat and always shook him out of his doldrums. It's no different now – she balances him.

He texts her again about Zany's idea of going together to those museums – it was nice of her to include Trish.

While he waits for Trish on Wednesday, he wonders how he'd have coped if she weren't here in Italy. She runs in, puffed – when is she not?

'Hi, Jakey!'

'Hey, Trish – only Flo calls me that, now.'

'And I don't even know her – must be telepathy.'

'You can meet her on Skype, some time,' Jake says. 'So, what's new? Chè passa, càra?'

'Let's go up,' Trish replies. 'I've got stuff to show you.' They start to go up the spiral stairs and meet Tom, coming down.

'You two?' he smiles. 'Joined at the hip?'

'No more than you and Suzanna,' Jake replies.

'Must see you, Jake.'

'Will do,' Jake replies. 'Been ages.' Whenever they pass each other, they never have time to chat; he must sort it out.

Once in his room, Trish notices the new decor. 'Awesome,' she says, admiring the newly painted boxes – stencilled with abstract shapes – which now hold T-shirts, note pads and art materials. On the wall, stuck with Blu-Tack, there are different-sized cypress trees, cut out of cardboard and painted various shades of green.

'I like,' Trish says, nodding to the walls.

'Ta,' says Jake.

'Takes me back,' Trish says.

'Meaning?' Jake asks.

'Your house, y'know. There was your mum's painting, your dad's writing, being creative, y'know – and that arty uncle.'

'And talking of art, Zany wants to find a date go to some Perugia workshop museums. Come with?' Jake asks.

'D'you want me?'

'Yeah. It was Zany's idea. One's about stained glass and the other's weaving.'

'I'd love it – if we can find a date. But you two go – I must –'

'Tell me... spit it out.'

'This could be a big one, Jake.' Trish always did make her ideas seem exciting. Jake envies the way nothing ever disappoints her. She spreads some pamphlets on the bed and takes out her iPad. She pats the bed, gesturing to him to sit down.

'These are photos I've taken. I'm convinced I've found new evidence of Jews living underground,' she says. 'I mean: underground, literally, and underground, as in secretly,' she adds. 'All thanks to your monk!'

'At Santa Maria?' Jake asks.

'The same. He took me down into the crypt and along a passage with kind of caves to either side. He pointed out etched Hebrew letters on walls, till he came to one particular cave that had a huge boulder against the opening, with an iron ring in it. Don't ask how it was ever fixed there.'

Jake interrupts her. 'Hang on, d'you want another drink? Coke – or coffee?'

'No, really, I'm fine.' Trish continues. 'In that last cave, the monk said there had obviously been an oven. He showed me a hole, with a kind of chimney leading up to the air. Afterwards, outside, he pointed out a grid, over the chimney exit.' She stops speaking for a moment, smiling at Jake.

'Yeah, and...? Why are you smiling?'

'It's you,' Trish replies. 'You look interested.'

'I am,' Jake says. 'So?'

'Oh, nothing.'

'Out with it.'

'I'm talking about Jewish stuff. So I'm surprised.'

'Oh, that. Well, you make it sound exciting,' Jake says.

'It is.'

The monk had shown Trish round the cave and she gathered that this was another of those hidden Jewish baking rooms. 'The ones in Pitigliano are well known,' Trish continues, 'and tourists visit them – but this may be similar. The monk kept saying "azzime", pointing to the ovens.'

'Meaning?'

'Unleavened bread.'

'Matzah?' Jake is interested now.

'There are signs of smoke on the walls and flecks of black dust in the angles. I scraped some into a plastic bag.'

'Why?' Jake asks.

'I think I can find out what it was – or is – with carbon dating.'

Jake sees, then, that it is Trish's enquiring mind that leads her to new experiences.

'What are you thinking?' Trish asks.

'About how you're so interested in everything. Always were.'

'But this is sick,' Trish says.

'Oh God, that word again – I –'

'You're so old-fashioned.'

'OK, OK. So when are we off to Pitigliano?' Jake says.

'Hey?' Trish is bemused.

'When?' Jake smiles.

'You're full of surprises,' Trish replies.

'I can't say no to you when you're excited.'

'Tomorrow afternoon, then?'

'Fine,' Jake says. 'After teaching Gianni... Oh, but I was planning on meeting Tom tomorrow. I'll have to think.'

'Do you want to come for a cold drink now anyway?' Trish asks. 'I'm meeting a friend at a cafe in a bit.' She stands up. 'Hang on, I've just realised, we can't get to Pitigliano and back in an afternoon, it's too far.'

'Oh. Never thought.'

'Let's make enquiries.' They will need Todi's tourist office.

In the meantime, they go to the cafe where Trish has arranged to meet her friend. 'How's your social life, so far?' she asks Jake as they sit down.

'Too soon to say,' he replies. 'Jeeves is a great guy. He's sound, dependable, y'know? Tom's OK – getting to know him better. Suzanna's not my type.'

'And Zany?' Trish can always hit the raw nerve.

'Whatever I think, she's out of bounds.'

'Says who?' Trish loves to probe.

'You know she is. Even more out of bounds than Dad was, for Mum, way back. *Why* does our family get into these messes?'

'Maybe cos you're creative,' Trish replies. 'But it's a generation on.'

'Some things don't change. Let's leave it, OK?'

'Sure. Fine. But what does Zany think?'

'No idea.' Jake wants to end the topic there.

'Ask her,' Trish says, with finality.

The two of them sip their cold limonata, drinking in not only the refreshing citrus flavour but also everything around them. As Jake stands up to go, she gives him a kiss on the cheek, which is accompanied by a wolf-whistle from nearby. One of her friends runs over.

'Trishy, are you deserting us for a *guy*?' For a moment Jake thinks she's said 'goy', the old, derogatory word for non-Jew.

'What? Not *me*, mate...' Jake says, immediately realising that he's misheard.

Trish's friend responds by hugging and kissing her and the two girls walk off, arms round each other, Trish nuzzling her head into her friend's neck. Before they are out of earshot, Trish calls back, 'Come over tomorrow at two to plan the journey, OK? You sort a date with Zany for Perugia and if I'm free I'll come.'

Jake puts up his thumb. He sighs, happy for Trish, slightly anxious for himself. He must get back to Zany, but he's still wary, even though the outing to Perugia was her idea. So he texts her.

'ZANY GR8 IDEA RE MUSEUMS. TRISH BUSY. SAYS WE CHOOSE DATE, SHE'LL COME IF POSS. DAY AFTER 2MORROW?'

Zany says yes. The week is improving. *Amazeballs! YOLO!*

NINE

At their next session, Gianni asks if Jake enjoyed the football match. At first, Jake doesn't tell him the whole truth – it's too complicated to explain in Italian. So he just says, as casually as he can, that they got worried about the Stremi.

Gianni laughs, gesturing with his hands as though to say, 'Oh, don't take any notice of *them*!'

Jake doesn't respond for a moment, then he says, 'È difficile.' He tries to explain. 'Mi'amico – my friend – he's, er,' and points to the brown table.

'A... si, è nero?' Gianni replies.

'Um... not exactly *black*.' And he mumbles through a description of Jeeves as best he can, then tries to say that the gangs are racist.

Gianni says, 'Non sono fascisti. No. Gl'italiani da Toscana sono campanalisti!'

Jake knows he's denying their fascist leanings but fails to understand the second part of the sentence. Gianni is smiling, so is what he said a joke?

'Campanilisti? What? You mean they live in bell towers or something?' Jake says, pointing to the bell tower of the Todi Cathedral. 'Campanile – bell tower. I don't understand "campanalisti".' Jake hopes he can sort this out without any ill feeling.

Gianni perseveres. 'Campanilisti. Ecco.' He draws circles on a blank piece of paper in some kind of map or plan, naming one circle, 'Todi', another one, 'Perugia', another, 'Pitigliano'; and in each circle he draws a rough sketch of a church and its bell tower. Then he draws a few little houses and stick people around each bell tower and within the circle. He draws a larger circle to enclose all the others which he labels, 'Toscana: Tuscany.'

'Man in Perugia no like man in Todi; man in Todi no like man in Pitigliano. Perugia like Perugia; Todi like Todi. Football same.'

Jake reckons that Gianni is telling him how Italians from small towns don't even tolerate people from neighbouring towns, let alone opposing fans.

Jake wonders what that has to do with colour, saying, 'Ma, colore?' Jake points to his skin then Gianni's skin. 'Stremi say colour not good.' This is becoming awkward.

Gianni just shrugs his Italian shoulders, saying, 'Stremi? I no speak. No look. I no like. They "Campanilisti Grandissimi",' and he mimes 'big headed' or self-important, 'comè Mafiosi.'

'Like Mafiosi? Oh,' Jake says, surprised that a local person would class them like this. He knows that Gianni's bell-tower description shows a degree of intolerance and prejudice, even between one lot of townsfolk and another... so they'd never accept people of colour. But this is far too complex for their basic conversation level. He stands up to leave and tells Gianni they'll meet in a week. He can see that Gianni is trying to work out how to say something.

'Football. You come to big match? With me?' he says.

'O, per favore, si,' Jake says, hoping it will be a non-confrontational match. 'Grazie molto.'

'Roma–Lazio. OK? I find tickets? And friend?' Gianni presumably adds this invitation for Jeeves. *Roma–Lazio? OMG!*

'Jeeves? Non so,' Jake says, aware that he's unlikely to come; but maybe someone else will.

'Si. Benissimo.'

'Quando?' Jake takes out his iPhone diary. Gianni points to

a date in a couple of weeks' time. 'Bene. Grazie molto,' Jake says and they shake hands goodbye.

'Ciao.' With that, Gianni takes Jake's shoulders and hugs him. He wonders if he's cemented this relationship too soon – shouldn't he keep it businesslike?

'We – amici – you, me – friends! No?'

'Si,' replies Jake, hoping that, after the football match, they will still remain so. He has no idea how Gianni views real racist gestures, but he may soon find out.

For now, he hopes for the best and sets off to meet Trish. It is a lovely route, with different, beautiful views through any gap, and his iPhone is kept busy catching some of them on camera for a future painting.

He clambers up the rickety stairs outside Trish's building and knocks at her door. There's no answer, though he can smell coffee through the gaps. He leans on the door, it swings open and he falls over.

'Sorry – are you OK?' asks Trish, as Jake uses her little wooden box to help him stand up.

'Fine. How're things?'

'Great – here – I've made you a coffee. It's a long way to Pitigliano.'

'Impressive,' Jake says, nodding to the cafetière on the dressing table.

'It was bulky to bring but worth the hassle,' Trish replies, as she pats a cushion on her little box, for him to sit on.

'Shit, I've got a splinter from that,' he says, trying to lick it out of his palm. 'You'd better watch your clothes.'

'I know, it's very old... but I only wear scruffy denim,' Trish replies.

'Then watch your skin if you wear short shorts,' Jake replies.

'ROFL,' she says. 'Me, in those? Look, we have never looked at this box properly, have we?' She throws the cushions from it onto the bed and together they examine the worn carving on the lid. Jake opens it to look inside; it currently holds Trish's books and pamphlets.

'Useful,' Jake comments.

'But what for, originally?'

'You're the historian,' Jake replies.

'No idea where to start,' Trish says, closing it and replacing the cushions. 'Swig your coffee so we can go and sort out our trip.'

Jake puts his hand in his pocket and shakes around the euros inside it.

'Isn't it a bit late, for today?' he says.

'The tourist office is still open... But you don't really want to go, do you?'

'It's going to a *synagogue*,' he whines.

'Not fair. What's happened to you?'

'You don't want to know,' he says.

'Yes I do. You're getting annoying,' says Trish. 'Are we going or not?'

'OK. I'll tell you stuff on the way.'

'About time.' Trish looks furious, which is rare for her. They make their way through the town to ask about transport to Pitigliano. At the tourist office they find there are two spare seats on an American tour bus, which is going on a day trip to Pitigliano.

'Non é possible *today*. Is long.' The man points to his watch, shaking his head. 'Domani is good.'

'OK, so tomorrow it is, then.' Jake says. They pay for the seats and carry on chatting. In his mind, Jake postpones meeting his friends yet again. And when would he go to Perugia with Zany? He and Trish perch on a wall and chat while Jake starts telling Trish about his family issues.

'Dad's job took us from Manchester to London. Or so I thought.'

'I remember a bit,' Trish says, encouraging him.

'Sounded exciting. But it was really about someone at work – not just the job. The woman heading the team was the main attraction.'

'Oh, grim,' Trish says. 'Are they still together?'

'No. Only lasted a couple of years. I knew it wouldn't last; she was everything Mum was not. Christian, for a start, as in: not Jewish, blonde, willowy, business savvy and determined to pinch Dad from us.'

'What's that to do with going to a synagogue?' Trish asks.

'Dad always used to discuss things openly – about Judaism, how he converted, my Bar Mitzvah, all that – and then he goes and fucks off.'

'Hey Jake. He was a brill dad,' Trish adds. The look in her eyes says, 'And I'd love to have one.'

'Maybe. But, listen. Let's go back, rest up and I can bore you with this on the bus tomorrow, if you want. It'll be a long day.'

'Sure. Come on,' Trish says, as they leave the area of the tourist office. 'Meet here at 6am, yeah?

'OMG, that's early! Ciao,' Jake says. He plans a solitary evening, writing and sketching.

'Seeya,' Trish replies, with a high five – and they go their separate ways.

Jake nearly sleeps through his 5am alarm. He showers quickly, stuffs things into a bag and half-runs, half-walks to the tourist office where they will get the tour bus. He catches up with Trish en route and they board the bus, taking the two back seats, leaving the American tourists sitting together. They try to ignore the strident voice of the tour guide and the inane comments from the Americans.

They carry on yesterday's conversation and as Jake looks out at the gorgeous views from the bus, he recalls the more recent, painful arguments with his dad.

'When the news broke that Dad was leaving, I wouldn't

have any more "open honest discussions". He'd been anything but open and honest. He'd made such a deal about everything Jewish, then he makes out it's OK to give it all up. And all of us.'

'I see what you mean,' Trish says. Jake sees in that look that she's got baggage, too.

He continues. 'So one day, a few years ago now, I threw all my fucking teenage shit at him.'

'And – ?'

'You won't believe what I said.'

'Try me.'

'I said, "You gave me all that crap about Judaism, how important it was for my Bar Mitzvah, then you bugger off with another woman who isn't even Jewish. Nice one! You're a total hypocrite, Dad." I went too far.'

'Mm...' Trish mutters.

'Dad was furious. Incandescent.'

'Were you surprised?'

'No.'

'But he *was* hypocritical,' Trish says.

'Well, I ranted on about him not being around. But he just said, "When you want to talk reasonably, I'll be there."'

'Blimey,' Trish says.

'Worst evening of my life. So I decided to get back at the world. I stopped going to synagogue or Jewish youth clubs and refused to recite Kiddush on Friday nights in place of Dad. You know what else?'

'Shock me,' Trish replies.

'I took off this Magen David and chain, with him watching. My Bar Mitzvah gift from him.'

'And he still speaks to you, after all that?'

'Yep. We chatted yesterday. And I am wearing the chain again.'

'Was it nice, speaking to him again?' Trish asks.

'It was. Really good. I mean, we have spoken, kind of – but

not *chatted*.' He wonders how Trish will take this. But then, the father who left her was not her natural father. Telepathy gets in the way, as always.

'You want to tell me to call *my* dad, as well –' she says.

Jake interrupts her. 'I wouldn't.'

'You'd like to. I know you,' Trish says. 'Honestly, leave it. It's not the same.'

'Course it's not. Thanks for listening,' Jake says.

'No worries.'

As the bus trundles along, Trish is pensive, though at times taken in by the stunning scenery and the little places they pass through. It becomes hilly with steep climbs and ravines. Jake knows that her father is on Trish's mind but she shakes herself out of her reverie and gives him a couple of pamphlets. The long journey gives them the time to sort out exactly why they're going to Pitigliano.

'We're heading straight for what was the Jewish ghetto, then, are we?' Jake asks, now alert to the plan.

'Yeah, we'll have to, to get back to the bus later on,' Trish replies. 'If it takes less time than I think, we can look around the town afterwards. OK?'

'Sure, you're the boss,' Jake says. 'It looks lovely in the brochures. We can always come back again.'

Trish nods. 'Exactly.'

'Oh, look – that's it, perched on a rock, up there,' Jake says, pointing to crowded buildings which seem to be clinging on for dear life to the outcrop which supports them and saves them from the steep ravine to one side.

'It's – it's just stunning,' Trish says, filming it through the window.

The bus eventually reaches the stop and they climb off with relief.

'Feel a bit queasy – ages since I went on a hilly bus ride,' Trish comments.

'Me too. But just look at it! I've got to do at least one tiny sketch here. Fancy a drink?' Jake says.

'Let's just buy a bottle of water and drink it on the way,' Trish says – and they do. She points to the map in the guide book. 'Look. We want Via Zuccarelli. It's... um... Oh, "Sinagoga" is on the tourist signpost, there.'

'I'm your willing servant,' Jake says, gesturing to her to lead the way.

'OK, then. Come on.'

They walk down the narrow cobbled streets of the erstwhile ghetto, so narrow that daylight hardly gets a look in. The guide book says that many Jews fled here when they were evicted from Papal States. Others came here from the more restrictive ghettos of Venice or Rome.

'It says that this was a more "open" ghetto – doesn't look it,' Trish comments.

One turn brings them to the museum sign and, over an old gateway: 'Piccola Gerusalemme.'

Jake gasps. 'Little Jerusalem. I didn't believe you when you told me.'

'I'm so excited, Jake. Ta for coming,' she says, giving him a peck on the cheek.

'Actually, the street is no worse – I mean no narrower – than the others, really. Let's see what there is,' he says, as they go in.

An elderly woman sits behind a dusty counter and greets them. It is the entrance to both the synagogue and a small museum.

'Shalom, Signorina, shalom, Signore.' The mixture of languages takes them pleasantly by surprise.

'Shalom, buongiorno,' they say, almost in unison.

They buy two tickets. Trish takes out her pamphlet and indicates that she wants to see everything: the synagogue, ritual bath, kosher butcher, bakery, wine cellar and so on, which are all preserved.

'Va bene,' says the woman.

Trish points to photos, on the wall behind the woman, of the two-roomed bakery.

'E questo, per favore,' Trish says. 'See the synagogue as well?' She points to the entrance of the synagogue. '1598' is carved ornately over its entrance.

'It says it was rebuilt by the Pitigliano community, not long ago. Oh! It collapsed down the ravine in a landslide, apparently,' Jake reads from the guide book.

'Si, si. La sinagoga.' The woman gestures to herself and the photos, and comes round from behind the counter, indicating that she will show them round.

'Oh no, not a long-winded guide – in Italian,' Jake whispers.

Trish puts her finger to her lips and they follow on down some ancient stairs, into a series of caves.

As they enter the various well-preserved cellars, it's Jake who says, 'Awesome. Oh my God!'

The look of delight on Trish's face speaks for itself. Since everything is clear, with photos and wording around the room, they can understand the woman's description. Trish then asks whether they can see the bakery.

'Pane. Dove?' she asks, as she mimes kneading bread.

The woman beckons them to follow her through some more cavernous passages, passing an ancient kosher wine press, till they come to two adjacent caves. Over a door, carved into the stone, is a menorah, the traditional seven-branch candlestick. Jake gasps at the sight of it. Each cave-room has a hole in the wall where a bread oven used to be.

The woman points. 'Quà – pane, e quà – azzime, Pessah,' she says.

Turning to Jake, Trish says, 'Azzime is unleavened bread, matzah; she's explaining that it's for Pesach, Passover. Jake – what's up?'

'I'm… I'm gobsmacked,' he says, looking around. 'Makes you think.'

'There's lots more to make you think,' Trish says.

'What's that?' He points to a stick, attached loosely to the old table in the middle of the Passover bakery.

The guide mimes using the stick to mix the matzah mixture.

'They obviously made loads at a time,' Jake says.

'Probably for the whole community,' Trish replies.

'Is grandissimo – very beeg,' says the guide, miming the size of the bowl that would have been used. Jake nods.

They wander in and out of each room, and then the woman points to an old wooden lidded box, standing at about knee height. She goes over to it and lifts its lid.

'È una madia,' she says.

'Madia?' asks Trish. 'What is it for?'

The woman says 'pane' – bread – and mimes placing it into the madia. She closes the lid. 'Bene, nella madia,' she says.

'Trish, it's exactly like the box in your room,' Jake says in a shocked whisper.

'I know.'

'Did dough rise in it, or was it to keep bread fresh?' Jake asks Trish.

'No idea… We'll find out somehow.'

It is turning into a detective story. 'Let's go,' Jake says. 'We've still got the synagogue to see – and there's the journey back.'

'I know, but just a sec.' Trish drags him back to the Passover bakery and looks around. 'Madia?' she asks the woman. Seeing the madia in there, she asks whether matzah was stored in it – or whether it was only for traditional bread.

The woman shrugs her shoulders. 'Non lo so.'

'She doesn't know,' Jake says. 'I say that a lot to Gianni, cos there's so much I don't know.'

Trish doesn't want to be amused.

'Smile,' he says, but she doesn't.

'You don't think…?' Trish trails off as they go up a steep staircase to the beautiful, ornate little synagogue. It has all the familiar component parts – the ark with the ten commandments over it in Hebrew.

'I could even feel like praying, in a place like this,' Jake mutters.

'Don't start getting religious on me,' Trish says. 'I know what you mean, though.'

'Where's the ladies' balcony?'

'Up there behind that panel. Look how high up the women were!' she says as they climb the steep stairs to the gallery. 'They would have to be fit to get up here. No equal opps for the less able-bodied then, eh?'

'So, what happened to the Jewish communities from here?' Jake asks.

'Well, they came out of hiding, eventually. They were emancipated and did well. For a couple of centuries or so, everything was fine. Till – you know –'

'Mussolini?'

'Yep. The Nazis.'

'Y'see, more negative stuff.' Jake says. He looks at his watch. 'Hey, we'd better get going.'

'Yeah. But I've got to investigate my madia,' Trish replies.

'D'you think it is one?'

'Non lo so,' Trish replies, with the appropriate shrug of the shoulders. She thanks the guide profusely, saying they will come again. 'Ritorno. Grazie molto,' she says, shaking the woman's hand. Jake does the same.

'Shalom. A presto.' The woman waves them off.

'I think we made her day,' Trish says.

'Best thing I've done in ages,' Jake says, as they buy some fruit and crisps from a stall, to keep themselves going on the bus home. He spots some pastries, wrapped up in cellophane and tied with ribbons. 'I fancy these, too,' he says, buying two.

'Sfratti, Jew biscotti,' the shopkeeper tells him.

'Thanks,' Jake says as he pays.

'Jew biscotti? What was that for?' Trish asks.

'No idea,' Jake replies. 'He didn't say "Jew" in a nasty way, though.'

Since the bus's departure gives them more time than they imagined, they sit on the town walls and Jake does a couple of quick sketches. Trish gets up to go and buy some more nibbles and another drink. It is a beautiful day and they absorb their surroundings feeling very satisfied.

As they climb on board the bus, they are both tired and fall silent, against a background of the tourists' comments, like, 'Wasn't that just the cutest little town?', 'And that synagogue – so neat, wasn't it?' Trish leans her head on Jake's shoulder and is soon asleep. He strokes her cheek as a show of affection and wonders what she would think of that. He looks up the word 'sfratto' in his dictionary app. The translation is 'evicted'. *Hey? What the...?* But just then, he nods off himself and his mobile slips to the floor.

The bus jolts to a halt, waking them both. Trish spots his mobile.

'Ta. I was looking something up. What was it? Oh yes. Sfratti – this pastry – the word means "evicted". Weird or what?'

'Mm... Must look into that,' Trish says, as they make their way off the bus and along to her place. She fixes them both a sandwich and lets out a sigh. She puts the sfratti on a plate. It is a long, filled pastry roll which she cuts into rough slices. 'The ingredients of the filling are nuts, honey, cinnamon and spices,' she reads. 'Tasty.'

'Weird... it tastes like the charoseth that we make for Pesach, sweet and gooey. What's it got to do with eviction?' Jake says, taking another slice.

'I don't know. There was so much to take in today,' she says.

'Yes. Long journey for one day too. Can we go by train next time?'

'Pitigliano has no train station.'

'Aha.'

When they enter her room, Trish goes straight to her little box and, as she takes off the cushions, Jake says, 'I know you want to start on that now but – another time, OK?'

'OK, but I'm *sure* it's a madia.'

'Stop there, Trish. Switch off and relax for the evening.'

'I will. My mates are coming round,' she says. 'That was the issue, y'know.'

'What issue?' Jake asks.

'With my dad. I've contacted him a few times, over the years. Wasn't easy to find him. Anyway, when I told him I'm gay, he shut me out totally. All over again. The idiot,' she says, looking tearful.

'God, poor you,' Jake says and puts his arm round her.

Trish hugs him and cries some more.

'He's the loser,' Jake says.

'It's so good to be with you again,' she says. 'We're still good friends, aren't we?'

'Y'know that,' Jake says. 'Tell me more about your dad another time, OK?'

'You can guess most of it.' They hug before Jake picks up his things and leaves. He contacts Tom on Facebook, tells him he's exhausted and suggests meeting the next day, instead of this evening; it's already 8.30pm. He texts Zany. There's so much to sort out.

TEN

'*Exhausted?*' Tom is waiting by Jake's bedroom door as he arrives back. 'Have a shower and come out. That's an order.'

'I'm... wiped. Honestly. It took two hours each way. I just need...'

'To relax with us,' Tom replies. 'Go on.'

'OK. Ten minutes?'

'Will do. I'll wait downstairs.'

Inside his room, Jake leans against the door and sighs. He knows he'll be thought unsociable if he doesn't go out, and he hopes Jeeves will be around, too, so he can talk football. After a quick shower and a change of clothes, he joins Tom, who leads him towards a new alleyway. Halfway down, he sees flashing coloured lights, and as they draw nearer, he hears voices.

'Jake! Where've you been hiding?' It's Jeeves.

'Not hiding. Busy. Let's catch up?'

'Good one.' Suzanna leans out of the doorway to greet Jake.

'*Three* air kisses?' Jake says. 'Isn't that the French way?'

'It's *my* way,' Suzanna answers, making a gap through the leaning bodies at the door, into what looks like more of a nightclub than a bar. There is good music playing and Jake spots the girl he remembers as Xanthe, in an alcove. He waves to her. *Cute*, he thinks.

He half sits, half leans on a chair taken by Suzanna and Tom, with Jeeves standing against the bar. Tom tells them he's found a job in an agriturismo.

'It's a lovely old house, owned by the same family for generations. There are rooms for paying guests and it's an olive and dairy farm, too. So there's lots of olive oil on tap and great cheeses at lunch time,' he says.

'What d'you do, there? Make beds?' Jake asks.

'Sometimes, yes. No big deal. It's a fair bus ride away, so I only do three, sometimes four days a week. There's extra if I want. Coachloads of tourists come for olive oil and cheese tastings and I help with those.'

'And he brings me cheese and olive samples,' Suzanna adds.

'Yeah. The family is lovely and there are great tips,' Tom says.

'Sounds good,' Jeeves says.

'And, Jake, never mind *making* beds, they've invited me to stay over occasionally, to sample it. With a friend.' Suzanna winks, nudging him.

'And how's your footballer, Jake?' Tom asks.

'Great – and he's very generous. I'm getting into it and my Italian's coming on, too.' He turns to Jeeves. 'You found anything?'

Jeeves tells them that he's working in a shop. 'A small grocery,' he says, smiling, as ever. 'It's my vocabulary job: food, money and numbers learnt on the job – and conversations with customers.'

'Is it stimulating, though?' Suzanna asks.

'It's OK for now. I may look out for something else, later on,' Jeeves says.

'And thanks to Gianni,' Jake says, 'I can now take you to a football match, free and gratis.'

'Big deal. Who'd want to?' Jeeves asks, not smiling now.

'Dunno – but Gianni'd be with us. I can't refuse – I talked to him a bit, about the troublemakers – awkward – wish I could speak better Italian.'

'What's the problem?' Tom asks.

'Gangs of hooligans at Italian football matches,' Jeeves replies.

'And?' Suzanna asks, looking at them blankly.

'Some have swastikas and make fascist salutes and...'

'What?' Tom says. 'Everyone?'

'Course not – some groups.'

'So why go?' Suzanna asks.

'Good question,' Jeeves says.

'I know, I know,' Jake replies. 'But if I refuse the free ticket, I offend my pupil. He pays me well and I like the job.' Just then, he feels his iPhone vibrate in his pocket. He looks at it discreetly and blushes.

'LOOK 4WARD TO TRIP. WHERE R U NOW? Z'

She has read his mind. He texts a quick reply. 'COME 2 GINO'S BAR. I'LL LEAVE IF U WANT OR C U 2 MORROW?'

She replies: 'BIT LATE. PERUGIA B4 ART HISTORY 2 MORROW?'

'GR8. GO TO ART GALLERIES. ART HIST CAN WAIT. TRISH CAN'T COME THO.'

'SOZ BUT GD 2 CU Z XX'

Two kisses... sick!

'You look happy. Good news?' Tom asks.

'Yep,' Jake answers, revealing nothing. He can hardly contain the thrill of hearing from Zany, especially with the vibration of the phone, deep in his pocket. A small table becomes clear and they all squash round it, chatting easily.

'No one's asked about *my* job,' Suzanna says, pretending to be upset.

'Which is...?' Jeeves says.

'Waiting at tables,' she replies.

They all go quiet. Suzanna, a waitress?

'Don't be like that,' she says. 'I'm seriously into cooking and it's a fine-dining restaurant, not a little café. I watch the chefs before my shift and work two lunch times and one evening a week – love it. Most customers are Italian so it's great for language.'

'Su wants to run a posh restaurant one day,' Tom adds. 'And

she's been offered a job at the agriturismo if she wants.'

'Great start,' Jake says.

'Cool,' Tom says.

Jake interrupts. 'Listen, guys, it's been good catching up but I'm off. It's been a long day.'

'Doing?' Jeeves asks.

'Visiting the Jewish ghetto in Pitigliano – and the ancient synagogue,' Jake replies.

'How ancient?'

'Sixteenth century.'

'Where are they now?' Jeeves asks.

'Who?'

'The Jews.'

'Long story – tell you next time,' Jake says.

'Tell me, too,' Suzanna says.

'Will do. Jeeves, we need to sort the Roma football match some time – even though it's a while off,' Jake says, as he get up to leave. 'I'm out most of tomorrow.'

'I won't go,' Jeeves replies. 'I've decided.'

'Gotcha,' Jake says.

'What's tomorrow?' Jeeves asks.

'Ancient textiles,' he replies, as he leaves the club. He starts to walk home when he is tapped on the shoulder.

'Hey. Walking alone?' It is Xanthe.

'Not on purpose,' Jake replies. 'Walk with me.'

She joins him and they make idle chatter. Jake finds her interesting and lovely to look at, with shiny auburn curls that bob about as she moves. Maybe he shouldn't only focus his attention on one girl. As they head off down different streets, he wonders if that's a girl who *is* attainable. He rushes back, as though it were now that Zany and he were going out, not the next morning.

He closes his bedroom door, imagining for one crazy moment that Zany may surprise him by being there. *I'm going mad!* The thrill he feels is almost painful as he imagines her embracing him at the front door, running with him up the stairs to his room, where they would scramble to take off their clothes.

He knows that can never happen, but picturing it excites him so much that he can't go to sleep. It's a long time since he last had sex, but for now, going to bed with her has to stay where it is – in his imagination.

As usual, only his drawing or his computer can take his mind off the impossible. Flo, among others, has texted him: 'DONE ANY BINGE-WATCHING? ROTFL WATCHING INBETWEENERS AGAIN!' He giggles at her text speak. She asks to skype so he answers her: 'UR ADORBS. SKYPE NOW.'

She always manages to lighten both his mood and his thoughts. She is a cute kid and he's pleased that she's surviving life without him and with separate parents. She shows that mixture of childishness and too-mature common sense, typical of a ten-year-old girl who's had difficulties to deal with. He listens to her chatting – about her friends, her games, her kitten and the new dress Dad has bought her. She helps him unwind. After saying goodbye, he puts on his earphones to help him go to sleep.

Someone is knocking on his door. Shocked, he jumps out of bed, slinging his towelling coat on.

'It's me. Sorry to disappoint,' says Tom, 'but there's someone waiting for you downstairs.'

Jake whispers, 'Zany?'

'The very same. Shall I send her up?' He says this with an exaggerated wink. 'Right now, before you get dressed?'

'Yeah, sure… I mean, no, of course not. Can you tell her I'll be a mo?'

'Will do, m'lord,' says Tom, who leaves and runs down the stairs.

Jake would have loved to invite Zany up, there and then,

but first, he has a shower, gets dressed quickly and goes down to meet her in the hostel lobby. After his wild imaginings, he feels embarrassed to see her, as though she might know what has been going through his mind. He is sure she blushed before she saw him looking at her and he feels himself do the same.

'Hi. Long time no see,' she says, casually.

'True.'

'How're things?'

'Fine.' This is not a dynamic conversation.

'Doing any more artwork?' Zany asks.

'I am, yeah, and I'm doing up my room. Have a look?' Jake asks, with no ill intent.

'Love to,' Zany says, which surprises Jake.

He opens the door to his room and after they are inside, he closes it. She goes and opens it, a little. 'Just to be sure,' she says.

'Of what?' Jake asks, though he guesses it's so that they are not perceived to be entirely 'alone'. Rabbis do that, if a woman comes to see them, and this is just the same – all about perceptions and discretion.

'Oh, nothing,' Zany replies. 'I… um… just prefer the door open, that's all.' Jake knows it was unfair of him to quiz her.

'There you are: my new decor,' he says, gesturing to his walls. He leans back against the window ledge, making expansive movements with his arms. 'My domain. Welcome!'

'I love it, Jake. And you've got such a great view. My parents' house is lovely but it nestles in trees and bushes so we don't see much beyond it.' She approaches the window.

Jake holds out both his hands, saying, 'Come here, you.' She takes them and he stands straighter, away from the window ledge, and pulls her hands round his waist. Then he grasps her delicate shoulders and whispers, 'Oh that does feel good.' She tightens her arms round his waist. He strokes her hijab, trying to feel under it – even one wisp of hair would do – then strokes her up and down her back, feeling for the first time how thin she is, beneath the loose clothes.

He guides her head away from his shoulder and kisses her cheek. She reciprocates and in one dramatic gesture he kisses her on the lips, drawing back almost as soon as he does so, saying, 'Oh, I'm sorry. I shouldn't have. I can't help it, I think of you all the time.'

Saying nothing, Zany takes his head and, in turn, kisses him on the lips until he opens his mouth and she hers; they kiss gently but passionately.

He wonders how she knows what to do, if this is uncharted territory, and whether it is her first kiss ever. Of course there are films to watch, Bollywood romances and so forth. He doesn't want this to stop and suddenly remembers that his door is open. Anyone seeing them could get her into serious trouble. She could be in serious trouble already. He kind of shuffles towards the door, his arms still round her, still kissing, till he can kick it closed. He kisses her neck, her nose, her hands and wrists; she wriggles as close as she can, till he feels her knee rubbing against his shorts and her foot (from which she has kicked off her flip-flop) stroking up and down his lower leg. He wonders whether she has ever felt a man's skin before. She's certainly enjoying this one, he thinks.

He breaks away. 'Hey, young lady, this isn't on, y'know. You'll get me into trouble.' He smiles down at her as she looks up with her plaintive dark eyes.

'I won't tell,' she says, smiling. 'I think I've fallen in love with you.'

Another, very loud, knock on the door wakes Jake from this dream.

'Shit,' he says, as he hobbles to the door, where Jeeves is standing, fist at the ready, to knock again.

'I was so sound asleep, sorry.'

'I'll wait downstairs. Wanted to talk football.'

'Good idea, but later. What's the time?'

'Ten o'clock.'

'Jeeves, sorry, I'm hopeless. This afternoon?'

'Sure. Four o'clock – usual café?'

'Yep. Thanks mate,' Jake says.

'Enjoy your chat with Zany,' Jeeves says.

'What? How d'you know?'

'I saw her on my way over.' He winks as he leaves.

God, that dream! Embarrassing or what? Now, Zany's really here, and he's aware of the things he dreamt of. *Hope it won't show...*

He tries to go down the staircase calmly, but nothing can prevent his excitement at seeing her again. He can hardly stop himself from running up and giving her a hug.

Instead, he says, 'Zany – it's been ages. How're things?'

'Good. It's not exactly ages, only about ten days,' she says, looking up and smiling, as usual. Jake notices that at the top of her headscarf the jewels spell out a famous fashion logo. A logo on a hijab? As his eyes rest on the jewels, she fingers them self-consciously.

'Like them?' she asks. 'Dad wasn't keen on this much decoration but Mum bought it for me, so there was no argument.'

'Pretty,' Jake says, wanting to stroke not only those jewels but also her face, and more. 'You look good – you've caught the sun.'

'Is that sarcastic?' Zany asks.

'Sarcastic? Why – what? Oh God, course not. You *are* suntanned – your cheeks are pinkish,' Jake says, looking at them closely.

'It's OK. This rented house is good, there are lots of trees so we can sunbathe in privacy. There's a small pool, too,' Zany says, looking at him as she smiles.

'Lucky you.'

'It belongs to a cousin. And *your* cheeks are pinkish too,' she says, almost touching them with a delicately painted fingernail.

Jake blushes and jokes, '*Now* look how pink they are! Are you allowed to have a job, while you're over here?'

'As long as I'm nearby. So I'm babysitting the children on either side of our house.'

'Oh yes, you did say. And that's cool – the best way to learn a language is through children.'

'It is – not very studenty but I'm lucky. Most of my Muslim girl friends aren't allowed to study abroad. My parents were determined to find a way that wouldn't let me lose face.'

'In whose eyes would you lose face?'

'Oh, you know, the prying eyes of people in our home neighbourhood.'

'Your parents work things out.'

'Dad isn't keen. He thinks it will spoil my marriage chances, but Mum knows that attitude doesn't wash with me. So... enough about me. Can we go sketching?'

'Sure, but not now, I want to go to the art history lecture and I'm meeting Jeeves later.' Jake replies. 'Let's just catch up now and go to the Perugia galleries tomorrow? Sorry to mess you about. Is that OK?'

'S'pose so,' Zany says. Jake is pleased that she looks disappointed. They take a table in the sun at a café they haven't been to before.

'It's cheaper than our usual, isn't it?' Zany observes.

Jake nods and they order a drink between them and one big croissant. When the drink arrives, Jake doesn't pour any into the two glasses provided but puts two straws into the bottle, bending one towards Zany and the other towards himself. Zany studiously avoids looking at this process and cuts the crumbly croissant in half, licking some of the crumbs off her fingers. Jake finds this seductive and wonders if she means it to be.

'I licked my finger *after* I cut the croissant,' she says, as she leans over to hold the straw and suck from it. Jake does the same, so he can almost touch her lips with his – or her hand. He winks at her, unable to resist at least that; she winks back. That sends shock waves of expectation through Jake's body; he finds it strange that an act so devoid of physical contact can excite him like this.

Zany stops drinking first. 'So, tell me about the football, then.'

'Oh, that. Hm. It's got complicated,' Jake replies.

'More than it was already?' she says.

'Mm. Yeah, cos of Gianni. Those gangs are disgusting... overtly racist. But being Jewish doesn't show like dark skin.'

'Never thought about that,' Zany says. 'So how can you prove that someone's being anti-Semitic?'

'Depends who says what to whom. But you know about that kind of thing, don't you?'

'Not sure. I mean, it's pretty obvious I'm a Muslim. But if someone's Jewish, it isn't.'

'But what if you didn't wear a hijab?'

'Hm... I get what you mean – not so obvious, yeah. And I don't have to wear it.'

'It's not compulsory, is it?'

'Some say it is, some say not.' Zany replies.

'All this stuff is quite complex, really. "Anti" language is in the mind of the receiver. Jeeves definitely won't go to footie.'

'So why will you?'

'Gianni's offered me tickets for *the* match. I can't refuse.'

'Cos he'd be offended? What does *he* think about these gangs?'

'With limited English and Italian it wasn't easy to talk about it.' Jake explains.

'So – where did you go with Trish?'

Jake is sure he catches a look of envy in Zany's expression. 'Oh,' he says. 'That was epic. We went to what used to be the ghetto in Pitigliano – saw caves where Jews did their baking, in hiding.'

'Hiding from the Nazis?' Zany asks.

'No. This was in the sixteenth century.'

'The *sixteenth*? Why?'

'Cos the Pope didn't want them nearby.'

'Hey, but...' Zany is clearly baffled by this part of history.

'I'll tell you more while we're sketching, one day. Who told you?'

'About the ghetto? No one.'

'No, I mean who told you I went with Trish?'

'Xanthe. She's a friend of mine.'

'As Trish is friend of *mine*,' Jake replies. 'We've known each other almost all our lives.'

'Mm,' says Zany, looking down.

'Are you jealous?'

Zany simply shrugs. Which says a lot.

'But Trish isn't into boys, anyway.'

'You're kidding.' Zany looks up.

'I wouldn't joke about that,' says Jake.

'Was she gay when you were young?'

'No idea. We were just kids.'

'I don't think I could even mention homosexuality to my parents – well, definitely not to my dad. They think they're modern but they're really not.'

'That's their way.'

'Thing is, my grandparents will be here soon.'

'Swapping places with your parents?' Jake remembers.

'Yes.'

'So... what's your problem with Trish?'

'It's nothing to do with her, really, it's just... Well, you haven't contacted me much, that's all.'

'I didn't want to be pushy. I thought you'd prefer it if we just... kind of bumped into each other.'

'Well, we didn't. And *I* suggested the galleries. What if I hadn't?'

'I dunno… I kind of…'

'*What*? You weren't retiring before, were you?' Zany is now the pushy one. 'What's happened?' she asks.

'You really want to know?' he says.

Zany nods, smiling at him. He thinks she already knows.

'I fancy you.' That does it. His words linger over the table and envelop the girl he fancies like a smoke ring.

She looks down and smiles.

'I shouldn't have said that,' Jake says.

'You should,' Zany says, looking straight at him again. She slides her hand across the table and touches his fingers with the tip of one of hers, stroking them lightly. 'Why look so upset?'

'This will lead nowhere. Well, nowhere but trouble, you know that.'

'I don't know. We don't know anything… nothing's in our hands.'

'Whose, then? 'Jake says, returning her touch, wondering if her delicate hands are somehow controlled by others.

'You know.'

'Fate, d'you mean?'

'Something like that,' she says, as she takes his hands totally in hers.

It is electrifying; he wonders how hands alone can be so sensual and feels he's in his dream. He looks at Zany, whose face now radiates something extra: more vitality, more expression. It does not seem to him that she is leaving everything to fate at all.

'Why are you chuckling?' she asks.

'Only something I remembered,' he replies, lifting her hands, turning them over to stroke the palms, intertwining her fingers between his. Then, in a flash, he brings her hands to his lips and starts kissing her fingers, one by one.

She pulls her hands back sharply. 'What?' she asks, as much to digress as out of curiosity.

'Something my late great-grandmother once said,' Jake replies.

'Which was?'

'She said that life-changing events are rarely of your own making – that most significant things are out of our hands.'

'There you are, then,' Zany says, putting her fingers back on top of his. 'Have I changed your life?'

'Kind of,' he replies.

'Did you know her – this great-grandmother?' Zany asks.

'No, but she wrote an account of her life for us.'

'Brill.'

'It was.'

Whilst he's thrilled that touching alone can excite him so much, he senses the hopelessness of it all. With his elbows on the table, he puts his head in his hands. Zany leans across and again, she uses just one fingertip – to lift up his chin and make him look directly at her. Jake grabs that finger and her hand with it and nestles it against his neck. When he tries to use her hand to pull her nearer, she pulls back, shaking a forefinger at him, meaning, 'Oh no you don't.'

He takes the hint and stiffens, straightening up on his chair.

'Where can this lead, Zany? Only to an emotional quagmire, that's what,' he moans.

'Melodramatic, aren't you – good phrase, though,' she says.

'It isn't. My parents were in this kind of situation. And it *was* a quagmire.'

'Is one of them Muslim?' Zany asks.

'No, Mum's Jewish – but Dad wasn't, when they met.'

'Oh. Is that why they split up? They did, didn't they?'

'They did. But that wasn't the reason – you don't want to know, honestly.'

'I do, honestly.'

'Another time, then,' Jake replies.

'Well… can we go sketching again, after the museums?' Zany asks, happy to change the subject.

'Course, but it's so tricky –'

'What?' Zany is being quizzical on purpose, Jake thinks.

'Being together – you know. I shouldn't even have told you I fancy you. Now teach me how to resist you.'

'Why resist? Let's just see how things go,' Zany says.

'Oh, come on. I'm not used to fancying someone I can't touch properly or kiss, all that. It's tantalising. Meanwhile, I'm meeting Jeeves soon – and I intended to go to art history. Time flies…' Jake gets up to leave.

'When you're having fun,' she says. 'I also meant to go art history. Ah well.'

'OK, I'll get back to you,' Jake says and, as he starts to leave, he deftly leans over and kisses her cheek. He then runs off, shouting, 'Ciao, carissima!'

He hears Zany laughing and knows the feel of her skin will haunt him for hours.

ELEVEN

Jeeves and Jake sit on the rocks that Jake found on his very first exploration of Todi. Jake has his sketching things and it's a peaceful place to chat, but he can't concentrate. He suggests going for a walk together, instead of sitting. He breathes deeply, taking in not only the air but also the intoxicating view.

'What's up?' Jeeves asks.

'Nothing,' Jake lies.

'It's a big nothing that makes you so hang-dog. You're like a lovelorn Romeo.'

'Not a happy comparison,' Jake replies, knowing the fate of Shakespeare's lovers.

'I'm right, aren't I?'

'Partly. Listen, let's sort out the football first, OK?' Jake takes out a bottle of mineral water. 'Want some?'

'No, I'm fine.'

'So. What do I do? I'm teaching an Italian footballer. I need the pay and we get on. Can I refuse to watch his sport?'

'You've got to go, but I can't face it, sorry,' Jeeves says.

'D'you think the gangs are less active in –' Jake begins, but at that moment, a text comes through. 'Scuse a sec, OK?' He turns to look at the message. It's a reply from Trish. 'MEET AT 8PM, MY PLACE?'

'WILL DO,' he texts back.

'So... you can't go alone,' says Jeeves, returning to the football. 'Who else is there?'

'I'll find someone.'

'Can I help?' Jeeves asks, looking worried.

'What? Oh, with the other shit? Not really. I'm meant to be an adult, sorting myself out, all that,' Jake replies.

'If it's what I think it is – forbidden fruit – steer clear, old boy.'

'And if it's too late?' Jake pleads.

'It's only too late when you're married. For now, leave well alone.'

'As a Hindu, haven't you ever dated someone from another background?'

'All the time. There aren't too many of us around, so it's needs must. But, so far, I've never got embroiled. Once, when I was dating a posh English girl, Dad said: "Sanjeev, my boy, you are not in love, you are in lust. They are two entirely different things. Trust me. She is not a girl for the rest of your life."'

'What a thing to say! Was he right?'

'I'll never know. *She* jilted *me* before I could even think. *Her* parents didn't approve. Basically, I wasn't posh enough, never mind C of E,' Jeeves says, chuckling.

Jake looks with envy at this pleasant, easygoing guy, in tune with the world. He'd love some of his attitude to rub off on him. He asks Jeeves to accompany him and Zany to Perugia, but they can't arrange anything positive, because of Jeeves's work schedule.

When they part company, Jake wanders over to Trish's place. The aroma of her home-ground coffee permeates the ancient door-lock like the wafting of Bisto gravy smells in old adverts.

'Come in, sit down. What's up?' she says, behaving like a mother. 'Or what's down, looking at you.'

Jake is certainly feeling confused. If he were simply in love, that would be different. In his situation, nothing is simple, as he explains to Trish.

'It had to be love,' she says in response. 'I've wondered about your attachment to her, for a while.' She puts up quote marks with her fingers at the word 'attachment'.

'A while?' Jake asks. 'We've only been in Todi for "a while",' and he makes his own quote marks.

'Do I see a smile?' Trish says. 'You don't half choose them, JT. What can I do? How can I make it easier? Is it sex you want?'

'No. Well, maybe.'

'Missing it?'

'Dunno. It's been a while.'

'Well, I do know a cute girl with no complications – apart from being Russian Orthodox. Ha. But you'd get over that, what with her father being a zillionaire.'

'Would that help?' Jake asks.

'Money's meant to be an aphrodisiac – not that I'd know.'

'Be serious.'

'I am,' Trish says. 'But you're being *too* serious, that's the problem.'

'I'm the problem? The problem is that Zany is Muslim.'

'Surprise, surprise! You knew the score.'

'So, should I not have talked to her? Did I know I'd fall for her?'

'There's always a chance. But you're not getting married, are you?'

'Course not,' Jake replies.

'So just enjoy yourself – yourselves.'

'That's just it. I can't cope with the restrictions.'

'You knew about *them* from day one.' Trish is sounding irritated. 'Just let it roll.'

'That's more or less what Zany said. Except she said, "It's not in our hands."'

'Jake, it's in *your* hands.'

'It's not, it's in her parents'.'

'Oh. Um, no comment.'

'So, why don't I just break into song?' Jake smiles at last.

'Please don't.' Trish apparently remembers his poor singing voice from their childhood.

'Che sarà, sarà,' Jake sings. 'Whatever will be, will be.'

Trish stands up. 'Can I interrupt this aria to show you another discovery?'

'Not before I tell *you* something,' Jake says. 'Those pastries called "sfratti", meaning "evicted". Well, when the Pope's representatives went around banning Jews from where they lived, they would bang on their doors with a stick...'

'To evict them?' Trish says.

'Got it. Rank, isn't it?'

'So they baked pastries like the sticks? Weird. And they're still made, hundreds of years later.'

'See, it *is* all about persecution, I told you,' Jake says.

At this, she tips his chin with her hand, to make him look up. 'Please?' she says, giving him a peck on his forehead. 'Feeling better now? Come over here.'

Do all girls do that? Tip up my chin with one finger?

She pushes him to the corner of the room, past the bed and a fair amount of clutter, to see the box that they sat on last time he was here.

She pulls it out. 'Help me turn it upside down.'

Jake does so, with Trish steadying it, lest it tips too far.

'Look.' She points to some carving underneath the box.

'Can't make it out,' Jake says, tracing it with his forefinger.

'Well, for starters, it's Hebrew – look. An aleph, a zayin and a mem.'

'You even know Hebrew? You genius.'

'Only the letters, I told you,' Trish says.

'A, Z, and M. So...?' Jake queries.

'Azeem: unleavened bread, matzah, remember?'

'God, yeah – in that Passover kitchen cave.'

'Exactly. I think this box is also a madia for storing matzah.'

'As old as the stuff in Pitigliano?'

Trish nods, grinning. 'Could be.'

'How d'you prove it ?'

Trish is giggling with satisfaction. 'Look inside.' She opens the lid right back and takes hold of a torch, which she shines into it. 'See that? I mean, those?'

'Bits.'

'And that?' She points to some waxy lumps, in which some black bits are stuck. 'There, just where the base joins the side.'

'What is it?'

'Candle wax,' Trish says.

'Candle wax? Oh my God! From Shabbat candles?'

'Maybe,' she replies. 'Or festival candles.' They both squint down into the box at these two tiny clues.

'So, what now?' Jake asks.

'Over to the best archaeology department in Italy – Padua,' Trish says. 'It's too far to go there, so I've emailed them with photos. Not ideal.'

'Won't they have to see it in the flesh, kind of thing?'

'Eventually, yeah, sure.'

'Can they really identify food that's so old?'

'You've asked me that before,' Trish replied.

'Sorry.'

'Answer: probably, cos the crumbs are burnt, so carbon dating should do it. And matzah crumbs are better preserved than bread, cos there's no yeast.'

'Could be epic,' Jake says.

'It could. And that monk you met, here in Todi – he's helped me. He's excited, because he wants more research done on the carvings under his church. He thinks my madia could be connected, somehow. Another monk is helping translate my emails.' Trish is bubbling again.

'So the monk's a good guy,' Jake says.

Trish shows him various printed, translated emails. She has

to take a scraping of the crumbs and the wax, both separate and together.

'D'you know how?' Jake asks.

'No. So between Padua and our friendly neighbourhood monk, they've found someone to do it for me.'

'Brilliant,' Jake says, adding, 'Really.' He hugs her.

'Glad you're with me on this,' Trish says, returning the hug. 'Funny old world, meeting up again.'

'And funny that you've dragged me into Jewish stuff again.'

They sit next to each other, across Trish's bed, leaning their backs against the wall, just as they did as kids. Trish puts two scatter cushions behind them.

Jake sighs. 'Why's life so complicated? Why didn't you and me fall for each other? I mean, was there ever a time... or did you always know boys weren't your thing? D'you mind my asking?'

'Boys just didn't excite me.'

'Did it upset you, feeling different?' Jake asks.

'Not exactly. But I didn't know that girls could turn me on, till that book launch I mentioned. That was the epiphany moment when everything suddenly made sense. That author and her friends are still mates of mine.'

'Have you had any long-term partners?'

'A couple. No one-night stands, though. Not my thing, that,' she says. 'You?'

'Same here,' Jake replies. 'Had a long, passionate fling when I was on a kibbutz holiday. That was – well, fantastic.'

'But that's holidays for you.'

'Yeah, but I take time over relationships.'

'Not this one,' Trish says, nudging him so he almost rolls off the bed.

'This one? Oh, Zany! Mm. True.' Jake says.

'Maybe she's right.'

'In what way?' Jake asks.

'Che sarà, sarà. Whatever will be, will be? I like that,' Trish says.

'I don't. It makes me think that I shouldn't plan anything.'

'Mm… did you plan to drop your Judaism?' Trish asks.

'I didn't exactly drop it, I let it go.'

'Why – when?'

'I told you,' Jake replies. 'When Dad left.'

'Was there more?'

'I was furious that he went off with that woman.'

'Would it have been any better if she'd been Jewish?'

'Dunno. He just shouldn't have left Mum and us.'

'You were cross. Period,' Trish says.

'Sure. Dad was my idol.'

'No one's perfect.'

'I know that now. But listen, I'm teaching Gianni in the morning, so I –'

'Off y'go, then.' Trish gets up and pulls him up, off the bed. 'I'll keep you posted about ancient morsels.'

'And I'll keep you posted about a young one,' Jake says, winking. 'Ciao for now.'

Trish blows a kiss. 'A presto.'

He texts Zany. 'MUSEUMS TOMORROW LUNCH TIME? J X'

And she replies immediately: 'YES! XX'

TWELVE

Wow! Meeting Zany soon.

Jake is meeting her in Perugia later on. He is glad he has a session with Gianni beforehand to keep him busy. The lesson goes well but there is still time to kill, so he finds an Italian class at the university which will fit in nicely.

He arrives a minute or two late but slides a chair into the semi-circle already set up for a conversation session. The same attractive young woman who took the previous lecture he attended is leading this one. Her tight, low-cut top, short shorts and jewelled flip-flops are nothing like his tutors' clothes at home. But this is Italy, in early summer.

The tutor introduces herself: 'Mi chiamo Adriana.' As he plays with her name in his head and looks around, he doesn't realise she is addressing a question at him.

'Come si chiama?' she asks. *Phew, that's easy,* he thinks.

'Jake. Mi chiamo Jake,' he replies confidently.

'Jake. Buongiorno.' This is a doddle. However, then she carries on with a long, unintelligible question. The only thing he knows is that it's a question.

'Jake...?' she says, trying to encourage him to reply. He has to gain time by asking her to repeat the question more slowly. At least he can do that. She is asking him why he was late, to make him describe what he's been doing today. He struggles on, as do the other students. Bit by bit, his ear becomes attuned and, towards the end of the hour, he's understanding more easily.

He is also aware that Adriana is flirting with him, which is more of a challenge than the language. He wonders what the ethics are of befriending a tutor, when she's probably only a couple of years older than him. One thing he does know: his dreadlocks seem to be sexy; he has been considering chopping them off but shelves that idea for now.

By the time she asks him to join her for a coffee after the session, it isn't his own moral code that makes him refuse – rather, the knowledge that it would prove just as complicated as his current entanglement with Zany. He thanks her and declines politely, hoping to himself that he can still come back next week without too much awkwardness.

'Grazie, ciao,' he says to her.

'Ciao, Jake,' she says. 'A presto.' Does he imagine it, or does she wink at him when she says it?

He walks around a bit and finds the stained-glass museum where he's meeting Zany. He's early and sits on a wall to wait, but not for long. When she spots him, she runs towards him, smiling and waving. Jake sees she is as pleased as he is to be going somewhere together. They approach the old but ordinary stone building, climb the steps to the entrance and take a little guide book, then sit outside to look at it in the sunshine. They lean in towards each other, looking at the guide book, and Zany sighs.

'Happy sigh?' Jake asks, automatically putting his arm round her.

'Mainly,' Zany replies. 'It's good to be out – I mean properly out, doing something interesting, on our own, y'know?'

''Tis,' Jake says, gently stroking the hand she has on the guide book. She looks round at him and as usual her eyes, so close to his, make him forget everything around him.

As his mouth moves involuntarily towards hers, she pats his knee firmly, saying, 'Come on, you, we got work to do.'

She lets Jake pull her up; the importance of not holding hands seems to have faded over their time together.

They find that the working museum is just that – a place where stained glass is exhibited and old pieces repaired. It is run by one family who want to show that they're preserving the ancient art. They also show new pieces they have designed and made.

'I love this kind of place,' Zany says, enjoying the personal story told by family members.

'Me too,' Jake says.

'We like the same things, don't we?'

'Lucky us,' Jake says.

'Oh, that is awesome,' Zany says as they are shown a scene depicting two lovers. 'È bellissimo – meraviglioso!' she says to the guide.

'Grazie,' the woman says, before explaining that she made it, with her daughter.

'Wow!' It was commissioned by someone in the US apparently. Jake is pleased that he's understanding so much Italian now.

Zany reads his mind. 'I can understand most of what she's saying. So chuffed,' she says.

'Me too,' Jake says. 'And what a pair of lovers!' he says, blushing.

'They're not like us,' Zany says.

'Well they're nude, for a start,' Jake says.

The place is quite small so they soon complete the tour and emerge back into the sunny street.

'Hey, it's a lovely afternoon, let's give the embroidery one a miss,' he says.

'No way, we're here now,' Zany protests.

Jake is amused to find Zany being more assertive. He quite likes it and thinks she must be feeling more herself with him. So they wend their way through the streets, picking up a bottled water to share, and find the hand-weaving museum.

'It's more like a church,' Jake says, as they go in.

'It was one, once,' Zany says, looking at the guide book and the vaulted ceilings. It proves to be a small display with other rooms where there are working looms. The fabric is like that used in the vast hanging tapestries in old buildings and churches round here.

'Not much to see, really,' Jake observes.

'Worth coming, though, just to say we've been. We can impress the culture vultures.'

That is just what Jake was thinking. *She even thinks like me.*

'You're funny,' he says.

'That wasn't funny,' Zany replies.

'Well, it was exactly what I was thinking. And that was funny.'

'Oh. Ha ha. Come on, let's sit somewhere before we go back.' They see an archway and walk through it into a courtyard. They have no idea what it belongs to but no one stops them. They lean over the far wall together and look at Perugia's roof tops.

'I love the curly tiled roofs,' Zany says.

'And me. Impossible to draw, though,' Jake replies.

'My parents will be pleased I've done a serious trip like this,' Zany says.

'You won't tell them, will you?'

'It's OK, they'll think I went with a class or something,' she replies.

'But you didn't.'

'No. This was better.' She turns, smiling, to face him, wraps his arms round her waist and snuggles her head into his shoulder. 'It's been so cool, Jake.'

'Been? It's not over,' Jake replies. He pulls back slightly and kisses her lightly on her forehead and cheeks, but their lips find each other easily and they kiss, enfolded in each other's arms for minutes.

Zany gently pulls away, giving him a final kiss on his ear as they start off for the bus, hand in hand until they come out of the archway. They fall into their usual silence which drops down on them like a cloak as they know they are about to part. As they get to the bus stop, there's a wave and a shout from amongst the people getting off another bus.

'Jake! Come stà ? Where 'ave you been?'

It is Adriana. *Bloody hell!*

'I Musei Laboratorio di Vetrate e Tessitura,' he says, hoping his Italian will divert her attention from his being with Zany.

'Interessanti?'

'Si,' Jake replies. By this time Adriana has run across the road and is lost in the crowd.

'Ciao,' she shouts. All he can see is her wave.

'Wasn't that one of our tutors?' Zany asks.

'Yeah,' Jake replies as they get on their bus.

'She knew your name.'

'I went to her conversation session just before I came here.'

'Oh, so that's how,' Zany says.

'Must be,' Jake says, hoping he's not blushing, though in the hot crowded bus it wouldn't look too odd. He takes Zany's hand. 'It's been a great afternoon.'

'Agreed. There aren't many guys who like galleries and stuff,' she says, squeezing his hand happily.

'Maybe I'm a bit weird,' Jake says.

'Well, it's the kind of weird I like.'

'We're back already,' Jake says, as the bus arrives at the familiar stop. 'Can you come up?'

'No way.'

'How about sketching tomorrow?'

'Love to. Morning?' Zany replies.

'Prefer afternoon,' Jake says. 'Different light.'

'OK then. Two o'clock?'

'Fine. Meet at the cathedral.'

'Great. See you then. Ciao càro,' Zany says, as she goes off home. Jake watches her but she doesn't turn back.

Back in his room, Jake feels so good and, as usual, he sees that his mum wants to skype, so he does. On the screen she is standing in front of a partly finished mural.

'So, what d'you think?'

Jake likes the way his mum chats without asking a load of personal questions. She isn't as intrusive as his dad, though mums are meant to pry more. However, he is surprised to find that he doesn't mention Zany, without being asked directly.

'Love it, but...'

'Yeah?' his mum asks, moving her mobile camera along the wall.

'That colour scheme... it's not your choice, is it?'

'Course not,' his mum replies.

'How creative is it for you, then, if they're not your colours?' Jake asks.

'Not very, but it's still fun.'

'Cool,' Jake says. 'Y'know I'm in touch with Dad, now?'

'He told me. I'm glad. So's he. And what else is news?'

'The usual.'

'Which is?' *So she is intrusive after all.*

'Some lectures, coffee drinking, teaching – that's going well – some sketching... that kinda thing. Went to two museums today. Really good.'

'All on your own?'

'Course not. But listen. Trish has discovered something amazing in her Jewish treasure hunt.'

'Are you and Trish an item?'

'Mu-um, didn't I tell you she's gay?'

'Did you? Sorry, course you did. Ah well, she'd have made a great daughter-in-law.'

'Don't worry, my dreadlocks attract lotsa girls.'

'It's the charm that does it, Jake, not the hair.'

'Who knows?'

'So... enough interrogation for now,' his mum says.

'Speak soon, love to Flo.'

Jake finds his mum so good at understanding him and, unlike other mothers he's met, she treats him with respect. Even when he decided to give up on all things Jewish, she just ignored it. His dad liked giving him a voice, even when he was young, to teach him to express his views. At the time, Jake felt privileged.

But lying there on his Italian bed, he wonders when and if he will tell his mum about Zany. He mulls over the more recent, painful times, which he's told his friends about. After the Dad trouble, he remembers writing in his diary, 'They were the best of times, they were the worst of times.' *Pretentious git that I was, showing off to my diary*. And Dad has forgiven him. He wonders whether all dads do that. *God, I need to grow up.*

THIRTEEN

Next morning, Jake sees a Facebook message from Tom: 'Long time no see.' So he quickly slips on some shorts, crosses the corridor and knocks on Tom's door. Hello-hugs are now the order of the day; Jake acknowledges how much closer their relationship has become, over these weeks.

'Hey, Tommaso! Come stà?' he asks.

'Benissimo, Jacobo,' Tom replies, laughing. 'How've you been? Where've you been? And with whom?'

'Fine, everywhere, and none of your business,' Jake replies, smiling.

'OK, so get dressed, pronto, then later, you're coming on an outing.'

Jake is intrigued, but he's meant to see Zany again.

'What d'you mean?' he asks.

'At our agriturismo, the boss couple want me to practise my hospitality skills and they've invited Suzanna to help in the kitchen.'

'Nice. What's it to do with me?

Tom looks pleased with himself. 'Get ready and I'll tell you more in ten or so, OK?'

'See you in the PC room,' Jake says. He is working out what to do about his arrangement to go sketching with Zany. Just as he finds a table with spaces at it, Suzanna sweeps in with an entourage of admirers: all girls, in every combination of student garb, from tiny, frayed shorts with a bare midriff and stretch top, to full maxi dresses. Watching his mum and Flo, as she grows up, he can't get his head round the different things women wear in the wrong season. For him, it's enough to wear less in summer and more in winter. He stands up.

'Hi, JT,' says Suzanna. With a flourish, she vaguely introduces him to the girls, who aren't staying and who say 'Ciao' to them both as they leave.

'They were all off somewhere when I bumped into them. You waiting for Tom?' Suzanna asks.

'Yeah. There's an outing or something. There he is.'

'Yo, Tom!'

'Right. It's like this,' Tom says. 'Every so often, the farm-cum-guesthouse has groups of tourists to look round. After it, they have a taster of their produce: olives, figs, avocados, ham from their pigs and cheeses from their cows. They make their own bread and serve wine, too, but they don't actually have vineyards, they're next door.'

'Sounds good,' Jake says.

'It is. Till now, I've been setting it out, waiting on tables, serving the wine and stuff. When Suzanna came over last week and they heard she likes cooking, they offered her a job there too. So now, they want us to practise laying on one of the spreads by ourselves.'

'This is today? I mean, when?'

'They have two sittings. They suggested we invite our friends to the afternoon one, to make up the numbers.'

'Can I let you know?' Jake asks.

'If it's soon. Gotta give them numbers and also, we've got to get over there to start work. What's the problem? Are you teaching today?'

'No, sketching.'

'The farm's an awesome place to sketch, it's beautiful up there. Why not bring your friend Trish? And I've told Jeeves.'

'You're not sketching alone, are you?' Suzanna asks Jake. 'I can tell. Who's the other artist, then? Come on, tell, tell!'

'Zany,' Jake says.

'Aha,' Suzanna says, grinning. 'So you two *are* an item, now, hey? I *thought* there was something going on.'

'I wouldn't say we're an item. We've arranged to meet at two, that's all.'

'So, invite her,' Tom chips in. 'The owners will lay on a minibus if we get enough people together. It takes half an hour to get there.' Tom takes hold of Jake's shoulders and shakes him affectionately. 'Will you come?'

'I'll text Zany now.' Jake goes into the back room of the hostel to send the message. Her reply is instant.

'SOUNDS GR8! NO MEAT OR ALCOHOL, OK? CU XX'

Are those kiss-kisses or the usual ones at the end of a text?

'Hi,' Jeeves says as Jake returns to the dining room. 'Coming on the outing?'

'Yep, plus Zany,' Jake replies. Addressing Tom, he says, 'Er, sorry, but neither of us eats meat.'

'Nor me,' Jeeves adds. 'And only goat's cheese for me, too.'

'OK,' Tom says. 'You'll be a challenge.'

'D'you need any more people?' Jake asks. 'I can ask Trish and her friends.'

'The more the merrier,' says Suzanna. 'But Tom and I have to leave now, to get everything ready, OK? The minibus will be at the door of the hostel at 1pm. It says "Da Maria: Agriturismo e ristorante" on the side. See you later, folks.'

Jake texts Trish and Zany; Trish replies that she'll come, with a friend. He goes back to his room to dress more suitably, thinking that Tom and Suzanna seem to have life sussed here.

This is the day Jake really starts to feel at home. It's been just over four weeks and he knows his group of friends well now. Today's trip is the first touristy outing he has made with them all – things are looking up. And Zany is coming. He grabs some fruit to stave off his hunger, decants more mineral water and, since he's early, sits on a bench and goes over some of his Italian vocab. Jeeves arrives soon after.

'Jake, put that book away. We're going out. Enjoy!'

'Done,' Jake says. He's so at ease with Jeeves. 'Oh, there's Trish.' He waves and she runs over, as do two other girls; they all greet each other warmly.

'Whose idea was this?' Trish asks, to no one in particular.

Jeeves is filling her in on Tom's plan when the minibus arrives. Jake panics as there are only five minutes before they are due to leave and he can't see Zany. She appears from a different alleyway than he expects and pulls one of his dreadlocks.

'Bet you thought I wasn't coming. Sorry, bit late. Trouble with parents.'

'What happened?' Jake asks.

'You don't want to know – to use one of your phrases,' she says. 'Hi Jeeves, long time no see. Hi, Trish. Good to see you.'

Zany has such an easy charm. Trish introduces her to anyone who doesn't know her as they all board the minibus. Even though Jake fully intends to sit next to Zany, he first makes sure Jeeves has company. The seats run across the van, three on one side, two on the other, with a tiny aisle. Jeeves goes along to a window seat, Trish goes in next to him and one of her friends goes next. Jake sits on the other side, next to Zany, without asking. She turns and looks at him, smiling.

But then she leans forward and says to Jeeves, 'Isn't this fun?'

'Yeah,' he replies.

'Trish, how've you been?' asks Zany. 'Jake tells me you're discovering things.'

'I am,' Trish replies.

Finally, Zany turns to Jake. 'Hi. You OK?' She's being so familiar – intimate, somehow. Jake spots nothing in her manner to reveal that she's had a row with anyone. He wonders what the argument was about. Him? The outing?

Still, their hands touch – that cannot be avoided, squashed up as they are. So do their thighs, however covered up they are: he's wearing chinos instead of shorts, as protection against possible farmyard mosquitoes. He knows she is stroking his little finger with hers and he returns that, with an attempt to curl his finger around hers. She doesn't resist... one finger becomes a hand... and so they sit, using their thumbs to stroke each other's hands.

Conversations with each other and their friends carry on around this sensual frisson. 'How's your job?' 'Great – yours?' 'Been to any lectures?' 'A few.' And so on. Jake finds it more and more difficult to concentrate on anything anyone says as he is increasingly sexually aroused – by a thumb stroke. Amazing. He looks at Zany, closer to him than ever. Despite their hands and fingers, her face reveals no passion, except her usual smile.

'Isn't that the most beautiful view?' she says, looking out of the window. She turns slightly towards him and says, 'Y'know, I still don't know that much about you. Haven't you got a sister?'

'Yes, Flo. She's much younger than me.'

'How old?'

'Ten. Growing up fast,' Jake replies. 'I loved having a baby sibling. I was a teenager when she was born.'

'Ah. I'm an only child,' Zany says.

'Oh. My name was her first word. Actually, she said "Akey". I was besotted with her,' Jake explains.

'And now?'

'Things change. S'pose I should've shrugged her off me by now.'

'She'd hate that, wouldn't she?'

Jake is quite at ease with Zany's interrogation. 'Dunno. She's got Dad to stay with and he spoils her rotten,' he replies.

'Bet she still needs you.'

'I think it's the other way round,' Jake admits. 'I've leant on her, really.'

'Is that cos your parents split up? Oh, not that again,' Zany says. 'Sorry.'

'Sitting like this, being "up close and personal" is OK, I reckon,' Jake says, squeezing her hand. She returns the squeeze.

'Just look at the view. Isn't it gorgeous?' Zany says.

'Stunning,' Jake replies. Then, with his mouth as close as he can to her ear, he whispers, 'Like you.'

She leans her head on his shoulder in silent acknowledgement but sits up again almost immediately and whispers, 'You shouldn't, you know.'

'Shouldn't what?'

'You know.' Zany continues the riddle.

'Nor should you,' Jake replies. 'We basically shouldn't be sitting this close, that's what.'

They both laugh and carry on looking at the view until, as everyone on the minibus falls silent, so do they. Before they nod off, they hold hands, properly. Then Zany's head falls naturally onto Jake's shoulder. She relaxes into sleep, her free arm drops across his lap and her nearest ankle wraps around his. He can hardly cope with this physical closeness, but eventually he too dozes off.

'Well, look at these two love birds!' Trish says, as the bus draws to a halt.

As Jake and Zany wake, they quickly pull apart any of their fingers or limbs that are entangled.

'Oh, there already?' Jake says, shocked and embarrassed.

'Yeah, look: "Da Maria, Agriturismo" – there, on the gate post,' Zany says, pointing it out. 'Looks like heaven. Come on, Jake.' She clambers off the bus and as she sees Tom, she says, 'You are lucky, this is idyllic.'

'It is, but we work hard,' Tom replies. He introduces everyone to Maria, owner of the eponymous establishment, her husband Giuseppe and their daughter, another Maria.

'They will give you all a tour of the orchards and vegetable plots first, and then the dairy. OK? Maria, grazie,' Tom says, gesturing to the young Maria to carry on. Maria speaks fairly good English but Jeeves asks her to stick to Italian, to challenge them. She points and gestures where necessary, starting with the olive grove, where the trees have massive bags of sacking tied loosely under them, in which the olives are caught.

'Ecco... per favore!' Maria says, 'These olives not ready.' But she does hand them a wooden bowl. Saying something they don't quite understand, she points to the bowl itself and then to a tree.

'Olive wood,' Zany says. 'Of course.'

After the olive grove, Maria shows them acres of avocado trees, small and leafy; and fig trees, which hold their silvery branches out and up, like a candelabra. Then a citrus grove, stretching into the distance; and off to one side, acres of vegetable fields. Each grove is bounded by cypress trees and Maria demonstrates their importance. She waves her arms and blows, holding her blouse to her, pretending she's in a gale. 'Il vento!' Then she mimes the way the wind stops as it reaches a row of cypress trees. Jake knows what she means.

'Windbreaks, yeah, great.'

'They're your trees, Jake. Take one for your wall,' says Trish, smiling.

'Will we have time to sketch?' Zany asks.

'Can't see it. Let's ask to come back one day, OK?' He can't tell why Zany look so disappointed. 'There'll be plenty of time,' he says, putting his arm round her.

'Never enough, though,' she says, enigmatically. The group follows Maria round the back of the farmhouse and hostelry, where there is a small dairy herd, with some goats in a separate field.

'I don't know much about cows,' says Jeeves, 'but they look pretty fit.'

'You're into cows, then, are you?' Trish jokes.

'I mean *healthy*,' he says.

'Benissimi,' Maria says, pointing proudly to her cows, leading the group round to a barn where the milking takes place and, at the far end, she shows them freshly made dolcelatte and goat's cheese.

'There's a lot going on,' Jake says.

Through a door to another barn they see an olive press at work. Maria explains that it is two hundred years old.

'Wow!' Jake says. He asks her how many people work on the farm.

'La famiglia.'

'Only the family? A lot of work,' he says.

'Si,' says Maria. 'Io, mia madre, mio padre, mio fratello e mia zia.' She starts to translate.

'No, let me,' Zany says. 'You, your mother, father, brother and aunt.'

Maria smiles with pride.

'Big family,' Jake says.

Maria sighs, saying, 'Benissimo,' and gestures to the surroundings. It certainly seems a great place to work.

'Come,' she says, in English. 'We eat and drink a leetel. Please.'

Zany, Jake and the group all follow her to the outside terrace of the house, where another group of tourists is gathering. A long table is set out, covered in a checked cloth, with glasses filled with wild flowers and grasses for decoration.

Tom and Suzanna are standing there, looking good in white tops, black trousers, and neckerchiefs and aprons striped red, green and white. With them is a woman who looks like a taller version of their guide. She smiles warmly and introduces herself as Alessandra, Maria's aunt.

'Tom and Suzanna really look the part,' Jeeves says. 'Hi there,' he says to them.

The pair stay in role: 'Buongiorno,' they reply.

They all sit down and once their drinks are served, whether

wine or locally made grape juice, they are invited to the tables of produce. Olives of all shapes and sizes, some stuffed with cheese, others with home-grown almonds, roll around on plates, with olive oil in jugs (looking like thick lime juice) by the home-baked breads. Bowls piled high with avocados and giant, glossy tomatoes lie amongst them; at the end of the long table are two massive platters. There's a variety of meats, salamis and slices of ham on one, interspersed with pink melon slices; and on the second, an expansive display of cheeses, also with watermelon slices. Other platters contain pieces of home-made apricot tart, accompanied by a labelled jug of their mascarpone cream cheese.

'Meraviglioso!' Trish says. 'It does look marvellous *and* I love that word,' she says, helping herself to the delicacies.

'Me, too,' Zany agrees. 'It's all wonderful.'

Jeeves, Zany and Jake select almost identical food, dictated by three different religions, though Jake enjoys his glass of local wine. He first squashes a dab of cheese onto a chunk of bread. 'Mm,' he says, savouring it for as long as possible.

'Just taste this,' Zany says, dipping the end of a grissini bread-stick into some olive paste and then into Jake's mouth. He grins through his tasting and rapidly nibbles the stick till his mouth reaches Zany's hand.

'Yum,' he says as she provocatively lets him suck her fingers, sticky with cheese, olive oil and other delicious tastes.

'Yum to my fingers or to the food?' she whispers, grinning cheekily.

'Both,' Jake replies.

Then, the older Maria claps her hands, saying, 'Momento, signore e signori, per favore.' Jake's group fall silent.

Giuseppe is ready to make a speech. 'Benvenuto – welcome to this farm. We 'appy to show you. We 'ope you enjoy food from our trees and our cows. Today, we say big "grazie" to friends Tom e Suzanna. Per favore –' He starts to clap, directing his applause towards Tom and Suzanna, who look on in delighted embarrassment, taking a little bow to thank their hosts.

Suzanna thanks the whole family in Italian, sounding like a native. Everyone claps them.

'She sounds really Italian, doesn't she?' Zany says.

'Dunno,' Jake fibs.

'Let's go and look at the food for sale,' Trish says. 'I think there's some fresh pasta and home-made sauces – should do for a few meals.'

Susanna tells them that the produce is almost cost price, as they are students. 'It's worth buying some staples,' she adds.

They crowd round the table. Maria explains that Suzanna made the apricot tart; and that tagliatelli are the best for bolognese sauce, as they hold the meat better than traditional spaghetti.

'Interessante,' Trish says politely, even though she is vegetarian.

Trish and her friends buy lots of pasta and sauces; Zany opts for two pieces of Suzanna's apricot tart; and Jake, a tub of mascarpone to go with it, when they eat it together. At least, he pictures them eating it together.

After the tasting, the students are told they have another forty-five minutes before the minibus leaves, so Zany and Jake take their sketching things and break off from the group.

'I spotted a great view,' Jake says, taking Zany's hand and pulling her round the back of the villa. She struggles to keep hold of her loose top, as well as carrying the things and holding Jake's hand.

'Slow down!' she shouts.

'You said we never have enough time,' Jake says.

She follows him down a path towards the cows and, off to the left, there's a barn. He kicks a couple of rocks over to the barn wall and, laying his sweatshirt on one, says, 'Herewith, your throne, your majesty,' inviting Zany to sit down with her back against the barn. He joins her and sighs.

'Every view is more beautiful than the last,' she says. 'Look there. The patchwork of the crops, the terracotta villages and cypresses in between.'

'Nature's colours,' Jake says. He sees a tear on Zany's cheek and wonders if he is imagining it, till he sees another.

He turns to face her and gently wipes her tears. 'Happy tears or sad ones?' he asks.

'Whichever they are, I can't see to draw through them,' Zany says, avoiding Jake's question and quickly taking out a sketch pad and pastels.

'My mum often cries when she sees something that takes her breath away, or when she hears particular music. It's cool to be moved,' Jake says, as he starts his drawing. Since Zany is left-handed and Jake right, they sit close; Jake puts his left arm round her as he draws and she leans into it, doing more sighing than drawing.

He puts down his pencil, twists round a little and takes her chin in his hand. He turns her face towards him and kisses her lowered eyelids.

'I'll kiss your tears away,' he says, tasting the salt.

'If you do that, I'll cry even more,' she says, so Jake simply brushes her tears away with his finger, enjoying the feeling of her skin.

He is so carried away by this intimacy, he wants to push Zany's hijab back, but changes his mind. However, a tiny wisp of gossamer hair escapes from it, which he twists round his fingers and puts in his mouth. He senses that she is aroused by these erotic touches, which he imagines she has never experienced before. He pulls her towards him and, as their lips touch, his mouth opens – but then she really starts to sob.

'Jake, what'll happen?' She stiffens and shifts herself away from him. 'My dad quizzed me over and over again before I came out today. He guessed there was at least one person I wanted to see – that it wasn't just about fields and farms. And that it was a boy.' She wipes her tears with the side of her scarf.

'Hang on, you're the one who says it's not in our hands. "Whatever will be, will be," remember?' Jake says.

Zany is quiet for a moment, then she says, 'But I think Dad will take it into *his* hands and then I *do* know what will be.'

At that moment they hear someone shouting, 'Come on everyone, the minibus is leaving!'

'You see, there's never enough time,' Zany says, trying to stand up again. Jake helps her.

Back on the minibus, everyone gradually settles into afternoon quietude. He and Zany get closer together again, Jake sliding a hand behind her back and rubbing two fingers up and down, feeling the warmth of her body through the very fine fabric.

'Feeling better?' he asks her gently, taking her hand.

'For now,' she replies.

They all nod off during the last part of the journey, some helped by the wine they've drunk, and wake as the minibus judders to a halt. They hug goodbye – all except Jake and Zany.

'Speak tomorrow, OK?' Jake says, as she makes off in the opposite direction.

She only nods, waving, with her back to him. He is filled with dread

He goes back to his room and tries to make the best of the evening by working on the pastel drawing he began at the farm. Smudging it with his fingers is relaxing, till he remembers the apricot tart.

He leaves the drawing to one side and sets out a lonely little plate of tart, plopping a big blob of mascarpone on top. Dreamily, he makes patterns in it with his plastic spoon and sprinkles on some cocoa. Somehow, making it look fancy helps him feel less alone. He can only hope that Zany is eating hers at the same time.

FOURTEEN

As the lesson next day is winding down, Gianni orders coffee for them both and places some tickets on the table. Tickets to a football match.

'Roma–Lazio.' Jake reads the teams on the tickets. 'Wow,' he says, trying to appear thrilled with such a gift, but inside he is petrified.

'Like Manchester United! You see best football in Italy.'

And the worst teams for hooliganism – the gangs control everything except the actual football. What can he say?

'Benissimo, non?' Gianni says. 'Good football for my good friend.' He takes hold of Jake's hand in both of his, gripping it delightedly.

'Grazie molto,' Jake says. He picks up the tickets to look at the date, though he knows he will be free. Few dates are set in stone for him, here in Todi. What excuse can he find?

'You 'appy? No look 'appy,' Gianni says.

'I am happy,' Jake lies, 'but I don't know who to bring.'

'Bring? What "bring"?' Gianni asks. 'Amico?'

Jake shrugs his shoulders pointedly.

Gianni pouts, pretends to cry and says, 'Ah. Jake 'ave no friend?' stroking his arm in sympathy for a friendless young man. They both laugh.

'I have friends,' Jake says, 'but they don't all like football.'

'Roma–Lazio? Magnifico – everybody want to come!'

Jake tells him he will text his friends to ask and does so,

writing first to Jeeves, then to Tom. Jeeves refuses point blank; Tom says no because he's working at the farm that day. Finally, he thinks of Trish. Pleased with the idea, he texts her.

He waits for a reply. 'Let's speak some more English for five minutes,' Jake says, pointing to his watch. He focuses on telling the time and, within the five minutes, Trish replies with a cautious 'YES IF YOU'RE SURE.'

'It's from my friend Trish. She says she'll come.'

'*She?* A girl like football?' Gianni is clearly bemused and a little amused, too.

'In England, girls like football.'

'She want to see Roma?' asks Gianni.

'See the sights? There won't be time, will there? Will we be going by train?'

'Ah no. I take you. Please. My car big and fast,' Gianni says. 'We leave at nine in the morning. Is good. We have time. But we must stay one night. Is too much cars.'

'Traffic,' Jake corrects.

'Si. Too much traffic… And next day, maybe you see Roma.'

'Thank you so much, Gianni. That's very kind. But I must go now. See you next week, OK?'

'Si – but you must speak Italian,' Gianni says.

Jake goes back to the hostel to meet Tom, with a spring in his step. Then he realises what he's done: said yes to the ultimate Stremi-controlled football match in the whole of Italy. *I must be mad.* He sends a text to Trish saying he'll call her later.

Tom and Suzanna are already at the door of the hostel when he reaches it, as arranged, and Jake guides them along an alley to a tiny, packed trattoria with checked cloths, bentwood chairs and a rotund *padrone* who greets them with a massive handshake. Over a delicious minestrone 'made by my wife', as the owner explains, they try to catch up.

'What's going on with Trish's stuff?' asks Tom. 'Y'know, her research?'

'Oh, you mean the sixteenth- and seventeenth-century bit?' says Jake. 'Well, the popes didn't want Jews living near them, so they were sent to live in ghettos in various little places.'

'Did *everyone* hate Jews, then?' Suzanna asks. 'Oh my God! Sorry, that's sooo rude.'

'It's OK. Not *everyone*. Anyway, some of the Jews of that time were settled in Pitigliano, where we went, and they were well protected by the local Orsini Count. They survived there for centuries.'

'But what about anti-Semitism?'

'It's always come and gone in waves.'

'Disgusting,' Tom replies.

'I'm not focussing on that. We're discovering so much and it's all fascinating.

'Aha,' Suzanna says, frowning in an effort to grasp the concept.

'Trish is brilliant at researching things,' Jake laughs.

Then he sees a woman waving as she approaches their table, so the subject is dropped. It's Adriana, the lecturer. He stands up and gives the statutory kisses, admitting to himself that it's pleasant to feel her silky hair against his cheek and to touch female flesh, even if it is only her upper arms.

He introduces her around and pulls up a chair for her. She sits seductively, crossing her bare legs, which are tanned and glossy. Her skirt is hardly bigger than a belt and her tight, floral T-shirt has thin straps which reveal the ones from her bra. 'Odd fashion, that,' Jake thinks, while watching her bracelets twinkle as she hitches up a slipped strap. 'Bit like the guys who let the tops of their underpants show.'

What with Zany's mode of dress and even Trish's, he has missed being able to observe the female form for the last few weeks. But what, he wonders, is Adriana's interest in him? Is it ethical? And why should he care?

She confidently introduces herself to the others – Suzanna

has been to one of her sessions but Tom hasn't seen her before. Tom and Jake pull faces at each other, as though to say, 'Should we be socialising with her but isn't she gorgeous?'

'Parliamo Italiano?' Suzanna asks.

'No, we are not in class now, but if you want,' Adriana replies, in perfect English, with a flashing smile.

'Preferably not,' Jake says.

'But your Italian is good,' she says.

He replies by blushing and wishes he didn't do that so easily.

Between them, they establish that Adriana is not a permanent member of university staff but a final-year language student herself, brought in for these short-term courses. In Jake's mind that confirms that socialising with her is probably OK.

She is easy to talk to and when Tom and Suzanna take their leave, Jake and Adriana are left deep in conversation, until eventually they air-kiss goodbye.

A text from Zany, soon after, asks who the girl is. Jake doesn't know what she means, so he tries to find her. When she texts him her whereabouts he sets off running, using his iPhone as a satnav. He runs down the alley, trying to find her, but despite her description, he fails. He keeps asking her again but each time he follows the directions, he ends up running out of breath and patience.

'STOP PLAYING GAMES!' he texts.

Then he hears female giggles behind him and she is there, with Xanthe and another girl. Jake thinks they're being childish.

'Hi there,' he says. 'What's up?'

Despite the giggles, Zany looks upset and a bit embarrassed.

'Did you have good company in that cosy little café?' she asks.

'That's really provocative! I was with Adriana, the language tutor from the uni. Tom and Suzanna were there too.'

'Not when I saw you, they weren't.'

Jake is angry. Zany is making him feel like a criminal, in

front of her friends. Then Xanthe suggests that they leave Jake and Zany to 'have a little chat', as she delicately puts it.

'See you guys around,' she says, dragging her other friend away from the warring pair.

'Come on, Zany,' says Jake, 'let's just stroll round the block. I can't afford another coffee stop and I haven't much time.'

'Sure.' Zany is less strident, now that her friends have gone.

Silence follows. Jake breaks it. 'What's your problem?'

'You know,' she replies.

'I don't, to be honest.' Jake says. 'I was with Adriana. I'd also been with Tom and Suzanna, but they'd left by the time you spied on me. That's it. End of. Why should I have to explain all this?'

'But you were kissing,' Zany says.

'We said goodbye! That's not kissing. It's what people do, it's a greeting. No passion, no lips.'

Zany blushes. 'Hm. Maybe I over-reacted. Sorry.'

'Maybe you're a bit jealous.'

'Well, I – er – maybe.' She starts to cry. 'It's so difficult.'

'Come on, sit down.' He pats the space next to him and she sits down and rests her head on his shoulder.

'There's more to this than seeing me with Adriana, isn't there?' he asks. Her tears land on the hairs of his arm. 'Look, they're like dew drops,' he says, licking them off. 'Salty ones.'

'I'm so mixed up,' Zany says. 'I hate seeing you with other girls but I know you aren't mine – or can't be.'

'What about leaving it in God's hands, all that?' Jake says, wiping her tearful cheeks with his finger. 'That's what we were doing.'

'Fair enough.'

'But you can't expect me not to talk to other girls, surely?'

'Suppose not. But it's –'

'Oh, your parents?' Jake sees that he's right. 'What's happening?'

'My grandparents are coming soon, for the changeover. Remember?'

'Yeah, they swap houses with your parents.'

'Yeah. So it always gets tense when they're coming, cos they're even less modern than my dad. Mum tries to keep the peace.'

'Families. I can picture how it was for my mum when she fell for my dad, now.'

'What do we do?' asks Zany.

'I don't know. What will be, will be, remember? Che sarà, sarà, in fluent Italian.'

'You do make me smile,' Zany says. 'And the rest.'

'Good. I will be in touch.'

'You won't leave it to chance, then?'

'Probably not,' Jake says.

'Promise?'

'OK,' he says as he helps her up, recalling how he feels with his arm round her slender waist. He gently rubs his hand up and down her ribs through diaphanous fabric, before letting her go. She loosely touches his hands as she leaves.

FIFTEEN

Someone has been trying to skype him. Zany? Already? Jake responds on his iPad but he sees two faces he doesn't recognise. A handsome gentleman with a shock of thick grey hair, possibly of Indian or Pakistani origin, and a woman whose beautiful, slender face is framed by a silky hijab with a few jewels on it. She smiles tentatively; the man does not.

The man says, 'Hello Jake. Let me introduce myself. I am Munir Chaudry, Zainab's father.'

Zany's parents! What the fuck?

'Hello. What a funny way to meet,' Jake says. As ever, he hates Skype for allowing people to see and be seen, especially as he is blushing. He self-consciously runs his fingers through his hair, of which he knows they probably disapprove.

Mr Chaudry answers. 'Yes, it is. That is why we want to invite you here, to meet you properly. It is Zainab's birthday so we are making a small tea for her. Will you come?'

Jake has no idea whether Zany is part of this. 'Well,' he stammers, 'I – er – that's very kind of you. I –'

'Very good,' says Zany's mum. 'A week on Sunday?'

'Is that her actual birthday?'

'No, but it's a good day. The children she babysits will be able to come with their parents, you see.'

'Well, thanks. Is it a surprise party?'

'Not really, but we wanted to invite you ourselves. This is our first time on Skype.' In Mr Chaudry's smile, Jake sees Zany's.

'It's fantastic for keeping in touch,' Jake says.

'Yes, we are going to try to teach our parents to use it as well,' Mrs Chaudry says.

'Good idea,' Jake says. 'What time do you want me?'

'Say, three o'clock? Our daughter will tell you how to get here,' Mr Chaudry says.

'We look forward to it,' says Zany's mum. Jake now sees exactly where Zany's good looks come from – they are a very attractive couple.

'Me too,' Jake says, not at all sure he does.

Zany's dad closes the conversation: 'Well, until then, goodbye, Jake.'

'Bye. And thanks.'

His wife simply smiles, with lowered lids. Jake switches off and begins shaking. *What's this invitation for?*

He skypes his mum but she doesn't answer. Then, he skypes his dad – so *he* will have to be the first to know.

'Jake, a lovely surprise. You look worried though. What's up?'

'I don't know. I must be mad to call you,' he says, feeling idiotic. Guys like Jeeves just get on with their lives.

'I'll tell *you* if you are,' his dad says. 'Cheers! I've just poured a whisky.' He lifts a glass and sips from it. 'Sorry I can't share it, you look like you need some.'

'Never got a taste for the stuff,' Jake replies.

'So, go on.'

'Well… I think I take after you,' Jake says.

'The good looks, you mean?' his dad says, grinning and stroking back his greying hair in a pose.

'Ha. Not that. Choice of women.'

'Is this a conundrum? Meaning what?'

'I mean, unsuitable.'

'Your mum wasn't unsuitable, she was and is a fantastic person. Recent choice wasn't too good, though.'

'Mm.'

'Out with it, Jake.'

'She's Muslim.'

'Ah. That kind of unsuitable. What's she called? Is she beautiful?' Jake's dad looks quite unfazed by Jake's revelation. His dad used to be in theatre and still has the skills.

'Zainab – Zany. Yes, she's beautiful – well, at least, her face, hands and feet are,' Jake says. 'I haven't even seen her hair, it's covered. I've seen a couple of wisps of it.'

'Like Uncle David's wife, Hannah? Hers is, too.'

'True. But that's different.'

'Well, why?' His dad is playing devil's advocate; he always has.

'You know very well why. Cos David's wife is Jewish.'

'So, I was just establishing that –'

'Dad, you aren't making this easy. You know that me and Zany is *far* more complicated.'

'No more complicated than me and your mum,' his dad says. 'I'd never met a Jewish person – let alone a girl – before her, y'know.'

'That's why I called,' Jake says. 'For help.'

'What's to say? Mum and me were brilliant when we were hanging out together, just we two. But once her parents got involved…'

'Grandpa Jo and Grandma Malkah? *They* gave you stress? Really?'

'Stress? That doesn't get near it.'

'Can't imagine them being difficult, you know,' Jake says.

'Glad you weren't there!'

'Ha, thanks for that, Dad.'

'I'm telling the truth. So, do you and Zany get on?'

'Brilliantly. I've never got on so well with a girl. Apart from Trish – and that's different.'

'It all depends.'

'On what?' Jake asks.

'Whether it's a holiday romance or a potential marriage,' Dad says.

'Marriage? No way – we're students.'

'Is that how her parents see it? A Muslim girl is fairly protected, judging from the families we know. Like "good Jewish girls" used to be.' His dad uses his fingers as quote marks.

'It's because of her parents that I'm calling. They skyped me to invite me round next week.'

'Oh.'

'For Zany's birthday, they said.'

'Nice.'

'They "want to get to know me". D'you think they mean that?' Jake asks.

'No idea. Let me think, OK? God, this is history repeating itself.' Jake's dad leans back in his chair and takes another taste of whisky, drumming the fingers of his other hand on his desk.

'That's making me nervous,' Jake replies.

'So don't look. Trouble is, Skype demands immediate answers. Not like good old letter writing; that gave you time to think.'

'Well?' Jake asks.

'There's over a week before then but I think you should go.'

'Why wouldn't I?'

'You might feel you're being thrown to the lions.'

'Mm. They were very polite.'

'I'm sure they were – and will be. But they can't approve of their daughter having a relationship with a boy. Any kind of boy.'

'I know.'

'Jake, let the dust settle, think about it.'

'That's the trouble. All I do is think. Mainly at night!'

'Ah, so you *are* like me, then,' his dad says, before they sign off. 'I'll get your mum to call you, too. If I have any other thoughts, I'll email, OK?'

'Don't bother Mum for now, all right?'

'Sure. Bye.'

'Ciao. Ta, Dad.'

That's how it has always been between Jake and his father; they throw ideas back and forth. Even now, his parents are there for him and don't tell him to sort himself out. Yet he seems to be hurtling over the same precipice as his dad. *Why do we make the same mistakes?* Despite their different religions, though, their marriage was not such a mistake – they were a great match and good parents. He has no intention of marrying Zainab, so it might well be interesting to meet her mum and dad.

He texts Zany asking her to skype him, but doesn't say anything about her parents. He doesn't want to freak her out if she didn't already know. Just then, inconveniently, his mum's face appears in the Skype icon.

'Can I call you tomorrow, OK?' he says, keen to free up the app. 'Seeya!'

'Sure, love, seeya,' his mum says, blowing him a kiss.

There is no reply from Zany. Then Trish calls, just as Jake is thinking that an outing will help clear his head; he spends too much time inside his head of late. She wants to take him to meet the monks who are helping her. *Good timing.* Walking in this beautiful place should do it and he hopes to find new vistas to sketch.

'So what's up?' he asks her.

'They've found out more, apparently,' Trish replies. 'The monk who speaks English called me. But it will be much easier if we go and see them, talk in person.'

'Sure. No worries.' He arranges a spot to meet Trish, who seems to know where she's going. For once, he has the time.

He takes the same uphill path he took in that first week here, which seems so long ago. He can't believe that such a short period has affected him so much. Maybe, he thinks, life would have changed even if he were at home. He doubts it. He turns left at what he takes to be the brow of the hill, and Trish is there, waiting on a wall.

They join up and find yet another uphill climb ahead of them. He can't understand that – he thought he was familiar with Todi. At the peak, they come to a long, church-like building.

'Wow! This is a hidden find.'

'I know,' Trish says, looking chuffed.

It is church-like only in its stonework – otherwise it's more like an old hospital or boarding school. It has rows of small windows set symmetrically in the wall, both on the ground floor and one storey above. Parts of the building are ruined, so Jake imagines it is unoccupied.

The entrance to the building is an archway, as you might see in a church or even in an old college, so he is hardly surprised to see a grassed quadrangle through the archway. He is more surprised to see monks wandering round it, in quiet contemplation. Trish half hides herself at the entrance to the building – which he now assumes is a monastery – and takes a quick photo with her phone, for her records. Jake takes one himself, to help him sketch it later. They sit on the outside wall looking in for a few moments.

'I often try to imagine how monks spend their lives to any degree of satisfaction,' Jake says.

Then one of them waves. Jake looks round for the monk for whom the wave is meant but hears, 'Giorno, Trizia. Come stà?' He recognises the monk from that first day's exploration, in Todi's cathedral. The monk breaks off from walking round the quadrangle, carefully avoiding the grass, and approaches Trish and Jake through the arch. He shakes their hands, and as he asks how they are, Jake tries to make up for his diffidence that first day.

'Bene. Benissimo, grazie,' he says. 'È bello.' He gestures to the elegant building and surroundings.

'Ah, parla Italiano?'

'A little,' Jake says.

'You spik good, now. I spik leetle English. And you, Trizia? You spik, now?'

'A bit,' Trish replies.

'Come, I show you,' he says.

They follow the monk round the quadrangle and through another door opposite.

'It's beautiful,' Trish says, gasping at the vaulted ceilings and mosaic-tiled floors. Jake thinks he recognises some famous paintings on the walls, mainly of the nativity or the Pietà, and resolves to swot up on the New Testament.

'How old is this monastery?' he asks, forgetting to speak Italian. The monk is striding too fast ahead and doesn't hear the question. He soon stops and opens a door, beckoning them inside.

The room is a library and reminds him of the library at Chetham's Music School in Manchester, which is also from the sixteenth century with a churchy look to it. The monk tries to hurry Jake and Trish along the glass display cases. Why the rush? Maybe it is nearly time for prayers, or their early midday meal. Jake knows that monks have rigid meal and prayer times, so he hurries too, but Trish is walking slowly, looking up at the ceiling and round the walls.

'Ecco,' says the monk, pointing through a glass case. 'Torah, no?' And sure enough, it is a parchment fragment with faded lettering that looks like Hebrew. The description below says it's part of the book of Jonah and shows how the fragment could be fitted into a portion of a Torah scroll. 'Interessante, no?'

'Si. Meraviglioso,' Jake says, using everyone's favourite word.

'And this one. Look 'ere,' the monk says, pulling Jake by the arm and ushering Trish to come nearer. He unlocks a cupboard with a key that dangles with others on his rope belt. There, not yet properly displayed, are photos – taken from above – of Trish's madia, open and showing the crumbs and the drop of wax. The monk grins excitedly. He beckons to another monk, who speaks fluent English.

'Trizia, you wonderful girl!' says the second man. He explains that while Trish's madia is probably from the sixteenth or seventeenth century, the crumbs may actually be more recent. Another mystery, then?

Trish is literally open-mouthed but silent – how rare – at this revelation. Jake is excited too and puts his arm round Trish, saying, 'You *are* a wonder. That little box is a real treasure trove. Trish, the new Wonder Girl.'

The English-speaking monk describes the monastery, which they no longer live in, apparently. He then tells them that Todi Castle, about fifteen kilometres away, was once their monastery but it is now simply a tourist site. So they had to move all their precious artefacts into this building. It once housed the leading priests and bishops of the area, who took in orphans too. Jake nods, acknowledging why there are rows of windows – they were once for the bedrooms.

For now, the part of the building which is in good order serves as a library, storage for all their precious things and a venue for conferences of all kinds.

'What a lovely place for a conference,' Jake comments. 'So where do you – the monks – live, if it's not here?'

'In a house near the cathedral. There are only six of us left in Todi. The others you saw were here for a meeting. But now, my friend Fra Pietro here wants to tell you more about the things Trizia found.'

Pietro has been nodding and smiling as his friend talks, obviously getting the gist of what he is saying.

'Come,' he says and takes them into a smaller room where they can sit down. He brings some freshly made lemonade with slices of lemon and sprigs of mint.

'Meravigliosa,' Trish says as she takes a sip.

Fra Pietro laughs. 'Tutto è meraviglioso,' he says. They all laugh at their paucity of Italian vocabulary.

'So,' Trish says, 'you said you had new information about

the madia and the matzah.'

Pietro has letters from Padua's department of archaeology addressed to himself and Trish. Looking over her shoulder as she reads, Jake sees that the professor in Padua is excited by her find.

'La madia is four 'undred year old. Very, very old. Si. Old like me,' the monk says, laughing and doubling himself over like a much older man. 'But azzime – matzah – no so old.'

'Oh.' Trish is almost speechless but manages to ask, 'But why are the crumbs not as old as the box?'

'We find out soon. And you come visit me at Todi Cattedrale, per favore?'

'Of course we will,' Jake says.

'Thank you so, so much,' Trish says as they make to leave. 'I'm so excited.'

'We are also,' say Pietro, who hands Trish photocopies of all the documents for her to study later.

'I must ask you more thing, per favore,' Pietro says. 'Giornale – the newspaper, 'ere in Todi, want you.'

'Want me?' Trish says. 'Why?'

'They interested in the story. Is importante for Todi. And for us – and you.'

'Va bene. OK, Thanks.'

Trish and Jake leave the monastery. Once they are out of the building, Jake mumbles, 'More publicity? "Jewish boy discovers relics with local monks?" Good one. All I need.'

'Shut up. Who says it'll have anything about you?' Trish says. 'But… I would like you to come with me for the interview.'

'Maybe,' Jake replies.

So Trish's enthusiasm has paid off. Jake envies her determination; she looks the happiest he's ever seen her. They find their way back down the hill and go to her room.

'You are so clever, Trish, well done you!' he says.

'That was just the most amazing day of my life,' Trish says, as she flops down on a floor cushion.

'And the building was beautiful,' says Jake. 'So, let's look at the stuff they gave you.'

Trish pours some of her wonderful coffee and together they look at a copy of the letter the monk showed them, parts of which his colleague has translated into English.

'Look at this,' says Trish. 'They think that because the crumbs were burnt – like the edges of matzah often are – they could carbon date them. They would have got very burnt in those old charcoal ovens.'

'Wot, no thermostats?' They laugh. 'So the dating has nothing to do with the candle wax, then?' Jake asks.

'Not the dating, no – but the wax kept the crumbs in situ, in the madia.'

'Right. So they said that the crumbs and the wax aren't as old as the box. How come?'

'Not sure yet, like the monk said. That's the remaining mystery. It's been sent to some expert somewhere,' Trish says. 'But can you believe it? Students renting this room have been dumping their stuff in that box, sitting on it, God only knows what else.'

'And all the time it was priceless.'

'With a story. A Jewish one,' she says, with tears in her eyes.

'Are you OK?' Jake asks.

'Sure. But it's so moving – another link in the Jewish chain.'

'I still don't know why that part excites you.'

'Jakey, where's your soul?' Trish nudges him. 'You will come with me for the interview? It'll probably be at the cathedral.'

'I'll come with you, sure,' Jake replies. 'But no way I'm part of the interview.'

'You are so,' Trish says. 'You were with me in Pitigliano.'

'Come off it – I'm a hanger-on,' Jake insists.

'Well, will you keep hanging on till after the interview? Please?'

'I can see the headlines: "British girl and Jewish friend find Jewish artefacts, blah blah."'

'Oh, Jake, stop it. I told you, it's not about you.'

'Mm.'

'Get the chip off your shoulder,' Trish says.

'Well, it'll be like public exposure.'

'Jake – you're not that kind of lad.'

'What?

'Exposing yourself!' Trish giggles, rolling around on the bed, just like she did when they were kids.

'Grim joke!'

'Sorry,' she says, laughing.

'I do love Trish like this,' Jake thinks. 'She's so attractive. If only...'

'Penny for them?' she says.

'You're so fanciable.'

'That's what Xanthe says.'

So Xanthe is a lesbian too? All the best girls... But he moves on. '*I've* got some news,' he says.

'Good, for once?' Trish asks.

'Not really.'

She sits up and tries to look serious. 'Out with it.'

'Zany's getting jealous when I'm with other girls. And – her parents have invited me round.'

'Oh. Good and bad.'

'Mm. Good that she's jealous, *if* our relationship could go anywhere. But bad with her parents chafing at the bit.'

'Isn't it good they've invited you round?' Trish says.

'They say it's for her birthday, but there must be an agenda. Not hidden, either.'

'Which is?'

'They say they like to meet all Zany's friends but the other bit is: as long as they're not Jewish boys.'

'No, they're against *boys*, period. Any kind. Come to that, a Jewish one may be better than some.'

'Still,' Jake says, 'her grandparents will be over soon. I bet that's affected the timing.'

'Aha. Cos they'll be less broad-minded.'

'I'll have to bite the bullet. Whatever will be...'

'... Is out of your hands,' Trish adds. 'So let's plan the press interview, OK?'

'OK. Something exciting. But can it wait till after the football match?'

'I'll call them and text you the date and time.'

'Fine. I usually teach Gianni on Tuesdays though. Oh, that reminds me, I need to talk to you about the football match. Gianni's offered us a lift there. I'm sorry to drag you along but I can't get out of it. And I've never been to Rome.'

'Me neither. I've hardly been anywhere. Wow!' Trish says.

'Don't know if we'll manage to see much of the city.'

'Well, I'm not being "dragged" there, anyway. I like footie,' Trish replies.

'Didn't know you watched,' Jake says.

'Watch? I play in a women's team at uni.'

'God, Trish. There's nothing you don't do. Are you good?'

'Don't laugh. I'm the reserve goalie.'

Jake laughs. 'Oh, sorry, but, well, y'know...'

'I know. Me diving for balls in the mud. But back to Rome. We'll have to stay the night, won't we? You can't drive anywhere after an evening football match.'

'Right, yeah, that's what Gianni said. Rome will be chaotic. I'll text you all the travel details.' He gets up to leave.

'Hope Xanthe doesn't mind my being away overnight.'

'Or Zany.'

'Why would she? D'you sleep with her?'

'Course not.'

'You prude,' Trish laughs.

'Hey, I just meant she'll miss me,' Jake says, blushing. 'Ciao.'

SIXTEEN

'How things have changed,' Jake thinks. At one time, he followed the others around. But these days, when he goes to meet Tom, Suzanna and Jeeves, he can use his local knowledge to take *them* somewhere special. And it's his choice today.

As they approach Jake's chosen trattoria, with red, green and white awnings outside, Suzanna says, 'Cool, this.'

'Just wait,' Jake says, leading them inside.

'Not indoors, on a day like this, surely?'

'Follow me,' he says, as he takes them through the café and up a narrow staircase at the far end. It leads to a terrace, with one of Jake's favourite views in the whole of Todi.

'Meraviglioso!' Tom says, taking a deep breath as he leans over the railings. 'How did you find this?'

'Came with Gianni, after a lesson.'

'Epic,' Jeeves says. They order cold drinks and some amaretti.

'To die for,' Suzanna says as she bites into one of the soft, pink macaroons. 'Do the green ones taste any different?' she says, taking one. 'No – but still divine.' The four of them empty the platter quickly.

'So tell me: you're still determined to go to the big Roma–Lazio football match?' Jeeves asks.

'Yep,' Jake replies.

'I just don't get it.' Jeeves is bemused.

'Because Gianni's taking us. He knows Rome *and* the stadium.'

'Is it true Trish is going with you?' Tom asks.

'Yep. That too – she plays footie, y'know.'

'It's crazy to take her,' Jeeves says. 'Even if she plays. And not cos she's a girl, but cos she looks *alternative* – and that's not derogatory – you know she does. She'll draw more attention than *I* would.'

'He's right, y'know,' Tom adds. Suzanna nods her head, emphatically.

'So?' Jake is despairing. 'I can't get out of it. I couldn't tell Gianni I'm turning down tickets to a Roma–Lazio match.'

'Then I'm coming, too,' Tom says. 'A tall, white Anglo male. That'll redress the balance. If there's a ticket.'

'But you don't like football,' Jake says.

'So? I think you need me. I'll swap my shifts at work.'

'Fantastic!' Jake is touched. There's more to Tom than he knew. 'What a mate, thanks. I'll check everything with Gianni tomorrow and I'll text you.'

'OK,' Tom says.

'Take care of him,' Suzanna says, putting her arm round Tom.

The group catch up with each other's activities, starting with Jeeves's promotion to manager at the shop for the next two months, while someone is on holiday.

'Your Italian must be fluent, then,' Suzanna says.

'It's coming on,' Jeeves says, with his usual humility.

Jake is completely at ease with them all at last and truly feels part of a group of good friends. Trish will keep him busy, his time in Italy is looking up, and he knows he can win over Zany's parents. But he wonders whether to cut his hair before meeting them. As they get up to leave, the man-hug between Jake and Tom has special significance.

It has been a while since Jake has been to any of the extra lectures and he is just in time, if he runs for the bus, to get to an art history one. He needs it because, although he knows his art, his upbringing has made him familiar with only the Old Testament, not the New, and this has left him lacking background. It's hard for him to understand much of European art, based as it is on

New Testament events. That is his noble reason for going to this lecture. He is also aware, of course, that Zany may be there. He hasn't seen or heard from her since her parents asked him round.

He dashes to the lecture hall and, since he's late, tries to slide unnoticed into a front seat.

'Buongiorno!' the lecturer says, with a wry grin, as he passes the attendance sheet over for Jake to sign. *Hardly a discreet entrance, then.* Jake returns the greeting and attempts to look his most attentive. Works of art are shown on the screen in what proves to be an excellent PowerPoint presentation, unlike some other lectures he's been to. It also touches exactly on the gaps in his knowledge.

Just as he begins to concentrate, he feels a poke in his back. He ignores it but it happens again. Turning round slowly, not wanting the lecturer to notice, he sees Zany, two rows back, holding a ruler. He winks, she smiles, unable to speak till the lecture is over.

He can't wait to leave but first he says 'Grazie molto' to the presenter, who nods his approval and says 'Ciao'.

Jake leaves, following Zany.

'We must talk,' he says, as he catches up with her.

'About what?' Zany asks.

'You know, the invitation.'

Zany stops walking. 'They asked you? Oh God, they meant it, then.'

'They skyped.'

'I wish I'd never taught them to use it,' she says.

Jake wonders aloud how her parents could have invited him without Zany's knowing.

'They told me they would and I begged them not to,' she replies. 'I give up, I really do.'

'But it's for your birthday – it's nice of them.' Jake says. 'They *look* nice, too. It'll be fine.' Jake is reassuring her because he needs to reassure himself.

They wave down the bus and hop on. 'Let's go somewhere

for half an hour,' he says, 'somewhere quiet. Not a café.'

'There's nowhere where we won't bump into anyone, you know that,' Zany says, already with tears in her eyes.

As they reach their stop, Jake says, 'I know somewhere. Come on. I won't hold your hand, in case anyone does see us on the way.'

They trek uphill in silence, until they reach the monastery. He leads Zany across the quadrangle, through the arch on the opposite side and into the corridor towards the library. On his previous visit with Trish, he noticed a beautiful garden beyond it. He tries a door leading off the corridor and – just his luck – it opens directly onto the garden.

Zany gasps. 'Oh, isn't it amazing? How do you find such lovely places?'

They walk through rose arches and pass walls covered with bougainvillea. Oleander bushes line the path and they go through a brick arch at one side, which reveals a sloping lawn where clumps of blue and white agapanthus lilies seem to grow wild. Jake knows how hard his mum tries to grow those at home; they definitely thrive in the Mediterranean. Jake takes Zany's hand, pointing out a big gazebo – like a little house – overlooking a pond.

'Come on,' he says. 'It's a folly.'

'And it's a folly to go into it,' Zany says, smiling at last.

'So you've heard of follies, too?' Jake asks. 'I've sketched lots of them in stately homes and parks. My uncle loved them. I suppose an architect would, wouldn't he?'

'Weird coincidence, that. I've got an architect uncle, too,' Zany tells him, lightening up for a moment.

They go into the structure and sit on the stone seat, looking out at the pond. Within seconds, their arms are round each other and they hug as they have never done before. As he pulls her tightly towards him, Jake is aware of the shape of her breasts against his chest, despite the layers of soft material which mask them. He strokes the fabric that enfolds her, the better to feel her shape, and crumples up some of the folds in his hands.

She sighs, wriggling against him enticingly, and whispers, 'We mustn't, Jake, we...' Suddenly, she takes his face in both her hands and kisses him on the lips, with a passion he never knew she had. Jake wraps himself even further round her and rubs his right hand up and down her thigh, trying to gather up the material that covers it. However, he stops short of touching the flesh he reveals. Their tongues enter each other's mouths and, as Zany tilts her head back, her hijab slides off.

Jake knows they have crossed a line – not only because of the hijab but everything else. It is he who pulls the scarf back up over her shiny black hair, which he has seen for the very first time. *At least I'm showing a sense of propriety over that.*

'You're beautiful, with it or without it.'

'Thanks,' Zany whispers. 'But Dad was right.'

'About what?'

'He says that forbidden fruit tastes sweetest and, once you have the first taste, you can't stop. And it's true. I want more and more of you, Jake.'

'The feeling's mutual. But we can't. So that's that.'

'You're so understanding.'

'We've no choice. At least till after the visit,' Jake says.

'I don't know whether there'll be an *after*,' Zany says.

'Hey? That's crazy. They may really like me.'

'They may well like you, but...' Zany trails off, looking out at the pond. 'Anyway, you still haven't told me about your own family. All that hassle. You keep saying you will.'

'Oh that,' Jake says.

'We can't keep on about me all the time.'

'What should I tell you?'

'About your dad leaving, your sister, all that.'

'Well, when Dad left, he thought we'd all be chums – that me and Flo could accept his woman as some kind of mother-substitute – but he lived in a dream world.'

'Were they happy? Him and his woman?'

'Not for long. I knew Catherine wasn't interested in me or Flo, except to curry favour with Dad. Flo went along with it, for the outpourings of presents, but they didn't come with outpourings of love.'

'God, Jake, you sound like a poet, the way you speak sometimes,' Zany says. 'What about your mum in all this? Poor her.'

'Course, poor her. She was too tied up sorting out a new home base – with a toddler and me – to even breathe, let alone think,' Jake says.

'Not nice.'

'No. But we're OK now. And I think Mum knew it was coming.'

'The breakup, you mean?'

'Yep. Hey, we'd best make a move.'

They walk back hand in hand till they reach the arch in the walled garden, after which their hands drop to their sides as they carry on in silence. The word 'breakup' swirls round Jake's thoughts, its meaning playing tricks in his mind.

'We'd better start back now,' he says. 'I've a lot to sort out for this football match. Gianni's planning the journey but I've got to know what it'll cost and stuff.' They start off down the hill together.

'Mm. You're a bit mad to go, y'know,' Zany says.

'I do know. Another folly. But Gianni will look after us. So I may not see you till the visit, OK?'

'Oh.' Zany's disappointed.

'Well, I'll try.' As they reach a place they recognise and start to move off in different directions, he strokes her cheek gently with the back of his forefinger. Zany takes it and puts it to her lips.

'You're lovely,' he whispers.

'And you're crazy. Bye,' Zany says, wrinkling her nose as she smiles. The next time they meet will probably be at her parents' house.

SEVENTEEN

Gianni has got hold of another match ticket for Tom and suggests going on a prebooked football coach, as there are now too many of them to fit comfortably in his car. Jake doesn't fancy being on a coach full of Italian football fans but really, it's not up to him. They are meant to have another lesson but there is hardly time; organising the trip to Rome and the match take precedence. He checks that both Trish and Tom can afford the price of one night in a small hotel, then he arranges with Gianni to book the rooms.

"Ow many room? One for you and Trish; one, me and Tom?' Gianni asks, more confident in English now.

'Oh no,' Jake says. 'One room for Trish, another for Tom and me together.'

'Trish non è *amica*?' Gianni winks, unable to make out Jake's relationship with her.

'Si, mi'amica, ma... not my girlfriend... non innamorata,' Jake says, struggling to differentiate between the types of 'girlfriend'.

'OK. Two rooms. One for boys, one for Trish.'

Jake is surprised that Gianni would share a room with them but realises he isn't one of the highly paid footballers with money to burn. Everything is sorted; they will meet at 9am on Thursday, returning the next day.

'I come to 'ostel,' says Gianni.

When Trish and Tom hear they are going by coach, they

are relieved; they all know that to drive into a capital city – renowned for impossible traffic – for a football match was crazy.

'It's going to be an expensive day out,' Tom adds. 'I'm going to work extra days at Maria's for the next two or three weeks.'

Thursday dawns. Jake texts 'CIAO CARA XXXX' to Zany. She doesn't reply straight away, which worries him. But the excitement and anxiety he feels for the trip take over, as he, Tom and Trish climb aboard the coach. Gianni is already sitting on the wide back seat and pats the spaces either side of him.

Suzanna and Xanthe climb aboard to hug and kiss their respective partners goodbye. They take a delight in meeting the famous Gianni; he enjoys the fuss which, as a player for a minor team, is a novelty. He laughs as they ask for his autograph.

'Gianni Travesi? I not famoso!' he protests, but he signs their notepads anyway. Before Xanthe and Suzanna get off the coach, Tom takes photos of everyone with Gianni, as well as a selfie, which he sends to friends. Jake takes a couple, too, and sends them to his parents, Flo and Zany. The girls wave frantically from the pavement as the coach revs up; then they are off.

On the way, Trish tells him that the monks are paying her to help with the restoration under Todi Cathedral. 'And with their library collection, too.'

'Where does their money come from to pay you?' Jake asks.

'No idea. Church benefactors or something, I suppose.'

The coach stops at a couple of small towns on the way, where more Italian football supporters get on. The Perugia fans recognise Gianni; however, not everyone does. Jake, Tom and Trish all practise their Italian with those sitting near them, who are intrigued by a trio of British youths en route to Rome. None appears to be part of a gang; however, the coachload becomes more rowdy after the beers they have brought along and, gradually, he and his friends keep more and more to themselves. Gianni joins in with some of the banter, which helps prevent them from being isolated. It's hard to find a balance between drawing attention to themselves and appearing unsociable; they know they are lucky to be with Gianni.

Arriving at the coach park on the outskirts of the city, Jake is excited. This is his first time in Rome, but it's a shame that there's apprehension as well. Gianni knows the way to the hotel, which he chose as it is walking distance from the coach park and the stadium. However, it is a long way from the sights of Rome.

'Can't wait to do a tour,' Tom says. 'It's pleasant out here, but doesn't feel quite like I imagined Rome.'

'Is no Roma. Roma centro over there,' Gianni says, pointing vaguely somewhere. 'We look tomorrow. Three hours to see, then go back on different autobus,' he explains.

'Good plan. Tutto benissimo. Grazie molto,' Trish says.

'We at 'otel,' Gianni gestures, crossing the road to a small hotel.

'Albergo Olimpico – now there's an original name,' Jake says. He begins to worry that, if it is a hotel built for the stadium, it may attract other, unfriendly fans; but on approaching the smiling reception staff, he relaxes a little.

'Gianni Travesi! Benvenuto a nostro piccolo albergo,' the receptionist says and, turning to Jake and friends, 'Welcome to this leetle 'otel. Very 'appy to see you.' They are shown the cosy bar with a breakfast room alongside it.

Jake, Tom and Gianni take a room card each and Trish takes hers.

'And we 'ave good vee fee.'

'Vee fee?' Tom says, frowning. '*Vee fee?*'

Gianni takes out his mobile and points to the internet icon.

'Oh,' Tom says, 'Wi-Fi! Sorry, stupid of me.'

Gianni laughs. 'We go eat something, yes? Before the match?'

'Great,' Jake says. 'Meet in the lobby in ten minutes?

'Sure,' Trish says, following him, 'but I want to see your room first.'

Jake still cannot believe that Gianni is happy sharing a room with two virtual strangers, but finds the room has plenty of space for three beds, with a sink in the bedroom and en suite shower room. 'Benissimo,' he says. Looking through the window of this fourth-floor room, he says, 'Hey, that must be the stadium.'

'Yeah,' Tom says, following Jake's gaze.

'Was it built for the Olympics, Gianni? Is it new?'

'New and old,' he replies. 'Lot of build, build. New in 1990.'

'My guide book it says it was once called Foro Mussolini,' Trish says.

'No Mussolini now! Is gone long time,' he says, protesting somewhat.

'Of course,' Trish reassures him. She leaves to go to her room on the floor below. 'See you guys.'

'Shall I come with you?' Tom says.

'Don't be daft. I'll manage. But don't keep me awake later – I'm right underneath you.'

The guys all wash quickly. 'Va bene. Andiamo.' Tom says.

'Yes, we go,' Gianni replies.

'Actually, "Let's go" is better, Gianni,' Jake says.

'You no my teacher today,' Gianni protests, putting his arm round Jake's shoulders. 'But... *Let's go!*' He winks as he says this.

'Sorry,' Jake says. 'No teaching.' They leave their overnight things on their beds, taking with them only the basic essentials and putting valuables in the safe, which their room cards can open.

Once in the lobby, where Trish is already waiting, they all log on to the 'Vee Fee' to send quick 'Arrived safely' messages: Jake to his parents and Zany, Tom to Suzanna. Trish is wearing a loose, sleeveless T-shirt over her cut-off shorts, the ones with fraying hems and home-made tears in the legs. Her T-shirt, like the ones they are wearing, has no identifying logo on it;

rather, a tie-dye abstract, front and back, in murky blue. They all agreed that logos might attract attention. She's hardly a style slave, Jake thinks, but at least today she's wearing something underneath: its green straps show. He is also wearing a loosely fitting T-shirt – his first Italian purchase, in fact. All the ones he tried were loose on him; this was the smallest he could find but it still flaps around. He doesn't know if he is too thin, or whether Italian men are all thick set.

He has tied back his dreadlocks in one of Flo's stretchy bands, but is not sure if tying them back draws less attention than leaving them. For today, somehow he thinks so. *Should I cut them off before going to Zany's?* He wishes he hadn't thought of that; anything to do with Zany makes him anxious. And his anxiety needs no encouragement, when he isn't exactly relaxed about the football.

As Gianni takes them into a small, friendly trattoria with smells of oregano and freshly baked pizza wafting around, a sense of wellbeing and camaraderie returns.

'Gianni! Come stà, amico?' says a huge guy who, by dint of wearing a once-white apron that just about goes round his middle, is clearly the padrone of the establishment. He pushes his way through to reach Gianni and everyone is given an expansive hug.

'Eenglish? Benissimo. You see football. Good. First, you eat my pizza, no?'

'Si. Per favore. The best pizza in Rome?' Tom asks.

'Si, si!'

They savour the smell and appearance of the pizzas coming out of the glowing oven, and Trish says, 'Gianni, this is our treat. Thank you.'

'Treat?' Gianni doesn't understand. 'Ah, you tweet? Twitter?' He hands her his mobile.

'No, no,' Trish smiles. 'A *treat*, not a *tweet* – it's like a gift. We pay for your pizza and drink.'

'No, no.'

'Si. Grazie molto. For arranging the trip,' says Tom.

'You must not...'

'We must.'

Gianni concedes. They eat and drink and finish with two shared portions of tiramisu, which bears no resemblance to any tiramisu they've ever had before. Trish scrapes the plate. 'It's yummy,' she says.

'Yummy. Mm. I like "yummy"!' exclaims Gianni. 'Good word. I learn. Jake, why you no teach me yummy?'

At that moment, the patron comes over again. 'You like?' he asks them.

'The best tiramisu in Italy,' Tom says with his usual charm.

But the owner guffaws and pats him on the back so forcefully that he nearly brings up his dessert on the tablecloth.

EIGHTEEN

Gianni points urgently to the clock, so they pay and leave. He gives Jake, Trish and Tom their tickets, in case they lose each other in the throng of fans that has built up outside. Gianni puts on a vivid orange baseball cap, pulled down low – partly so their group can see him in the crowd and partly to prevent his being recognised by anyone else. He's also wearing massive, mirrored, wraparound sunglasses, which partly hide his face. He may not be mega-famous but he has told Jake he still gets spotted. Jake couldn't fit into any cap he tried over his mop of hair; but Trish looks cute in a loose-fitting baker-boy cap. Jake and Tom take Trish's hands protectively, though she seems the least nervous of the three.

At the entrance, they buy some bottled water and muddle through the crowds, showing their tickets, along with their passports as ID. The guy at their gate says, "Giorno, Gianni,' as he checks his ID. It was Jake's suggestion that Gianni wore his disguise, to keep attention off this motley crew. The less attention the better. But Jake realises it must be strange for Gianni not to have autograph-hunters prowling.

Trish looks round in wide-eyed fascination; her experience of professional football matches is limited and Jake's pleased that, having been so good as to come, she seems to be enjoying the atmosphere. So far, Tom also looks happy and unconcerned.

That is, until they enter the ground. As they come out of their staircase into the light of the ground, the first things they see are the big swastikas on banners draped over a barrier in the opposite *curva*, where the seats bend round to the goal end. Trish gasps audibly and puts her hand over her mouth. Tom whispers, 'Oh God – it's true.' Gianni, all too aware of what they are looking at, beckons them to follow him to their seats. Since the hooligan fringe always sit in the curva, their own seats, in the middle of the opposite side of the pitch, have all too good a view of them.

As they move into their seats, Jake puts up his finger to his mouth, to say 'Sh' to his friends. They decide that even speaking English, let alone making shocked comments, would draw too much attention to themselves. He has also brought a little notepad and pen, in case one of them wants to say something significant during the match.

'Is good, no?' Gianni says, gesturing to the seats. By now, he must be wondering why they are all so quiet.

'Si. Benissimi,' Tom says, adding, 'Grazie, Gianni.'

'Everybody 'appy?' Gianni asks. 'Roma–Lazio. Best, no? Like Manzester United–Manzester City?'

'Si,' Jake replies, always amused by Gianni's inability to pronounce 'ch' in English words, even though the sound does exist in Italian. The football may be as good; the atmosphere here, dominated by the visual display of fascist symbols, is unimaginable. He thinks of his grandpa Joe and uncle Ernie, both of whom fled the Nazis, and is relieved they are now dead, so they will never hear of this experience.

Jake and his friends pass their programmes to and fro, trying to translate things for each other and trying not to look constantly at what they don't want to see. Excitement builds till the teams run from the tunnel and the crowd stand and cheer. Jake then sees what he has dreaded. Whole swathes of the crowd in the opposite curva stand and give the straight-arm salute, some holding and waving their swastika-adorned banners. Trish goes pale; Tom nudges Jake, hard. Gianni simply cheers for the footballers.

'Va bene,' Jake says, trying hard to focus attention on the

football, 'Lazio play in Man City colours, pale blue; Roma in red, like Man United. Got that?'

'Yep,' Tom replies. He then swigs some water and passes the bottle to Jake and Trish, who do the same. At least it cools the heat they feel from mild panic and stops them saying anything out of turn.

'Ecco,' Trish says, at last drawing breath. She offers the bottle and an open tube of mints to Gianni and they all take one. 'Come si chiama?' she asks Gianni – remembering their agreement to try to speak Italian – and pointing to a Lazio player who dribbles the ball skilfully down the wing. She is right to pretend to watch the game, not the distractions, Jake thinks.

''E is best player for Lazio. Name Gianni,' he says, smiling. 'I not so good player.'

'Lazio gioca bene,' Tom says, praising the team's play.

A voice comes from behind. 'Roma best!'

They all turn round, afraid at first, only to realise that a couple of people behind them are clearly Roma supporters but are being friendly.

'You Eenglish? At football in Italy?'

'Yes,' Jake replies. 'Siamo studenti,' he explains.

'Bene. Benvenuto a Roma,' they say and lean over to shake hands with them all. Gianni does the same but says nothing. As they all shake hands, a roar goes up: a Lazio player has scored in that split second.

'Must watch. No let Lazio win, per favore,' says the fan behind Jake.

'Va bene,' Jake says.

Tom writes on Jake's pad: 'We're among Roma supporters. Hm.'

The first half of the match is fast and furious, end-to-end football and Jake is seriously enjoying it, after a while away from Premier League football matches.

'Good match,' Trish says.

'It's not always this good,' he replies.

'I've never liked live football as much as rugby,' Tom says, 'but I'm getting into it.'

'Good, no?' Gianni asks.

'Si,' Jake replies. Half-time comes and his unease returns. He doesn't even want to venture to the gents, for fear of meeting a fascist gang, just as he... well, just as he reveals his Jewishness in full flow. But Gianni needs to go, so Jake goes with him. Tom says he'll accompany Trish to the door of the ladies.

There are clearly some gangs around. Jake hears a rumble under the noise of the fans: a couple of groups by the gates are banging drums – not rhythmically or musically, but with a dull beat, in unison. *'Gli Stremi'* is printed across the chests of their T-shirts.

Jake nudges Tom and whispers, 'That's them: The Extremes.'

'What? Who? Oh, them,' he gasps, looking at the group. There are other gangs in the passages near the toilets – and all chanting together. A couple of them flick Jake's hair as he passes, whistling as they do. He knows his hair draws attention from conservative people; but the friends all make it safely back to their seats for the second half.

Jake relaxes more into the game as it goes on, knowing that they have managed the impossible. He turns and smiles at Gianni, putting his arm round his shoulders – or as far round those broad 'goalie-shoulders' as it will reach.

'Happy?' he asks.

'Si. But I 'ope Lazio win,' Gianni whispers, tossing his head in the direction of the Roma fans behind him.

'Aha,' Jake says, knowing not to say more.

The match changes tack in this half; there are more tussles, more ugly tackles with more yellow cards. There have been two good goals from each team, leaving Lazio in the lead, 3-2, when a Lazio player is given a yellow card and starts gesticulating at the referee. It is his second one, so the ref then pulls out a red card. The player should leave the pitch, but gangs in the curva erupt in screaming protest.

Jake sees swastikas amongst their waving scarves and then, red flare smoke not only engulfs the curva but emanates from other blocks of seats as well. Gradually, the whole pitch is in a red, green and white fog and through it, on one of the big screens, Jake can just make out a group of Roma players surrounding the ref, angry at the disruption to play. An announcement is made that the ref is calling off the match.

There is uproar from fans everywhere. Now Jake has reason to worry. Trish and Gianni remain silent and she looks particularly pale. They stand there, frozen in their inability to take sides. Jake whispers to her, 'You OK?' to which she whispers back, 'Tell you later.' The people behind Jake pat him and Tom on the back, shouting their disagreement with this uproar; Tom and Jake turn and shrug their shoulders in sympathy. Gianni simply acknowledges them with the occasional 'Si' and 'No', giving little away.

This is the worst thing that could have happened. They cannot believe the apparent power held by the Stremi, forcing a referee to call off a match. The end leaves Lazio in the lead and Jake hears the people behind muttering, as they leave, 'Sempre Lazio. Sempre Lazio.' *Always Lazio. Does this often happen, then?*

Gianni rubs his thumb along the fingers of one hand, indicating that money has changed hands. Bribery? Surely not. Jake's age-old sense of fair play is blown away, as he nudges Tom – who nudges Trish – to make them see Gianni's gesture, which he makes low down, between his knees and Jake's. None of them speaks.

Gianni starts off quickly up the steps. Jake takes Trish's hand, squeezing it firmly, and Tom puts his arm round Jake's shoulder as they leave, letting him know he's there. And Jake finds Tom's huge frame very comforting. It's strange, not talking, as they would do usually, but they all know that any word out of turn could be problematic.

The further out they go, the more they can hear the gangs' chanting and the beats of their drums. As they pass them and their banners, one of the people who was sitting behind spots Jake and shouts out to him: 'Inglesi! Studenti! Is good football? No. Lazio, Lazio – sempre Lazio! Is no good. See! Manchester United always win? City always win? No.' And they point to the Stremi.

'I wish they hadn't spoken English just here,' Tom whispers, echoing Jake's thoughts, 'pointing them out and drawing attention to us as well.'

'Stay with me, per favore,' Gianni whispers, stepping up his pace. Jake wonders if anything was overheard. Every so often he looks behind him but sees nothing suspicious. They keep up a speed – walking, not running – out of the vicinity of the ground.

'Not far to go, hey?' Trish says, squeezing Jake's hand. Her turn, now, to be reassuring. Poor girl, Jake thinks.

'Good job you chose a hotel nearby,' he says, patting Gianni on the back. Gianni still says little, having pulled his cap well down over his forehead; he's kept his sunglasses on, even though the sun has long since gone down. He gestures, 'Sh,' and marches on. Jake is anything but reassured. Has anyone followed them? He shrugs off this crazy idea.

Trish talks about her shock at seeing the Italian flag colours in the gangs' smoke bombs. 'Reminded me of bloody Hitler. He coloured Berlin's fountains red, green and white, when Mussolini went to Germany,' she says. 'And I thought... Oh God...' Tears roll down her cheeks. Jake puts his arm round her while Tom marches on alongside Gianni.

Once the entrance to the hotel is in their sights, Jake is relieved and, at that moment, the friends are all smiles again. But then, just as they are about to set foot inside the safety of Albergo Olimpico's porch, they hear taunts. Jake feels his hair being pulled and, as the elastic band comes off, he flinches. 'What the fuck?' It must be some splinter gang of Stremi, he thinks. They start to flick at Trish's cap and they jeer at her piercings. In a split second of sanity, Jake guesses that those English-speaking fans were overheard by this gang, as they passed them on the way out.

Oh God, they've followed us to the hotel! At the threshold of the overhanging porch, the gang start shoving and pushing them, hissing comments – presumably so they won't be heard from inside the hotel. Gianni tries to keep the friends with him. But the gang keep attempting to ruffle Jake's dreadlocks or to stroke Trish's punk-shaved head and Jake makes out something like: 'These English with their crazy hair.'

They come even nearer, pushing harder, while Tom, Gianni and Jake keep pushing them back, with disastrous results. The gang grab and thump anything they can – arms, hair, hats and then T-shirts. The friends all have trouble keeping their balance. Jake says, 'God! They've torn my T-shirt. And –' He is petrified as he knows his Star of David neck chain is now visible. It was well hidden under the back of his T-shirt when he got dressed. He looks round at the others and sees the thugs tugging at Trish's T-shirt. She's shouting as they rip that too, yet Jake manages to think, 'Thank goodness she's wearing something underneath.'

It seems that Tom may be too big for the bullies, who is left to defend his friends. But it proves impossible, even for him, and he is then punched from all sides. He comes nearer to Jake, whispering, 'Did you hear that?'

'Not properly,' Jake replies.

'Good. Best not to,' Tom says. 'I heard, "Yid, yid" – put it that way.'

'Look, just take care of Trish, can you?' Jake continues to try to protect himself from the shoving, but he is knocked to the ground and bangs his head against the wall. Meanwhile Gianni is fumbling with his mobile phone, trying, Jake assumes, to contact the police or the hotel.

He hears the taunts directed at Trish, as they have now

realised she's a girl, despite her hair and clothes: 'Eh eh… ragazza/ragazzo, bella/bello,' accompanied by laughter and wolf whistles. He sees them elbow her hard and she falls over. That's the last thing he sees before he blacks out. He will later be told that when Gianni hears their abuse, he pounces on one of them, dropping his mobile and leaving his emergency call incomplete. Gianni is then punched hard and slumps down. His sunglasses fall off and one of the gang recognises him.

'È Gianni Travesi!' As they realise they've attacked an Italian footballer, they run off. Jake comes round a bit, just then, and sees Tom running over to protect Trish, but Gianni is sprawled awkwardly, out cold.

'Gianni! Oh God, Gianni!' Tom calls, as he bends over him. He then takes out his own mobile phone but realises he doesn't know how to call the police. Jake can't get up, but with blurred vision, sees Tom move Trish to sit down against the wall of the hotel. She looks about to faint from pain. Jake tries to move to pick up Gianni's phone but passes out again while he's trying to work out why no one from the hotel has noticed the furore.

Tom, regaining composure, shouts, 'Hey, they've run off. Why?'

'Cos they recognised Gianni – and you called his name, too,' Trish says. 'Ow, my arm!' She holds the injured arm across her stomach. There's no sound from Gianni. At that moment the hotel staff run out and the police sirens approach.

Jake wakes to find himself in a hospital bed. Gianni is next to him, a frame lifting up the sheet over his legs, with Tom next to him, and Trish across the ward with a flimsy curtain half-round her for propriety, a bandage round one wrist and arm. They all start to talk about what they remember – all except Gianni, who is doped up on painkillers.

'I honestly thought we'd be OK with Gianni,' says Jake. 'He looks badly injured. Shit, shit – I'm really sorry.'

'He's got a suspected concussion, and a mashed-up ankle,' Tom tells them. It transpires that Tom came round a while ago; Trish never lost consciousness, though her arm hurt a lot; and Jake drifted in and out.

'Grim. And for a footballer,' says Trish.

A nurse comes in and says that they can all go back to Todi in two days. They learn that Tom has a twisted knee and bruising; Trish's X-ray on her wrist showed a break, and Jake has suspected concussion. However, scans cannot show concussion, only skull fractures – with no fracture or internal bleeding, he is being assessed more by symptoms. His headache is gradually disappearing so the medical staff feel sure he is OK. Gianni did have symptoms of concussion and his scan showed a fracture to his ankle – more tests will clarify exactly how bad it is.

'I think six weeks no play,' Gianni moans.

The nurse asks whether they would agree to a short press interview. They decide it would be best to do so, if only to make sure things do not get printed that they would not want.

'Good job we decided to come by coach, instead of letting Gianni drive,' Tom says. The group make frenzied attempts to contact their friends here and family at home, once the hospital has given them the Wi-Fi password. Later, they skype some of them, giving a visual reassurance that despite everything, they are OK.

Jake feels guilty for taking his mates to the match at all. This is grim. It's worse than his most vivid nightmare and he owes them all, big time.

'Mea culpa, mea culpa,' Gianni mutters, the moment he is properly awake.

'It's not your fault,' Tom says.

'Si, it eez.' Tears trickle down his cheeks. Poor guy, the macho footballer, so upset; Jake feels for him. Trish gets up from the armchair by Jake's bed and goes to wipe away his tears.

'Poor Gianni,' she says, as she lifts up the spouted feeding cup in her one good hand and helps him take a sip of water. 'OK?' she asks.

'Grazie. Si,' he replies. He isn't OK, of course. He is devastated and turning, painfully to Jake, says, 'Per favore, you still my teacher, Jake?'

'Si, of course!' Jake says, smiling. Jake knows he will carry on teaching him but what matters is how long it will take before Gianni can play again. Or whether his transfer to Wigan will be delayed, or even cancelled. *That'd be my earnings out the window...*

Jake calls Gianni's family for him. Like many Italian young men, Gianni still lives with his parents, unlike young Brits who can't wait to leave home. As yet, Jake still has not received a reply from Zany which, in the circumstances, upsets him.

They all gradually start to recover and, although Gianni has to use crutches and Trish has her wrist strapped up, they know they are lucky. Interviews with the police come and go; they hold out little hope of the thugs being traced. There remains the matter of their belongings, left behind at the hotel. Just as Jake is thinking of this, the hotel manager arrives.

He says he is heartbroken that his receptionist didn't call the police more quickly. He explains that she was too scared, as she was alone at the desk. Gianni mumbles to him, looking angry. Jake can understand something like, 'That's no excuse for not helping,' and the manager simply carries on apologising. He promises to refund their room charges and says he has persuaded Gianni's football club to pay for a coach to take them back to Todi.

'That's great. Grazie, signore,' Jake says.

The manager goes over to Gianni, who is less chirpy then the rest of them.

'Gianni, per favore you come again to Albergo Olimpico? Please.' He looks very upset, holds out his hand to the footballer and they shake on it. Gianni assures him that he will come back.

Before the manager leaves, he asks permission to retrieve their things from their bedrooms and safes. They are amazed that after all that has happened, they can remember the combinations they used and they hand over their key cards. They slowly collect themselves and those who can, try to get dressed. But the bloodstained clothes in which they were admitted to hospital are in no state to be worn. The sight of blood shocks them – only then does it dawn on them how near they were to catastrophe. A man at the door of the ward who is chatting up the nurse approaches them – he's from the local press.

'Permesso?'

'Oh no, please, no fuss,' Tom says. He holds his hands over his face as a massive camera lens is pointed at them all.

'No way – no photos!' says Jake.

The journalist backs off, turning instead to the footballer. 'Gianni?'

'No,' he says; he turns his back on him, wincing with pain as he does so.

In the end, they have a short interview and, instead of a hospital photo, Jake says he will send a group photo of himself with Tom and Trish from his iPhone, when they look happier. Gianni has one of himself that he uses for publicity – though not usually this kind of publicity.

Eventually, they are free of the hospital. The hotel manager arrives with all their bags and their valuables from the safes. They dress in fresh clothes, though Trish and Gianni need help. They are all helped into a large people carrier. Gianni needs a lot of help up and down the step and sighs with relief as he is lowered into a seat specially draped in a soft throw, which he pulls round himself.

By each seat is a picnic lunch with a small bottle of rosé wine; an envelope attached offers a free night's stay at the hotel.

'Great. Grazie,' Jake says, echoed by the rest of them. The

driver explains that he's taking the circuitous route from the stadium area to show them at least a little of Rome before reaching the ring road.

It is a beautiful day which, in other circumstances, would have been a perfect touring day, but still, they cross the River Tiber and pass the Borghese Gallery – or, at least, the driver points out its park.

'I want show you Colosseum but is not possible. Scusi,' the driver shouts.

'At least we can say we crossed the Tiber,' Tom says.

'I've managed a couple of photos through the window,' Jake says.

'Hm, tricky, with one hand,' Trish says.

Gianni is quiet and sullen. With every jolt on the journey, he winces – in more pain than he admits. Trish, always positive, fishes out her guide book and maps, and tells them all, at intervals, where they are and how far they have to go. Otherwise, the journey passes uneventfully and they snooze, on and off. Jake tries to keep an eye on Gianni, who sleeps fitfully most of the time.

'I feel totally spaced out,' Tom says. It's unusual for Jake to see him at all vulnerable. 'Everything seems unreal.'

The last two days have been so far removed from Jake's previous weeks in Italy that he wonders how they will all settle back.

'Look, is that Todi, on its hill over there?' Trish says. 'Mind you, all the hill villages look alike.'

'Si, è Todi,' Gianni says. He smiles – the first for a long time.

'Benissimo. I'm exhausted, don't know about you lot,' Tom says. The coach draws up and the driver comes back to help them. What service. Tom helps Gianni out of his seat and onto his crutches. Jake takes his and Trish's bags and, once they're at the door, he's aware of a commotion.

A small crowd is there and flashlights glare. A reception

committee. There are two cute little dogs, jumping and fussing, a few people Jake doesn't know... and then he sees Suzanna, Xanthe and Jeeves. No Zany. The unknown people are clearly Gianni's parents and there are two other guys. Apparently, one is a journalist from the local paper, the other, Gianni's football trainer. Once the journalist has checked all their names and clicked his camera he agrees to leave them alone, with persuasion from the trainer.

Jake watches Gianni and his parents greeting each other emotionally and effusively and he feels jealous, for a moment; the dogs have to be lifted for a snuggle with Gianni, lest their jumping knocks him off balance. Jake ruffles their furry heads.

'Carlo e Carlotta,' Gianni says, though Jake can't tell them apart.

'Cute, or what?' Trish replies. Gianni smiles as Trish kneels down to stroke the dogs.

'Cute Carlo e Cute Carlotta, ' he says, laughing.

Jake turns to Jeeves, Xanthe and Suzanna – who is a little tearful. There is hugging and kissing all round. Gianni's parents have a shopping trolley for the luggage, the trainer has a wheelchair for Gianni, so the meeters and greeters run alongside, the little dogs frisky.

'Where did that journalist appear from?' Jake asks, to no one in particular.

'Papers communicate – anyway, nothing much happens round here.' Trish says. 'Must be big news, locally, with Gianni involved.'

'Not keen on publicity,' Jake grumbles.

'Finding a madia fades into insignificance,' Trish comments. 'And I haven't told you about the sfratti, yet,' she adds mysteriously.

NINETEEN

With the whole group gathered back at the hostel, Jake wonders what will happen next for everyone. He and Tom will cope, back in their routine – their injuries are minor and their rooms so close. But he turns to Trish, sitting happily in Xanthe's arms in the vestibule, and asks her how she will manage with only one useable arm.

'I'll be her other arm,' Xanthe says. 'Won't I, Trishy?' They kiss and Jake sees Trish at her happiest, in that moment. *Good on her.*

Gianni's mum comes up to Jake and puts her arm round him.

'You teach Gianni. Benissimo. Grazie molto. 'E like Eenglish.'

'And I like teaching him,' Jake replies.

'You come eat one day? And your amici?' she says, gesturing to his friends.

'Well, that's very kind. I...'

'You come. My mamma make good food,' Gianni pipes up.

'OK. Si. Soon, per favore,' Jake says.

'Me, too, per favore,' says Tom.

'I tell Gianni, 'e tell you – cosi?' and she jabs her finger on the palm of her hand.

'Si. By text? Bene, grazie,' Jake replies. So they all hug Gianni and his mum before they get into their car, where the dogs and his father await them.

The invitation to Gianni's parents reminds Jake starkly of

his forthcoming visit to Zany's. He didn't expected her to come to the station, as it would be too public, but he had hoped she would be waiting for him at the hostel. Xanthe has told him that she tried to contact Zany but failed. Jake hopes, then, that she at least read his messages from Rome. A new anxiety hits him and he realises he is still vulnerable after the fracas.

'We're off!' Trish says, standing up with Xanthe. They hug goodbye and he sees that she is tearful.

'It's been a weird couple of days,' she says.

'Weird flatters it. It was the pits,' Jake says.

'But not all of it,' Trish says. 'What about the hotel manager and the trattoria?'

'And the tiramisu?' Tom adds.

Trish gets up to leave for her place, with Xanthe carrying her bags.

'Are you OK walking?' Tom asks.

'I don't walk on my hands,' Trish calls, as they set off.

Jake says a few placatory words to Tom and Suzanna, feeling a sense of obligation. Whose idea was the match in the first place? *I cared more about keeping my job with Gianni than our safety. Shit. I totally screwed up.*

At that moment, Jake receives a text from Zany. Tears of relief start to appear, which he rubs away quickly. She tells him she hasn't had her mobile, just over these crucial days, without saying why. She wants him to send a selfie to show he's all in one piece... And then she arrives, to surprise him. Thank goodness. Her concerned look is welcome.

Tom and Suzanna hug him, say hello to Zany, then excuse themselves saying Tom's exhausted. Suzanna suggests they should check up on each other over the next couple of days.

'Sometimes the shock comes later,' she adds. 'A presto.'

'Seeya,' Jake says, echoed by Zany.

Zany turns to him and holds his face in her hands, examining it to see if he's really OK.

'Just a few scratches,' she says. 'Wow. You got off lightly. I mean, from what I've heard, you could have been badly injured.'

'I know. It's awful for Gianni: he feels guilty and he's off football for a good few weeks. Listen, I have to go up to my room. Will you come with me, just this once?'

'Till I'm sure you're all right,' she says, taking his bag for him.

However much Jake fancies her and wants more of her, at this moment he has no energy and is beginning to ache everywhere. Bruising appears after the event, he has read. They climb the stairs slowly, keeping to his pace. In his room, he flops on the bed.

'I never thought this room would be a welcome relief,' he says.

'I'll unpack your stuff,' Zany says, putting her own bulky bag on top of his desk.

'No, don't – some of it's bloodstained. But it's great to see you.'

'Likewise,' she says, with her smile that could win a national competition. Jake pats the bed. 'Come and sit down.'

Zany wags her finger from side to side. 'You're not in a fit state – and the answer's no, anyway.'

'In fact, what I need is a shower,' Jake says, as he struggles painfully to get off the bed. 'God, I ache all over. Please will you wait till I come back, to make sure I don't pass out or something?' he asks. 'Won't be long.'

'Sure,' Zany replies.

Jake grabs his towel, wash bag and some clothes from a drawer and limps out of the room.

'Oh, you wonder woman!' he says as he comes back. Zany has unpacked his things and folded everything neatly on top of one of his boxes. On his desk there is a paper plate of cheeses, olives and a fresh, buttered roll, with an ice-cold bottle of Orangina, all from her insulated bag. She has even put a bougainvillea flower into an empty yoghurt carton.

'I pricked my fingers plucking that,' she says. 'I didn't know bougainvillea had thorns. And the... those other clothes... are in the bin, by the way.'

'What a treat, you... oh Zany, you are a love,' Jake says, as he goes up to her and kisses both her cheeks. He tilts her chin up towards him and they kiss each other on the lips with the same insatiable fervour they had before, till Zany pushes him away gently.

'Not now,' she whispers.

'Hm. When, if ever?' Jake replies. He sits on the edge of the bed and eats Zany's little feast. 'Mm, tastes good,' he says. Then he lies back.

'I'm going to leave you, now,' Zany says. 'And I've put off the visit to my parents by a week. You need to get over all this.'

'Thanks. That's great. When'll I see you next?' Jake asks. But he remembers no more till he wakes early the next day.

It is Sunday and four days have passed since the match, though it takes him a while to work that out. He still has his clothes on but his flip-flops are neatly placed by his bed, his covers are over him and the blinds are closed. *Zany – she must have tucked me in. And I missed it!*

He takes out his iPad and looks for the *Times* sports report that his mum told him about, when she last emailed him. It is easy to spot – he wishes it weren't. 'Italian player and three British students injured after Roma–Lazio match,' reads the headline.

He skims through the first lines of the article until he finds his name.

Jake Taylor, one of the students involved in the fracas, is a pleasant lad with dreadlocks and a winning smile – although there were not many smiles as we discussed the chaos that ended the match or the attacks that followed. [Ha, never knew I had a winning smile.]

According to Taylor, he and three fellow British students attended the game as guests of their friend, Perugia goalkeeper Gianni Travesi. All four were followed from the stadium and attacked close to their hotel by members of a hooligan gang.

'We think they noticed us at half-time because we looked different from the other fans,' said Taylor.

Despite being knocked to the ground, he and his friends fought back. Asked if taking on twenty hoodlums was a brave choice, Taylor replied: 'Bonkers, not brave! It was the worst day of my life.' But it had not put him off Italy, he insisted, 'Only Italian football.'

This kind of violence unfortunately remains all too common around major matches across Italy, with little preventive action being taken by the authorities.

God, that's about me. As Jake tries to get out of bed, his back hurts; he sees a note under his door but it's hard, bending to pick it up. 'Come stà, amico? Sono OK. Tom.' He must have been up early; but Jake needs to call home before anything else.

This is when Skype is wonderful, because his parents and Flo can see that he isn't badly injured. They make it a conference call. *Almost a united family again.*

'There are better ways to get yourself into *The Times*,' his dad says.

'So you've seen it. Hm.'

'Yeah and the photos.'

'Gianni's so fit,' Flo says, 'even with crutches.'

'Are you really OK, though?' his mum asks.

'I am, physically,' Jake replies. 'But the gangs are horrendous. Seeing swastikas waving around was…' he wells up, trying not to cry.

'Take it easy,' his dad says.

'It's not for myself, I keep thinking of Grandpa Joe and Uncle Ernie. I… I'm glad they aren't here to know about it.'

'How do they get away with it?' Mum asks. 'What actually happened at the match, before the… before they got to you?'

'They objected to a decision the ref made. You read the paper. One of the Lazio players should have been given a yellow card. The team objected and the gangs supported them – simple as that.

'Unheard of!' Jake's dad says.

'Not here,' Jake replies. 'I felt bad for Gianni.'

'How is he now?' Flo asks.

'He may have fractured his ankle; it's very painful but his parents are looking after him – he lives with them. And his mamma has invited us all for a meal.'

'Lovely. What about Tom and Trish? They only went along for the ride, didn't they?' Jake's dad asks.

'Yeah. They're such good mates. They enjoyed the journey, the buildup, the meal together, all that – they even got into the football...' On the screen his parents look worried. 'We all had suspected concussion and the sods broke Trish's wrist.'

As Jake talks, the attack seems part of another existence. Till now, he must have subconsciously distanced himself from the reality of being beaten up by fellow human beings.

'You've gone pale,' Flo says. 'You're not OK, are you?'

'Yeah, kind of... I will be,' Jake says, realising that it's all only just sinking in.

Their chat is interrupted by a knock on his door. A voice shouts: 'Read all about it, read all about it!' and Tom barges in – Zany having left the door unlocked – with a pile of newspapers in his hand.

'One copy, or a hundred – one each for all your fans?' he asks. 'Hello there, Jake's family,' he says, waving to the Skype camera. He holds up the local newspaper, showing the photo of their football outing group.

'Epic!' Flo gasps.

Jake looks at it. Here, in a small Umbrian town, he and his friends are front-page news.

'Fame like this we don't need,' he says.

'Why not?' Tom says. 'It's about time these hooligans were outed.'

'It depends on the slant given in the paper,' Jake's dad says.

'Let's see the page again,' his mum asks. Jake holds it up for her. 'I can't actually read it but that's not the best mug shot, Jake.'

'Gimme a break, Mum, I wasn't modelling. Anyway, guys, I'm going for now. I want to get back to routine stuff here, OK?'

'Sure. Kisses.' She and Flo blow kisses on the screen.

'And here's one for Tom,' Flo says, blowing another.

'Love you,' his dad says – and it seems as though he's saying it to Jake's mum as well. *I wish.*

'Seeya,' Jake says, accompanied by a wave from Tom at his side.

'Bye, Tom,' say his parents and Jake closes Skype.

'Coming for P.C.?' Tom asks, his usual, upbeat manner seemingly unaffected by the events of the past days.

'Not till I've read this,' Jake says, opening out the paper. 'I need to know what the locals say, before I face the fans. I've read the *Times* version online.'

'Fine. See you down there. How d'you feel? D'you ache?'

'Yeah. I could hardly get out of bed. I slept like a log, still in my clothes.'

'Did Zany stay?' Tom asks, winking.

'Not like *that*. She brought me a snack, y'know. She's cool. I fell asleep before she left – don't even remember saying goodbye.'

'YOLO! She's sweet.'

'Seeya. Ciao,' Jake says as Tom leaves. His mobile pings.

'FAMOUS NOW? AWESOME. PARENTS SAW PIC IN PAPER. R U OK? ASLEEP B4 I LEFT! Z XX'

Jake replies: 'AM OK BUT BRUISED. SOZ DIDN'T SAY BYE. WILL TXT SOON J XX'

He turns to the newspaper: the Umbria freebie, delivered in

piles, weekly, to the hostel. In the photo, they look a pathetic, motley crew, just off the coach: him with his dreadlocks, Trish with her piercings, Gianni on crutches and Tom looking cool. As he thought, as well as Gianni's local celebrity, the papers feature Jake's Jewish identity. He feels awkward about the emphasis on his being Jewish, though it is right, considering the attitudes of the Stremi. He can't hide it away, even if only for the sake of his grandfather and uncle's experiences in the 1930s. He's relieved that no inference is made about Trish's sexuality – only her haircut.

At that moment, he decides to cut off his dreadlocks. He sees them through other people's eyes, in the newspaper photo. He knows it will be better for Zany's parents, too, though that is not the main reason. He is just wondering where to find a decent barber when there is another knock on the door: it's Jeeves, looking shocked.

'I've seen the paper. I hadn't heard. Why did no one tell me? Are you OK?'

'Yeah, mainly. How did you not know? You were in all the group texts from Rome.'

'Hang on.' Jeeves looks at his mobile. 'It's there now. What the – ? I went exploring, with you guys out of town. Must have been out of range.'

'Shame,' Jake says.

'I really thought you'd be fine, with Gianni and everything. I won't say *I told you so*.'

'You did. Seriously, thank God you didn't come.'

'Yeah. Was it as bad as the papers said?

'Yep. Only worse.'

'Glad you're safe,' Jeeves says. 'Come for P.C. with me?'

'In five minutes, OK?'

'Sure.'

Jeeves leaves and Jake sees that an email had arrived from... Adriana? *Oh my God!*

'READ THE NEWSPAPER – CAN I SEE YOU? ARE YOU INJURED? A XX'

Now that's fame for you. 'I'LL BE AT YOUR LECTURE THIS AFTERNOON,' he replies, having checked his timetable.

'BENISSIMO,' says her immediate reply.

Jake has breakfast with Tom and Jeeves, dealing with the barrage of comments from his fellow students who are waving the newspaper around. He knew it would happen and he only hopes they see how serious the actions of the Stremi were. Jeeves is upset, even while being relieved that he wasn't there.

'But you knew how it would be,' he says.

'And you know I went for Gianni. He did arrange it well, y'know. Friendly hotel, eats where they knew him, all that.'

'Hm…' Jeeves says.

'He'd seen a match called off before but never, ever the kind of attack we suffered.'

'Will you keep on teaching him?' Tom asks.

'Course. Why not? Specially as his mum has asked us all for a meal.'

'There's always a plus side,' Jeeves adds.

'Sure. Maybe some good'll come of it,' Tom says. 'That hotel guy was cool.'

'Who?' Jeeves asks.

Jake tell him all about his kindness. Then Jake gets a text from Trish. 'She's asking how we feel,' he tells the others.

'Hey, I almost forgot about her broken wrist,' Tom says. 'She's far worse off than we are and I never called her this morning.'

'It's OK,' Jake says. 'Xanthe's moved in, to be her nurse.'

'I'll look in on her later. I'm not going back to work for a couple of days. The guys there have been really sympathetic.'

'Well, I'm off to a lecture later. I need to get back into everything,' Jake says. 'D'you mind if I go now? I need to clear my head.'

'OK,' Jeeves says. 'What's the rush?'

'Well, I meant that literally.'

'What?'

'The bit about my head. See you.' Jake winks. He enjoys being enigmatic and his friends clearly don't know what he meant. Getting the name of a good barber from the guy at the hostel desk, he sets off without a second thought.

The feeling he has, as he goes into the sleazy little back-street shop, takes him back to when he was four and had an inexplicable hatred of barbers. His mum took him to a ladies' hairdresser for a while, where it felt less threatening. Trying to cut it herself was worse. *Maybe that's where the name 'dread'-locks comes from,'* he thinks, smiling to himself.

The barber greets Jake, then turns and flaps a newspaper around.

'Ecco! Nel giornale! Eez you?'

Jake knows now that getting his hair cut may have the added benefit of people not recognising him so easily. He sits in the chair while the barber does the usual thing: he pulls Jake's hair out horizontally, lets it drop through his fingers and shakes his head, as though he has never faced a worse challenge. Jakes reckons it must be fun, for once, to be able to change someone's appearance so dramatically.

Alberto, the barber (who wants to be on first-name terms), asks how short Jake wants his hair, using the sharp points of his scissors on a lock of hair, at three different lengths – 'Così? Così? Così?' – grinning all the time with glee at the thought of leaving him shorn.

'Così,' Jake says, pointing at the length he wants, in serious danger of having his finger snipped off. While Alberto snips, he sings Italian arias, joined by his assistant – and they sing well. 'Not quite *The Barber of Seville*,' Jake thinks, grinning as he relaxes more than at any other time at a barber's. He tries to make sense of the rest of the newspaper but hair keeps falling onto important words. When the barber stops singing for a moment, he points to the paper.

'Non buono. Football no good, Italy no good, Stremi no good,' he says.

Jake decides it's best not to comment, particularly as Alberto waves the open scissors to gesticulate while he speaks.

'Studente?'

'Yes I'm a student.'

''Ow you know Gianni Travesi? Mi'amico. Ee come 'ere for cut,' the barber says.

'Oh. I teach him English.'

As the usual barber banter goes on, Jake trusts that the haircut will be fine, although he does tell Alberto when to stop. He is surprised when he agrees. The barber flicks the soft brush round Jake's neck, then shakes the hair off the cape with the drama of a toreador swirling his red cloak in front of a bull. Jake smiles. He's quite enjoying his morning and, looking in the mirror held behind him, he's pleased with the result.

Alberto agrees to Jake's taking a selfie of them both; then Jake pays, tips him and leaves. He feels that, perhaps, his nightmare memories of Rome have been brushed away with his hair.

He sends the photo to Flo, Trish and Zany and awaits their response. Trish is the first to reply, saying she loves it and to get in touch properly soon. Jake knows she will have some news, but he will wait till after the lecture to phone her back. 'WILL CALL U LATER OK? X' he texts.

He is certainly cooler like this as he takes the long way round Todi to Adriana's lecture. He can't help fingering the nape of his neck, or running his fingers through the short hair that remains. Zany texts in response to the photo saying, 'HARDLY KNOW U. PARENTS WON'T! BTW NOT GOIN 2 LANG LECTURE 2DAY Z X'

Jake is ashamed to feel relieved by her absence. When he reaches the lecture hall he is unexpectedly anxious. Whether because he's facing people after the unwanted publicity, or because of the haircut, he isn't sure. But as he spots Adriana preparing her papers, he knows it is partly because he's excited to see her again – and guilt over Zany is mixed with it.

'Jake, come stà?' she shouts from her position at the bottom of the tiered lecture hall, as Jake comes in at the top. She makes to go up to meet him as he comes down.

'Va bene,' he replies, embarrassed to be singled out like this.

'I am sorry to read about the football. Terrible, terrible. You 'ave time for coffee after this?' She looks at her watch.

'Si,' Jake says, blushing – and he knows his blush extends to his neck, which, of course, is now plainly visible. 'Afterwards, OK.'

Jake notices the intensity of her stare, the way her face changes with her smile, and wonders… As he sits down, not too near the front, he sees a text from Flo about his haircut. 'AH WELL. STILL LUVYA. FLO X'

Adriana's language session begins. He's starting to find it easier to answer questions in Italian and to understand the passages she gives them to read; it hasn't come gradually but all of a sudden. She asks questions about the passage, then goes off at tangents connected to the subject matter, and Jake relaxes into it. He feels good about the language, his hair and Adriana – who is definitely pleasant to watch.

As the session ends, he leaves from the back of the lecture hall, rather than going down the steps to meet her, and waits outside.

'Allora, Jake,' she says, giving him the three-kiss welcome. Once again, he notices how good it is to greet a girl whose arms he can feel and whose hair brushes his cheeks. Adriana, for her part, notices the contrast: 'Where is your 'air?'

'Gone,' he says, surprised but pleased that she is so personal.

'It feel good?'

'Very,' Jake replies, not too sure what else to talk about.

They go for coffee. Adriana orders two cappuccinos and sits next to him, rather than opposite.

'You 'ave bad time in Roma, no?' she says, looking at him with concern. She then puts her hand on his knee. 'Povero

Jake.' The frisson he feels as she touches him – even if it were an instinctive comfort move – is electric.

He puts his hand on hers momentarily, saying, 'It's OK, thanks,' then wishes he hadn't moved his hand away.

'Not OK. Italian football bad news,' she says. She is now holding her coffee in two hands, Jake sees with relief. 'Is big problema for Italy. Make me angry – and sad.'

'Si, yes, it is bad. I was frightened at the match but after...'

'I read in the paper. I cannot believe. They 'it you, they say things, bad things, si?'

'Yeah. Very bad.' He doesn't know whether to explain about his neck chain and certainly can't explain the issues over Trish.

'Is this... the problema?'Adriana points to his visible Magen David. 'This star, yes?'

Jake wonders what to say next.

'I know this star,' Adriana says. 'I see it before, you no need to worry with me,' she says. And he isn't at all worried, except about how much he is attracted to her. Their chat rarely rises above small talk, but he is touched by her empathy over the attack.

Neither of them suggests another meet-up and their goodbye is no more affectionate than before. 'A presto,' he says. She says the same and they go off in different directions.

Jake decides to go straight to Trish's. He hasn't seen her since their ignominious return from Rome and he knows she has something to tell him.

He starts to bound up her rickety staircase as usual, but feels a sharp pain in his lower back; he rubs it and realises it's bruised. The after-effects of his fall are still emerging, then, just as he thinks it's all forgotten.

'Hi, Jake, good to see you,' Trish says as she opens the door. 'How're you feeling, now?'

'OK but bruised.'

'Like your hair, though. What made you do it?'

'I didn't like myself in the paper,' Jake replies.

'Hardly the best photo of any of us! Come and sit down.'

Jake gently takes hold of Trish's wrist. 'How is it? How're you coping?'

'It isn't painful, really. This is a kind of splint,' she says, pointing to her bandage. 'Much lighter than plaster.'

'Aha. But it was awful, wasn't it, in Rome?' Jake says, noticing Trish welling up.

'At least we were in it together,' she says, with tears starting to trickle down her cheeks. It strikes Jake that, until the attack, he had never seen Trish cry before, even when they were young.

'Hey. We'll get over it.'

'We shouldn't have to,' Trish says. 'It's not fair. But kinda... odd.'

'Why?' Jake asks.

'We were both picked on for looking like English weirdos, weren't we? Different ones, but, you know...'

'Same only different,' Jake interjects. 'We were beaten up – "picked on" is a bit too kind.'

'It was real prejudice. And hooliganism.'

'Those gangs know every "ism" in the book,' Jake says, trying to lighten the air. He notices a new coat-stand has appeared since his last visit, with piles of clothes on it.

'Like it?' Trish asks, seeing him looking. 'Xanthe picked it up in the local flea market. Useful when she stays over.'

'Bet she's helping a lot,' Jake says. 'Feel better now?' he asks, wiping a tear from her cheek with the back of his hand.

'Yep. It comes and goes.'

'Me too,' Jake says. 'So, what's your news? You texted me.'

TWENTY

'More twists to the same story,' Trish says. 'Pietro, our friendly monk, has been trying to discover where my madia came from. I mean, how did it hole up here? Whose was it, between the sixteenth or seventeenth century and now? All that.'

'And…?' Jake is used to Trish's way of slowly drawing out her news.

'Well, you know this is a very old building –'

Jake interrupts her. 'Yeah?'

'Well, there's a whole other chapter in the Jewish story.'

'You could write a book,' Jake says.

'I will do, one day,' Trish replies. 'Are you sitting comfortably? Then I'll begin.'

'Get on with it,' Jake says, smiling.

'Soz. Well, many Jews survived the seventeenth-century ghettos, thanks to various dukes.'

'Which ones?

'The Orsinis and Medicis, guys like that,' Trish says, 'but I'm scrolling on a few centuries, till the 1930s, to Mussolini and co. '

'Go back a mo first please.'

'Why?'

'I didn't think the Medicis were such good guys,' he says. 'Didn't they make Jews wear red badges?'

'Yeah, but they kept them safe,' Trish replies.

'Mm…'

'Well, fast forward to Mussolini. He got started before Hitler and cronies. So, early in the 1930s, lots of farmers around here sheltered Jews – hid them, y'know.

'Like my uncle Ernie. He was hidden on a German farm.'

'I remember, yeah,' Trish says.

'God, she remembers everything, this girl,' Jake thinks. 'And?' he says.

'The monk reckons that this madia was hidden by one of those families. My building – this one – was once what the French call a *grenier*.'

'A grain store,' Jake adds. 'It's never seemed like a proper building.'

'Exactly. You've seen, it's mainly made of wood – not like other places round here.'

'Come on, spit it out!' Jake says.

'It's a long story,' Trish says.

'It has been, already,' Jake adds.

She explains that the monk showed her an old map of the area. In the 1920s and 30s, there was little between Trish's building and the nearest farm.

'He thinks the madia was secretly used by a Jewish family – kept up here, in amongst the grain, to hide it from any *fascisti* doing the rounds.'

'During Passover, you mean?'

'Probably, and –'

'This is a long one, Trish.'

'Sh. I've covered hundreds of years. You must hear this. He's found relatives of a local farmer. They remember hearing that he once hid Jews.'

'Trish, you're amazing.'

'It's not me, it's Fra Pietro. Come and see him again with me?'

'Sure.'

'Tomorrow?'

'Yep, fine. What about that newspaper interview?' asks Jake.

'I've postponed it – been in the papers enough for now.'

'Maybe. Anyway, I'm off. It's all great.'

'See you at the cathedral at... when?'

'11.30?'

'Great. Benissimo.'

'A domani.'

'A domani.' They hug goodbye.

Back at the hostel, Jake is suddenly overwhelmed with tiredness so he goes to his room for an official siesta. His bruises feel more tender and his back aches; he lies on his bed and closes his eyes. *Good idea, siestas.* However, he can't relax and just as he thinks he'll sleep for a while, his whole body tenses up and he feels his heart pounding and missing a beat every so often. He takes his pulse and knows it's much faster than usual; he is sweating even though there's a cool breeze coming through the window.

What the hell? He's panicking and goes to the window, trying to breathe slowly and deeply. It doesn't help. He takes his pulse again and it seems even faster. *God, I'm having a heart attack – young people sometimes just drop dead with faulty heart rhythms.* He tries to skype his mum or dad, then realises how crazy that is. *Grow up, Jake.* He goes downstairs and asks the guy at the desk how to contact a doctor.

'Non si sente bene? Doctor come 'ere.'

'Si, non bene. Grazie,' Jake replies. As he stands there, thinking he's going to faint, Jeeves walks in.

'God, Jake, what's up?'

'I think I'm having a heart attack,' Jake replies.

'No way, can't be. Sit down with your head between your legs.' Jeeves then pulls up a chair.

'They've called for a doctor.'

'I'll wait with you till he comes. Or she.'

'You're a good mate,' Jake says.

Jeeves hands him a paper cup of water and a hankie. 'Dip it into the water, then wipe the nape of your neck with it. Oh, you have got one!'

'What?'

'A nape. Sorry, joke.' Jake's haircut is still a talking – or joking – point.

'No worries, I get it,' Jake mumbles. He lifts his head up, carefully, feeling a little more human. A car skids up outside the hostel and a guy with a stethoscope runs in.

'You ill?' he asks, checking that Jake is the patient.

'A bit. It's my heart.'

'You 'ave room 'ere?'

'Upstairs,' Jake says, pointing upwards feebly.

The receptionist gestures to a door behind his desk. 'Come,' he says, raising the counter for them to go through into a little staff room.

'Sit, please,' the doctor tells Jake. Then he drags over a box. 'Feet on this. Do like me, OK?' He demonstrates breathing slowly. It works – Jake starts to breathe more easily. The doctor takes his pulse and says, 'Mm.'

'What?' Jake says.

'Is OK. You upset.' He gestures to Jake to lift up his shirt and listens to his chest, front and back, with the stethoscope. He is smiling all the time and seems a nice guy. Jake's head clears a little, once he knows he is still alive.

The doctor then attaches a blood-pressure monitor to his arm and says, 'Now we talk, OK? Parla italiano?'

'Only a little,' Jake says. 'Pochissimo.'

'I speak a bit more,' Jeeves says.

'OK. Come si chiama?'

'Jake. Sono studente.'

'Si. Jake, what you study?'

'Italian. I take Italian,' Jake says.

The doctor looks bemused. He takes some pills out of his bag, pours some into his hand and fakes swallowing them. 'What you take?'

'Oh! Niente,' Jake shakes his head. 'I don't do drugs.'

The doctor mimes snorting cocaine. 'This?'

'No!'

Jeeves looks on uncomfortably. 'I shouldn't be here,' he says. 'This is private.'

'Don't worry, I'm not a crackhead,' Jake says.

'We go to your room, please?' the doctor asks, unwrapping the monitor.

'Yep, I'll manage the stairs now,' Jake replies. 'Come with, Jeeves, for the language?'

'You'll manage, I'll wait here by reception. Text me if you need to. See you after the doctor leaves.'

'Fair enough,' Jake says and he goes cautiously up the stairs with the doctor. Once in the room, the doctor sits on the one chair and Jake on the edge of the bed.

'Is true, no drugs? No...?' he asks, miming smoking.

'No. No smoking of anything – not even tobacco,' Jake replies.

'Studente – no smoke? No drugs? I never see this before.' The doctor smiles. 'OK. So I think you panic.'

'But why?'

'You 'ave problem? Your back 'urting?' he says, noticing Jake wincing as he leans against his pile of pillows.

'Fa niente,' Jake says.

'Nothing? I see, please?'

The doctor takes a look at Jake's bruised lower back, buttock and thigh.

'Good colore... you fall?'

'Si.'

'You fight?'

'Not exactly,' Jake wonders how on earth he can tell the doctor what happened. 'It was in Rome, after the football.'

'Football? Momento.' He steps back to look at Jake, face on. 'Is you. In giornale. But you different.'

'I was in the paper, yes. But I've had a haircut,' Jake explains.

'Si, si,' the doctor says, nodding his recognition of Jake's face. 'I understand. I so sorry – scusi – gl'italiani not good. I no like this thing, Stremi, football. I am Italian, I am Toscano, but this bad for me. Was very bad for you, no?'

'I'm OK.'

'But this why you panic. You think bad things.' He twirls his finger round by his head. 'You sleep OK?'

'Not really. And now, I think more about the match than before. Mm,' Jake says, realising that bad memories do occupy his mind, certainly when he's alone.

'I no know the English words but sometimes bad things worse after – you understand?'

'I think so. Is it post-traumatic stress, d'you think?'

'I think, yes. Trauma, si. OK at beginning, not good later. Is difficult.'

'I've heard of it,' Jake says, remembering his mum's illness after his dad left.

'You want pills for sleeping?'

'Not really,' Jake says.

'I give you my number. You call. Anything, you call, please.'

'Thanks. That's really good.' Jake gets off the bed to see the doctor out.

'Momento. More panic, this you do.' He sees a paper bag in Jake's bin, left from Zany's snack, and takes it out. He shakes out the creases, puts it over his nose and mouth and breathes deeply for a while.

'You panic, you no carbon –'

'Dioxide. I've heard of it. A girl I knew had to do it.'

'Good. You know? You do. OK?'

'OK,' Jake says, frowning at the thought of doing it in public. Really girlie.

'Is funny, but importante. You 'ave bad time in Roma. But you 'ave good friends, yes?'

'Yes, very,' Jake replies.

'So... I go now. Your friend come back? I tell 'im.'

'No, I'll come down with you,' Jake says, opening his door

for the doctor, who stops to shake his hand.

'Good to meet you, Jake.'

'Do I pay you or – ?'

'No. Niente. Italian football, English student – is very bad. No pay.'

'Grazie molto,' Jake says, as he follows the doctor down the staircase. Jeeves jumps up anxiously from his chair in the vestibule.

'Are you OK, mate?' he says, putting both hands on Jake's shoulders.

'Yeah, yeah, I'm fine. The good doctor here sorted me out.'

'You good friend. Bad people at football,' the doctor says.

'But his heart?'

'I'm OK, Jeeves, honestly.'

''Is 'eart very good. Arrivederci,' the doctor says.

'Not *ciao*?' Jake asks.

'*Ciao* if I see you every day. I think you not need me again.'

'Benissimo, grazie molto,' Jake says and waves him off.

'Prego,' the doctor says as he leaves.

'Nice guy,' Jake says.

'Yeah. You gave me a shock, though,' Jeeves says.

'Me too,' Jake sniggers. 'Let's get some air.'

As they go outside, Jake's mobile rings. 'Can I just answer this?' he asks Jeeves. 'It's Gianni.'

Jeeves nods and leans against a wall as Jake takes the call.

'Buongiorno, Gianni, come stà?'

'Walking not good. But Mamma make me food and I rest in sun. You – 'ow are you?'

'Up and down. I hurt a bit. We must see each other.' He could not possibly explain these recent symptoms.

'Mamma want you to come. 'Ow is Trish hand? Povera Trish. Please you give me number: Trish number?'

'Sure,' Jake texts it to him.

'You come to eat Mamma's pasta, si? E Tom, Trish – and Suzanna – all friends. Please.'

'That's a lot of people,' Jake replies.

'A lot make Mamma 'appy. And other friends. You tell me 'ow many come. Si?'

'Well, I'll ask Jeeves, he's with me and… I may ask one more. A girl. Si chiama Zany.'

'Zany. Bene. Sei… six people, OK. And me, Mamma and Pappa. Nine is nothing for Mamma. In one week, at one o'clock? With sun and wine.'

'Wonderful. A *real* al fresco Italian lunch,' Jake says.

'Si. You text, say me who come. Va bene?'

'Yes. Ciao, Gianni, e grazie molto.' He turns to Jeeves. 'Lunch, thanks to Gianni's mamma. A week today, yeah?'

'Meraviglioso,' Jeeves replies. Jake texts the invitation to Trish, Tom, Suzanna and Zany. The replies come in straight away, except for Zany's. She contacts him on Facebook. She wants to know that they will be in a group – not just her, him and Trish. He answers yes.

In his text to Gianni, telling him the numbers and diverse dietary requests, Jake asks when he'd like to start English lessons again. Jake is running short of cash but knows Gianni still can't walk or drive. Gianni replies to say they could start next week, but at his house.

'USE TAXI. I PAY.'

'WILL BORROW BIKE – IF NOT TOO FAR,' Jake replies.

'Well, the lunch is something to look forward to,' Jeeves says. 'You feeling better?' he asks, looking worried.

'I'm fine,' Jake replies, not really sure that he is.

'Will you be OK on your own?' he asks, looking at his watch. 'I'm meant to be back at work by now.'

'Go, for goodness' sake!' Jake says. 'Don't risk the sack because of me.' His panic attack was so weird, he can't imagine it happening again. 'I'll go back to my room, face my demons and then maybe I'll go sketching.'

'Good plan.' Jeeves gently takes hold of Jake's shoulders and looks him straight in the eye in a paternal way. 'Text if you need.'

'Sure,' Jake replies. 'And thanks, mate.'

'For what?'

'Y'know.'

'A presto,' Jeeves says, as he leaves.

Jake feels vulnerable, now he's alone again, and goes back to his room with mixed feelings. He wants the security of his own room, yet fears the same sensation returning. *Panic attacks? Thought they were for girls.* He checks his pulse as he goes up the spiral staircase and then again, once he's sitting down in his room. He knows he shouldn't do this and spots three Skype icons on his computer screen. Mum, Trish and Zany. *Who first?* Each one brings a different stress level.

He emails each of them, saying he'll call in a hour or so. Procrastination won't help, he knows, but he gathers up his art things and sets off to sketch. Once he's settled on his folded coat, he breathes deeply and starts to work on an earlier piece that's still unfinished. He feels calmer; then a text arrives. Zany wants to know how he is and where. It would do him more good just to sit and sketch alone, but he can't resist telling her.

In the twenty minutes it takes for her to arrive, Jake almost completes his painting to his own satisfaction; a rare achievement. He doesn't hear Zany approach but feels her delicate hands over his eyes. 'Boo!' she says, in her childlike way. The quickening of his heartbeat feels like another panic attack starting. Jake takes her hands in his and wraps them round his shoulders so she is leaning over him, her face next to his. She takes her hands away and sits beside him.

'This is our boulder, isn't it?' she says, smiling and putting an arm round him. 'How've you been? You seem a bit – not yourself, somehow.'

'I was a bit off, actually.' Jake blushes. *Why tell her?* 'But I'm fine now.'

'A bit off, how?' Zany asks.

'I felt ill and the hostel called a doctor,' Jake says. 'Right now, I've got the finishing touches to do on this painting. Will you just sit by me?'

'Sure. Poor you.' She snuggles close to him, without impeding his ability to paint. He tears out a sheet from his pad, gives it to her with some pastels and Zany sits there, quietly sketching with him. Neither of them needs to speak and she realises instinctively that Jake needs a bit of peace.

Then he says, not looking at her, 'I had a panic attack.'

'Aha,' Zany says, unfazed. 'Not surprised.'

'Oh.'

'I've heard of them.' Zany remains non-committal.

'Thought I was dying,' Jake says. 'Honestly.'

'When those thugs attacked you, I bet you thought you *were*.'

'Yeah, but –'

'So, it's delayed reaction,' she says.

'You know about that, too?' Jake turns to her, even more impressed by her than ever.

'My auntie and uncle are both GPs and tell me a lot. I nearly studied medicine too, once – or maybe psychology,' she says. 'The mind fascinates me.'

'I thought you'd think I'm soft,' Jake says.

'You got beaten up in a foreign country. Soft? Come off it.'

'Thanks, Zany.' He turns and takes her face in his hands and kisses her gently, on her cheeks, her forehead, her nose and finally, her lips. 'What about the mind when it's in love? What then?'

'No answers,' she says, leaning her head on his shoulder and putting her left leg over his right one, rearranging the fabric of her loose trousers over her lower leg. Jake strokes it; even through fabric, he finds it sensuous.

'But you need to take care of yourself,' she adds.

'How?' Jake asks.

'Chill out, don't pressurise yourself, just, you know…'

'Che sarà, sarà?'

'Yeah.'

'You're so cool, Zany. It isn't only passion, y'know,' Jake says, clasping her hand in his.

'What isn't?'

'This – us. We really get on well, too – all that.'

'Mm...' Zany falls silent. 'Look, I must go, there's a lit class and then I've got my kids to look after.'

'Kids?'

'My babysitting job, remember?'

''Course – parli bene?'

'Si. It's coming on. I just about speak at the level of a five-year-old,' Zany replies.

'They say the best way to learn a language is with kids.'

'Good for fluency, not for adult vocab.'

'Listen, you go off now.' Jake doesn't want to talk about his visit to her parents.

'OK. But have you forgotten...?'

'What?'

'It's this weekend you're coming to my parents'.'

'God, it's come round quickly.' He fakes surprise. 'I hadn't forgotten about it, no. I was thinking about lunch at Gianni's.'

'First things first,' Zany says. 'Get the Perugia bus for two stops. Text me as you leave and I'll meet you off it.'

'Good one, Zany. Can't wait.'

'*I'd* put it off forever if I could,' she says. 'Seeya.' She kisses him lightly on his head as she stands up.

Jake stays there, touching up his painting even where there's no need. He knows, of old, that if he carries on he'll ruin it. He sighs and gathers up his things; the view is changing already as the sun drops. He loves the way colours can be so different through the day and decides to do a full day's images of this scene. He will come out at different times each day for a week, to capture everything from the morning mist to the evening's pink skies.

TWENTY-ONE

Thinking that a slight breeze might prevent any more panic attacks, Jake opens his blinds and windows, so his room becomes quite cool. He begins to plan the sequence of paintings, knowing he should first call his mum.

He skypes Trish first. She holds up her splinted, bandaged wrist: 'This is driving me crazy; it's so hot,' she says. 'And even though my fingers are free, I can't really hold much – least of all a pen. Thank goodness for iPads and laptops. We're meeting up tomorrow, why the Skype? You are still coming?'

'Yeah, sure,' Jake says.

'You don't look sure. You OK?'

'Just about.'

'What's up?'

'Well, first, I've got massive bruises from the beating.'

'You told me. Are they worse?' Trish asks.

'Much,' Jake replies.

'And?'

He knows Trish can ferret out anything he doesn't want to say. So he fills her in about his 'funny do'. As usual, she is quite matter of fact.

'Bet you've got a paper bag ready,' she says, as though it's an everyday occurrence.

'Right again. How d'you know?'

'A friend of mine had one.'

'Xanthe?' Jake asks.

'No, someone else.'

'Well, see you domani.'

'Good one – and you just smiled! Ciao,' Trish says.

Jake still isn't ready to skype his mum. Doing a face-to-face with her is different – she sees too much. If he looks strained, she sees it and if tired, she'll see that, too. Mothers... even worse than Trish.

So he emails her, saying he's got a bit of a reaction to the attack but that everything else is good. *(If she believes that...)* He tells her about Jeeves's friendship, his art, Trish's find and a bit about Zany. He ends by saying he'll eventually tell her all about the monk and the Tuscan farmer's family. He sends a copy to Flo and his dad, promising to skype them soon.

His bruises are aching again and he still needs the rest he was about to have when he felt ill. He's worried about lying down but can't help it. He sets his alarm for one hour's time and takes two paracetamol for the bruises with a large swig of bottled water. He's woken before the alarm by Tom, at the door.

'Jake, mate, have you... are you still alive?'

'Just about.' Jake feels dizzy from jumping up to open the door but asks Tom in. He recounts the doctor episode and although Tom is very sympathetic, Jake thinks he may not be much into emotions. Nevertheless, the company is reassuring – just what he needs to be shaken out of his self-pity. He grudgingly accepts Tom's invitation to pop out for a drink. The guys they meet up with are not ones they know well and their banter is light, which does do him good. He sleeps better that night, the paper bag ready at his bedside.

In the morning Jake feels bright, his bruising looks more colourful but feels less painful and he sets off to meet Trish at the cathedral. She is waiting for him with the monk. It is hard to believe that this man who has been so helpful is the same person Jake tried to brush off on his first morning in Todi.

'Buongiorno, Fra Pietro. Come stà?' Jake says, smiling. Trish grins her approval of Jake's charm.

'Bene, grazie. 'Appy to see you again,' Pietro replies, shaking Jake's hand with both of his. 'I 'ave informazione about madia. Come – come with me,' he says, leading them into the church. He goes into the vestry and points to Trish's madia there.

'It belong to a family ebraica. Mussolini come and fascisti. Pericoloso – you know what is pericoloso?' he asks.

'Dangerous; yes, we know it was dangerous for Jews,' Trish says.

'Many good farmers 'ere. They ask ebrei: "Please, live in farm with mia famiglia." So they OK. No fascisti come. Madia OK, also.'

'That's great, Fra Pietro. And in English we say "Jews" or "Jewish", not ebrei or ebraici,' Trish explains tactfully.

The monk nods. 'OK. Allora, I 'ave good news,' he says. 'I find famiglia – family from farm near Todi.'

'Wow, meraviglioso!' Trish says.

'Amazing,' Jake agrees.

'You want to meet?' the monk says.

'Meet them? Of course, please,' Trish says, hardly able to believe her good luck.

'I tell you a leetel. You can meet daughter of farmer. She is old. Not possible she come 'ere. You come with me?'

'To the farm, you mean? Of course,' Trish says.

'Si. You meet 'er. She remember she see famiglia ebrea – Jewish – in farm.'

'This is terrific. When can we arrange this?' Jake asks.

'Pronto. We go now – is OK?'

So Jake and Trish leave with the monk, who surprises them with his cute red and black smart car, into which they squeeze – Jake's long legs doubled up at the front, Trish, part sideways at the back. Fra Pietro drives a bit too fast for the car, Jake thinks, and a bit fast for a monk. Luckily it's not far to the house.

They learn that the elderly woman, Signora Luchesi, though very frail, still lives in what was her father's farmhouse. Her own daughter and grandchildren will be with her for the meeting. Fra Pietro's English improves as he goes on, so between them, they gather that the woman's memories are quite clear. Apparently, her daughter learnt what happened in the 1930s from her and from the diary she kept as a girl. 'Intriguing,' Jake thinks. 'And I feel better – it's good to keep busy.'

'Ecco la casa, quà.' Fra Pietro says, as he draws up by a dilapidated farmhouse. 'Ecco the granddaughter. Ciao!' he shouts from the window of the car. Trish takes a photograph of the house, to add to her records, with Fra Pietro in front of it. But Jake is staring at the young woman.

It is Adriana, the lecturer. Seeing her out of context, Jake's panicky feelings surge: what the hell is she doing here? His heart races as he gets out of the car, so he stops and breathes deeply.

Trish comes round to him and whispers, 'What's up?'

'Nothing. A bit dizzy – you go ahead.' He opens the car door again and puts his foot up on the floor, pretending to fasten his trainer laces, stalling for time. He peeps out at the monk and Trish greeting Adriana and a family group that includes an elderly woman.

OMG! She's Signora Luchesi's granddaughter… Of all the…

'It's Jake! Buongiorno. Welcome – a casa della nonna,' she says, laughing.

'You know Adriana?' Fra Pietro asks.

'Er, kind of, she's my teacher,' Jake answers.

'Si. We know each other well,' Adriana says. She introduces her brother Silvio, her mother, and her grandmother, Signora Luchesi. He notes that they are not as welcoming as Adriana: the protective Italian family? Jake's panic subsides, despite the surprise.

'Buongiorno,' he says, at his most charming. Trish greats everyone too and they are beckoned through the farmhouse onto a back terrace with a wonderful view.

Signora Luchesi eventually makes it to the terrace, supported by Adriana and a stick, which she uses to point, saying, 'Ecco la bell'Umbria. S'accommodi, per favore,' gesturing to the rickety garden chairs, whose wicker has known better days.

A small table has been set with glasses and what looks like fresh limonata, cheeses, olives and amaretti.

'Yes, Umbria is beautiful, specially this view,' Trish says.

However, Jake sees dark clouds gathering; they seem to roll around from time to time here. 'Ecco,' he says, pointing to the dark sky.

'Umbria – è bella, no?' asks Signora Luchesi.

'Very cloudy right now, though,' Jake says.

'And the hills look so dark,' Trish adds. 'Hey, is that why it's called Umbria, from shadows – ombre – d'you think?'

'Google it later,' Jake says.

'Umbria much piove,' says Signora Luchesi, obviously following the gist of their observations.

'It rains a lot? Ah, and there's a storm brewing,' Trish says.

They hear a distant roll of thunder and see lightning on the horizon. Jake imagines that they'll have to move indoors.

'Here, ignore the weather. Have some of this drink. It's made with lemons from that tree,' Adriana says, pointing to one of many citrus trees. 'The farm doesn't have animals any more but we have fruit and vegetables.' She pours them all a glass of iced limonata.

'Mm, benissimo, grazie,' Trish says, sipping some.

With the help of Adriana's fluent English, Signora Luchesi's old, torn diary and the monk, Trish and Jake gather the details of the family's story and the Jewish family whose lives they saved. And, of course, the madia.

'What is it?' Adriana asks Jake. 'You look bewildered.'

'I'm not,' he replies. 'I'm stunned.' He is also surprised by Adriana's familiarity. 'It's all such a coincidence.' In his head, he hears his great-grandma's words again: 'Things that change your life...' and so on.

'Stunned that it is my family?' Adriana asks.

'Yes, that… and also because of my uncle.'

Adriana translates for her mother, who wants an explanation. So Jake tells them how Uncle Ernie was also hidden on a farm in the Thirties; but he cuts it short, not wanting to divert attention from *their* family story. Trish is deeply involved in talking to the old lady, while looking at the diary.

'Coincidences…' Adriana says, smiling and flirting.

'… Make life interesting,' he says. At which moment the heavens open and it starts to pour with rain, so they do move indoors.

Adriana's brother Silvio and Fra Pietro now try to engage Trish and Jake with other details from the Thirties. Silvio confirms that there had been a madia which was hidden for their 'Passover bread', as he puts it.

'But the madia is much more than ninety years old,' Trish says.

'Si, si,' Silvio says. 'They stay in families for hundreds of years, usually for bread, but this one for matzah, you know?' he says in immaculate English.

Trish nods, grinning. She has all the information she needs, for now. She is so happy and Jake is happy for her. But in Adriana's company he is confused by his feelings. He sees Adriana's mother and brother observing the interactions between them and Silvio interrupts whenever Adriana and he talk to each other. Time passes and Fra Pietro points out that they shouldn't tire Signora Luchese. He suggests to Signora that they leave now and meet again another time.

'Bene, bene, si. Per favore.' She may be tired but has clearly enjoyed the meeting and the opportunity to reminisce.

'Yes, please, we'd love to come again,' Trish says.

'That would be good,' Adriana says.

'Is there more to that?' Jake wonders to himself.

They say their goodbyes and thanks and Fra Pietro drives them back.

'That was so, so special,' Trish says in the car.

'I think newspaper want to meet you,' the monk says. 'Is importante story, no?'

'It is,' Trish says. 'I'll think about it.' She is too late, since, as they arrive back at the cathedral, there are a couple of guys waiting with flashing cameras.

'Scusi, I tell them. Is good for Todi and me too, no?' Fra Pietro says.

'It is,' Jake says. 'You helped a lot.'

Trish glares at him a bit but shrugs her shoulders in acceptance as she agrees to talk to the journalists. After all, it's a far more positive, optimistic story about local Italians than the football one. Jake is proud of Trish's perseverance. Maybe Fra Pietro will turn Todi into a visitors' centre about Jewish history, to compete with Pitigliano.

What Jake can't work out is what to do about Adriana. Things are tricky enough with Zany, without even contemplating two-timing, something he's always disapproved of.

Trish finishes her interview and they both thank Fra Pietro profusely, acknowledging that this story is very good for him and his local standing. After they say goodbye to him, Trish begins to ask Jake about Adriana.

'I must catch up on my work,' Jake says.

'But what's going on with her?'

'Nothing, OK? I'm going to Zany's this weekend.'

'Aha. Dreading it?'

'Dunno. Listen, today was brilliant. You're brilliant – dead proud of you.' He kisses her goodbye and leaves for his hostel.

In the two days before going to Zany's, keeping busy is the only way to cope and to put his panic attack behind him. Luckily, he has a lot of work to catch up on and a lot of people to catch up with. So, on Facebook he suggests a get-together with Tom, Suzanna and Jeeves; he postpones skyping Flo, his mum and his dad; and he prepares some work for Gianni. He decides to email some language exercises to him: 'You do not have to finish these before I see you. Hope you are feeling better. A presto, Jake.'

Next on his 'to do' list is his own Italian prep, as he tries to drum in his ever-lengthening list of vocabulary; he wonders whether his new-found conscientiousness has something to do with Adriana. The last thing in his catch-ups is to complete more of his sketches; he wants at least one finished and up on his wall.

So the first of the two days passes busily but by two o'clock he realises he's had no lunch – not the best approach to feeling fit. He closes his books, takes a sketch pad and paints, and makes off down the staircase and out into the square. He sets off on a short, brisk walk, trying to breathe deeply, picking up a snack en route. As he sits on a bench to eat and drink in the sun, Facebook messages arrive from Tom and Suzanna: they'll meet him the next day – just one day before the visit.

He feels his pulse; it's fast, he's sure of it. He times it with his watch and, a short time later, compares it. It's faster still – he starts to feel dizzy. There's a surge of panic and he takes out the paper bag from his pocket and breathes into it, just in time. It's miraculous but leaves him feeling ashamed and vulnerable – what if it happens when he's with people? Worse still, at Zany's parents? He calls the doctor and makes an appointment to see him again at his rooms; perhaps there really is something wrong and it's not just trauma.

He stands up, ready to go back, but first climbs the hill to his favourite spot. Here, he stretches, breathes in the fresh air, hot though it is, and decides to take himself in hand. *You're too soft, Jake my man. Grow up.* Just as his strength returns, a text comes from Zany.

'R U FEELING BETTER? C U DAY AFTER 2MORROW. GRANDPARENTS ARRIVE SOON. TENSION MOUNTING. C U AT END OF OUR RD, 3PM? LOVE Z X'

God, and I think I feel tense. Zany must be under even more pressure. How can we sort it all out? He is now even more aware that everything may not be in their hands.

Back in his room, there's one painting Jake particularly wants to finish, not least because it was painted at his and Zany's favourite spot. He has told her he will give her a painting for her birthday even though it won't be finished in time. As he is about to finalise the details, he adds two blurred, silhouetted figures in the foreground, off to one side – the acrylics allow him to paint over paint. The figures are not recognisable but he knows whom they represent and Zany will also know.

He feels content for the first time in a week; as he walks back to the hostel, he makes sure to go past a place where the wood-fired oven produces magnificent pizzas to go. They are always a bit burnt round the edges but so tasty. He buys a giant one and takes it back with him in its insulated box.

As he's eating it – and realising his room will stink in the morning – he sees that his family are waiting to skype. And there they all are, the three of them together again.

'So, what's news of your bruise, bro?' Flo says. 'D'you like the rhyme? Let's see!'

'Cheeky,' Jake says, smiling. 'It's not for public view. But I wish I could give you some of this.' He shows them the pizza, taking another bite as he does so. The cheese drips off the end of his chin and he has to lift it away from his iPad. 'What a mess. It was baked just near here.'

'Which meal is that, then?' his mum asks. 'Lunch or dinner?'

'Dunno,' Jake replies. 'Just grazing. Hey, here's the first complete painting. Like it?' he asks, holding it up for them.

'Peng!' Flo says. Jake thought that word was only used to describe people.

'What a view,' his dad says.

'Did you use a palette knife?' his mum asks.

'For some of it, yes. And the view... yeah, it's one of many. Our... my favourite,' Jake says.

'And *our* meaning who?' Flo asks.

'Me and Zany, if y'must know,' Jake says, blushing.

'Is that you and her in the foreground?' Flo asks. Jake nods. 'Can't see her face,' she says, 'silhouetted from behind.'

'True,' Jake says.

'How are things, then?' his dad asks. 'Sorting?'

'Not sure. They put off the visit to this Sunday,' Jake explains. 'No idea what'll happen.'

'It's not in your hands, really,' his mum says.

'God, not another one,' Jake says.

'What d'you mean?'

'Oh, nothing.'

'Are you OK? It's hard to tell on this screen but you look a bit drawn. Anything else going on?'

'I've not been feeling great,' Jake answers. 'Since the football, really.'

'In what way?' his dad asks.

'Look, I have seen a doctor – lovely guy – and I'll see him again. It's all under control, OK?'

'You're an adult, Jake. None of our business really,' his dad assures him. 'But being attacked – well, I mean, that's just disgusting.'

'Yeah. Funny thing is, the doctor thought I was a druggie.'

'With all those students around – and he must see lots of them – he would think that,' his mum says.

'And I can't teach Gianni at the moment, unless I go to his house, cos he can't walk.'

'So your routine's changed, too,' his dad comments.

'All that, yeah. I've got good mates, though.'

'*The* best thing,' Flo adds.

'But Trish's discovery is just unbelievable. I've no time to tell you about it now, but I'll scan and send you her newspaper interview.'

'Isn't it online?' his dad asks.

'What? The little local paper? Doubt it... I'll see... Hey, it is.' He tells them the website. He feels better; he had thought speaking to the family would make him worse.

'Take care, Jakey,' Flo says. 'Ciao.'

'Ciao, la famiglia,' Jake says, blowing them kisses as he switches off his Skype screen. Night has fallen by the time his conversation ends, so he has an early shower and reads in bed, to the accompaniment of iTunes music in his ears.

He wakes the next day to a lurch of his stomach, not palpitations in his heart: only one more day till Zany's. There is the usual morning knock on the door. It can't be Tom; that crowd are all meeting at eleven. It's a female voice.

'Hello, are you there?' And another knock, so he opens the door. It is Zany. 'Can I come in?' She is very flustered. Jake lets her in and closes the door behind her.

'I'm not protecting your reputation this time, young lady. You chose to come here, your problem.' Jake says, hugging her close. 'God, I miss you when I don't see you.' He is in his pyjama shorts, which do little to mask his arousal; he wriggles away a little. But she wriggles closer, moving a knee between his legs. He puts a hand on her shoulder and gently pushes her back.

'Here, sit down for a sec, Zany,' he says. 'Just getting something.'

He leaves for the bathroom, but when he gets back, she has gone. *WTF?*

He sees a note on his desk: 'Sorry, I shouldn't have come round. See you tomorrow at the end of Mum's road.'

For God's sake. Shouldn't have come on to me, more like. This could easily drive me completely crazy. And I'm crazy enough already. Why did she come – did she really want to get off with me?

It is time to go and meet the gang, but Jake is sitting on the bed with his head in his hands, rubbing his face and eyes with his palms, trying to shake off his self-image of some doomed, tragic lover. He is involved with three problematic women, but in love only with Zany. He can't miss seeing his good friends, so he splashes his face again and again with cold water, pulls an afro comb through his hair and puts on some fresh clothes, as though to discard his passion.

'Everything's gone haywire since I had my hair cut,' he thinks. He breathes deeply and goes down to find his friends. It's a tonic to realise that they're pleased to see him; his old insecurity has disappeared. They exchange news and he tells them about the farm visit with Trish.

'We know about that, it's all in here.'

Of course. The local newspaper. He had forgotten that they would all see it, as it is left in a pile in the vestibule.

'Getting quite famous, you and Trish, aren't you, my man?' Tom says.

'It's a really amazing find. I didn't know anything about Italian Jews, to be honest,' Suzanna says.

'Didn't know that much myself,' Jake says, 'it's all Trish's work.' At that moment, Trish rushes in to the hostel dining room, waving something – and it's not the newspaper.

'Did you follow our radar?' Tom says.

'What? Oh. No, I came looking for you. You'll not believe this,' she says, puffed with excitement. 'I've been offered a research scholarship here, if I want it, starting in the autumn.'

'Researching what?'

'The Jews of Umbria and Tuscany, ancient and modern – something like that,' she says.

'Mental!' Susanna says.

Jake hugs her. 'Trish, that's awesome. Do you want it? I mean, staying in Italy and everything?'

'Not sure. I'm just flattered, for now. I'll have to get fluent in Italian first, obviously.'

'Obviously,' they say, in unison, mocking her a little.

'And it also depends on Xanthe.'

'Are you two an item, then?' Suzanna asks.

'Definitely,' Trish replies.

'Cool,' Jake says.

They carry on chatting for a couple of hours; it's therapeutic for Jake to relax like this, knowing that this group is there for him, no matter what. Jeeves arrives later on, hand in hand with a gorgeous blonde girl Jake has never seen before.

'Hi guys. Meet Luisa.'

'Hi Luisa. Lei è italiana?' Tom asks.

'No, I'm Swedish,' she says, in accentless English. 'But I work here, in the administration office of Perugia University.'

'So – join us,' Jake says.

Then Xanthe finds them, half an hour later, which makes the circle so big, they run out of chairs. The strange thing is that within the group, Jake doesn't miss Zany. He realises that she doesn't quite fit in, not really, however delightful she is. Would Adriana?

The day winds on but they separate eventually and Jake is pleased to see how comfortable Trish is in Xanthe's company; maybe she is the love of her life. And Jeeves? Is Luisa just a girl friend or *the* girlfriend? He suspects the former. He takes his leave and goes to his room to work some more on his Italian. But concentrating on that, with the next day's events looming, is impossible.

After trying to memorise more tenses and conjugations, he spends time working on another piece of art – the same view as the previous one, but seen in the evening light. He uses pastel, smudging it to capture the misty, blurred outlines. It looks so different but, for once, he's pleased with the result and wonders where to find some simple frames for the series. Probably in Perugia, where there's an art department.

'My first gift for Flo,' he thinks.

The evening draws in and with it, the church bells which announce the eve of Sunday; he's only gathered since he's been in Italy that the Catholic Sabbath begins the evening before, just like the Jewish Shabbat, which begins on Friday evening. He's often watched a procession of families going to church on Saturday evenings here, and after it, the *passeggiata* begins, when the young men of Todi stroll through the streets looking immaculate in their crisp white shirts – parading past the girls, also in their best clothes. It's so cute and old-fashioned.

Whole families are about, as they are on Sunday evening, too, but Jake has noticed that, although the youngsters are obviously looking to meet up with the opposite sex, they don't disown their parents as they might in the UK. There seems a lovely atmosphere and he decides to go out for a while and mill around, soaking up something so typically Italian.

He wanders around, in and out of the young people. Their camaraderie is impressive since there is not too much going on around here, socially. The students have a lot more to do, he thinks, remembering that he wanted to ask his mates if they'd like to go to a concert. The little theatre/concert hall is quite impressive for a small town like this. He texts them all but Suzanna texts back the information that performances finish in April. *Good idea gone wrong, then.* She does tell him, however, that the theatre is worth an visit. 'IT'S V ORNATE. WELL COOL.'

He passes the rest of the evening like this, thinking, texting, drawing poorly, till he can't put off going to bed any longer. At least he has a Sunday language session in the morning. The afternoon will be upon him before long.

TWENTY-TWO

Jake knows his compulsive glances at his watch, to see how long it is till he leaves for Zany's, are becoming obsessional, so he moves the watch face round till it is under his wrist. He smiles to himself as he lifts his arm to peep at it anyway. Five hours to go. His heart races, so he feels for the paper bag in his shorts pocket, but it's not there. Knowing it isn't there makes his heart go even faster. 'Breathe slowly, Jake,' he tells himself. He decides to buy something, from which he can keep the paper bag.

It's Sunday. *Shit.* Not one single little shop opens on Sunday – maybe a café? Buy a pastry? That's it. None of the nearest ones sell them in bags, only on a little piece of waxed paper or, at a charge, in a small cake box. He puts his finger to his pulse but with his watch turned over he can't time it. The panic takes hold and he sees no option but to run back to the hostel, which is further than he thinks, so he is doubly out of breath. In one narrow alley he sinks almost to the floor, sitting on his haunches, sure he's about to die. Or faint. He thinks he'll text the doctor for an earlier appointment but again, it's Sunday. *Should I call at the weekend?* He sits on the ground and puts his head between his knees. He knows he can't faint in that position.

A text beeps and he sits up, aware that he didn't die or faint and that he feels a little more normal. The text is from Adriana. 'R U OK? THOUGHT YOU WERE COMING 2 MY CONVERSATION GROUP.' Jake had not known it would be led by Adriana this morning; these extra Sunday sessions are only occasional and could be taught by any tutor. He is now grateful for his panic attack because he'd never have coped with being at Adriana's class just before going to Zany's.

He replies: 'SORRY. IF I'D KNOWN IT WAS U I'D HAVE TEXTED. AM OK. SOMETHING CAME UP. CU AT NEXT LECTURE. J X'

'How good a liar I am,' Jake thinks. However, this is the first time a panic has passed on its own, so he feels a bit more in control. What now? He sees people coming out of church and strolling around or sitting in cafes. He chooses a table near some young people and wonders whether he can practise his Italian conversation this way. Sure enough, before long they need the spare chairs at his table and start to talk to him. He struggles at first, gradually gaining confidence in Italian. They're a friendly group, a fair bit younger than him – not yet at college. They are intrigued by the life of foreign students here and Jake seems to be the first one they've met properly. He feels chuffed about that. When he gets up to leave, they ask when they'll see him again and say 'Ciao' like old friends.

Jake's mood is lighter as he goes back to shower and change. He puts on a cool, short-sleeved shirt and the only pair of long trousers he's brought with him. He can't imagine shorts or even cut-offs going down very well with the Chaudry family. Zany has warned him that the buses are less frequent on Sundays, so he'll give himself an hour to get there. He turns over imagined conversations with her parents as he gets ready.

Facebook has messages from his mates, wishing him luck for the visit, as well as one from his parents. Where they are concerned, Jake wonders what they really want the outcome to be. A little earlier than needed, he goes off to the bus stop and waits, but the bus doesn't come. It is late even for its delayed Sunday schedule. He looks again at the Google map on his phone and decides to walk it. He could still just do it. And if he follows the bus route, he might even flag it down.

So he sets off. 'This is the way to my destiny,' he thinks – in Petrarch mode. It's a fair distance, so he steps up his pace, still hoping to catch a bus along the way so he doesn't get too hot. Arriving with sweat marks under his arms would hardly make a good impression.

He hears what he thinks is the bus behind him, turns round to look and then runs towards the next bus stop, which is not far ahead. As he runs he sticks his hand out and points to the bus stop. He thinks that should be clear enough. But the bus driver apparently thinks otherwise.

'Grazie molto!' Jake shouts. He forces himself not to give the finger – and it's a good job he doesn't, because the bus screeches to a halt a little way past the stop and backs up as Jake reaches it. He gets on, says a meaningful 'Grazie molto' to the driver, showing his student pass, and sits down with relief.

Before he reaches his end stop, Jake sees Zany, waving and flagging down the bus. He thanks the driver and jumps off, quite pointedly not into Zany's arms.

'Hi, you,' he says. He feels awkward, as though her parents are already listening and watching. 'You OK? You left suddenly the other day, didn't you?'

Zany blushes. 'Sorry, I...' Her eyes start to well up.

'No worries – saved us from a fate worse than – well, maybe... Cheer up.'

Zany leads him up the street to a tree-lined path which seems to go nowhere till it opens out, revealing three large, modern houses in a cul-de-sac.

'That's ours,' Zany says, pointing to the middle house. 'We don't live in a grand place like this in Leeds, y'know.'

'It's lovely though,' Jake says, as they walk to the front door. He is surprised that Zany doesn't use a key but presses the doorbell.

'They want to greet you properly,' she explains. And they do. Her parents open the door and stand side by side, formally introduce themselves and invite him in. Her father shakes Jake's hand; her mother holds her hand across her chest and nods slightly as she says hello. He knew she would not offer her hand. She gestures to his sandals – which he's already removed, copying Zany – and offers him a pair of slippers from a box.

'Thanks,' Jake says, as he puts them on.

'They *are* washable,' Zany reassures him, smiling.

'Please, come in,' her mother says. Her father says nothing, apparently assessing Jake's every move. The room they go into is bright and formally furnished, with a large coffee table in the middle, on which there are drinks, platters of fruit and dishes of sweetmeats.

Zany sits demurely next to her mother on the settee; her father sits on one armchair and gestures to Jake to take another one. They sit, then, on three sides of a table with a door to the garden open in front of them. Jake wonders why they aren't outside, in this weather. The lounge walls are devoid of pictures or photographs but, of course, this is not their permanent home. However, there are two framed sheets of Arabic calligraphy on the wall behind the settee.

'A lovely house you've got here,' Jake says, breaking the silence.

'Yes. It belongs to my cousin – those are their Islamic graphics,' Mrs Chaudry says, following Jake's gaze.

'They're brilliant,' he says, getting up to take a closer look. 'Done by hand?'

'Originally, but that is a numbered print,' Mrs Chaudry says.

'You're lucky to have a holiday home like this,' Jake says.

'It is my daughter who is lucky,' Mr Chaudry says. 'She could not have studied in Italy if this was not here for us.'

Mrs Chaudry interrupts this line of conversation by getting up and asking Jake which drink he'd like: 'Fresh lemon juice or pomegranate from a carton?' She has a winning smile.

'Lemon, please.' Mrs Chaudry then offers Jake the choice of

fruits and sweetmeats, handing him a delicate china plate. He puts a handful on his plate, wishing he could take them one by one to fill the gaps in the strained conversation.

'I hope you don't mind my asking, Mrs Chaudry, but Zainab told me that your name, Malak, means angel. Am I right?' Jake asks.

Mrs Chaudry nods.

'Well, it's the same in Hebrew – *and* it's also like my grandma's name, Malkah. Mind you, that means "queen".' He wants to sound interesting but knows he's trying too hard.

'So we have things in common,' Mrs Chaudry says. 'Are you happy in Italy?'

'I am, yes. And I love the language.'

'But not the football, I gather,' Zany's dad says, picking out a newspaper from a rack – the paper that reported the attack.

'Well, the football's very good. Those guys are just disgusting hooligans. They wreck the game for everyone,' Jake says.

'And they're racist – it's terrible,' Mr Chaudry adds.

'And terrible for you. Were you badly hurt? The paper said you were OK,' Mrs Chaudry says.

'I was bruised and... pretty shocked,' Jake replies.

'And your friend, here. How is she?' Mr Chaudry points to Trish in the paper.

'She broke her wrist.'

'Oh dear,' says Mrs Chaudry.

'I see her again in the paper,' Mr Chaudry says, pointing to the farm visit. 'Hm, she looks an interesting sort of girl.' He gives a wry grin, then quickly adds, 'And of course, it's a very interesting story.'

'Have some figs,' his wife offers.

Jake takes one and chews it for longer than it takes to finish it. 'That's gorgeous – so juicy,' he says, blushing and not looking at Zany. *That describes her perfectly.*

'You are Jewish, aren't you?' Mr Chaudry asks.

Jake cannot imagine what's coming next. 'Why do you ask?'

'Well, as I understand it, from the Jewish families I know in my interfaith group, they also keep an eye on their kids, like we do. Am I not right?'

'It's very nice of you to think that, but I can't generalise. My parents do want to share my experiences and they are there for me – they love me. But they don't know everything I do, by any means.'

'Ah, but you are a boy – well, a man, actually.'

'I don't think they differentiate,' Jake replies.

'So, you have a sister?' Mrs Chaudry asks him.

'Yes, she's a lot younger. Maybe they will be more protective of her as she grows up, I don't know.'

'Aha, you use the word protective. In our family that word works two ways,' says Mr Chaudry.

'It does?' Jake asks, wanting to put off this agonising portrayal of Zany's life.

'Yes,' he continues, 'we love our daughter and protect her from harm; her behaviour protects our family reputation.'

'I see,' Jake says. A change of subject is sorely needed. At that moment the doorbell rings. Zany goes to the door and in run two little girls with, he presumes, their mother. Zany introduces them.

'This is Fatima, she's ten, and this is Shanida, she's six – and their mother, Signora Faisal.'

Jake says hello with a nod of the head, fascinated to meet a family who are both Italian and Muslim.

'Scusi. Buongiorno. Come stà, Signora Faisal?' he says.

'Bene. But I speak English; it's the girls who are learning,' she says. 'I'm pleased to meet you.' By this time the two girls have already run out into the garden with Zany and a big ball.

'Come and see our beautiful Italian garden,' Mrs Chaudry says. 'Zainab tells us you are an artist. Maybe you'd like to paint this, some time.' She leads the way onto a terrace, takes him round and points out interesting trees and shrubs.

'I love gardens and ours in Leeds is very small,' she says.

'But you make it lovely, though, Mummy,' Zany says, linking her mother's arm. 'You should see what my mother's done, Jake. She grows vegetables as well as flowers *and* she helps in the business.'

'Oh, Zainab, you flatter me.' Mother and daughter giggle to each other.

Mr Chaudry stops Jake as he is about to follow Zany and her mum onto the lawn. He puts his arm round Jake's shoulder, making him wriggle and blush.

'You see, Jake, life is like a garden stroll.' *What is he on about?* 'This is the path to the garden; this is straightforward. The path we follow in relationships is more complicated: lots of alleys leading in different directions. Know what I mean?'

Jake can only nod, hemmed in as he is by the older man's arm.

'You seem like a good boy. My daughter is a good girl but she is a bit too free, here in Italy. Maybe the sun is hypnotic, hm?' Then he smiles, and continues the tour of the garden in the opposite direction to the women, till they reach the small swimming pool, where they stand facing each other.

'It is only small, like I said, isn't it?' Zany says, across the pool, in her first utterance for ages. The children chase each other, throwing the ball and pulling Zany's arm to make her play games.

'Momento, ragazze,' she says to them. 'Aspetto!'

The girls are clearly fond of Zany – and she of them. Jake does enjoy teaching Gianni, but it looks as though her job is more fun; perhaps he takes his too seriously.

'Zainab and I take a dip late on, each day,' Mrs Chaudry says, nullifying any thoughts Jake might have had of mixed swimming. 'Before she starts her babysitting.'

'How's it going?' he asks Zany.

'Good.'

As Zany chats with the girls while moving towards him, Jake hears how fluent she has become. Mr Chaudry comes between them, inviting them to sit in the wicker chairs on the terrace. Jake doesn't relish any further intrusive comments and says he will have to go shortly.

'So soon?' Mrs Chaudry says. 'You must stay for Zany's birthday cake.'

'Of course. I forgot,' he says. The girls run up to the table, ready for the treat, and the younger one asks to share Jake's chair. He moves up and pats the cushion.

'Ecco! Per lei,' he says, as she clambers up onto it. Zany smiles across at him. He resists putting his arm round the cute little girl, thinking it may not be right. The cake comes out. It's actually a pile of Asian sweets like he used to buy in Rusholme, back in Manchester. All colours and shapes are heaped high in a wobbly pile, with a candle on the top. Mrs Chaudry lights it and Zany invites the girl to help blow it out – not that one candle will take much effort. They sing 'Happy Birthday', then her parents, the girls and their mother hug and kiss Zany. How Jake wishes he could, too. After a taste of the sweets, Zany wraps some up and gives them to Jake.

'Here, take them back with you,' she says.

Jake thanks her and takes his leave. 'It's been lovely meeting you all, really. See you, Zany,' he says, trying – and failing – to regain eye contact with her. 'Don't forget the outing to Gianni's.' He mentions it on purpose, to check her parents know about it. 'There is quite a crowd of us going.'

'Great. You know about that, Abba,' Zany says, making sure her father has really given his permission.

Fancy hearing 'Abba', the same word for Daddy as in Hebrew. Weird or what?

'We are invited to a real Italian meal, home-cooked and everything, remember?' Zany adds.

'You did tell me, yes. That will be nice. I will see our friend to the door,' Mr Chaudry says. Zany and her mother nod a goodbye. In the hall, Jake fishes out his sandals from the box and Mr Chaudry accompanies him off the porch.

'I know that you and Zainab are good kids. Just be careful which path you take, hm? Watch for those slippery cobbles, in case they lead to a brick wall. Don't you think?'

Jake cannot be expected to answer that. Then Mr Chaudry shakes his hand, which is sweating profusely. He's sweating all over, in fact.

'Zany and I are just friends, Mr Chaudry. Thanks for having me.'

'Our pleasure,' Mr Chaudry replies.

It has been an awkward couple of hours and Jake could not work out what Zany made of it. The half-hour walk back is good but he cannot sort out his muddled thoughts. Was Mr Chaudry warning him off – did he mean Jake should stop seeing Zany, with no regard to her views? He feels like Hamlet, asking conflicting rhetorical questions with no one listening but himself.

Jake tries repeatedly to contact Zany after the visit but not one message is answered – and he tries texting, Facebook, email, everything. The days from Sunday to Wednesday and lunch at Gianni's have to be lived and he needs to stay sane. Whilst he wants to report back to at least one member of his family about meeting the Chaudry parents, he decides a group email is best. Talking to them would be stressful.

So for now, he calls Trish, who suggests he comes over and that they go out for a stroll with Xanthe. 'We're joined at the hip at the moment,' she says, adding, 'and no sniggering. See you at eight?'

He leaves a message for Jeeves, then plans how he will fill the rest of the time before the outing to Gianni's. The next two days, Monday and Tuesday, he can take a few extra lectures and prepare more work for Gianni. If he keeps busy, he might survive without Zany. Or she might call, of course.

Trish and Xanthe are waiting on the street by the entrance to Trish's room and he gets two hugs for the price of one.

'Hi, you two. Lookin' good!' he says, but however upbeat Jake tries to be, Trish sees through it.

'Oh. Was it that bad?' she asks, as they start off down the alley.

'What? Well, how do I define bad?' Jake says, as each girl takes one of his hands to march him along.

'One to ten – ten's awful,' Xanthe says.

'Nine and three quarters,' Jake replies. 'The quarter's cos the food was tasty.'

'Aha,' Trish says. They stop walking to look in a trattoria window. 'This is open on Sunday evening ready for the passegiatta. You can buy ready-made salads and stuff to take away. Good idea?'

A tap on Jake's back is from Jeeves. 'Hey, found you – how're you doing?'

'Great,' Jake says.

'Been to Zany's house yet?'

'Yep.'

'Oh. I can picture it now,' Jeeves says. 'Kindly cordiality, lots of tasty nibbles but veiled warnings from her dad.'

'Right on every count,' Trish replies, for Jake.

They order takeaway deli food. Since Jeeves is vegan, the girls are vegetarian and he is too, mostly, they choose four salads between them in little cartons, with portions of tiramisu and panna cotta.

'It's still warm outside – why don't we perch on a wall to eat it?' Trish says.

'I know a spot. Hope you've not got your best clothes on,' Jake says.

Xanthe and Trish laugh.

'Haven't got any,' Xanthe says. 'Be our leader, Jake.' So

Jake takes them to his favourite hillside spot and points to the boulders on which to perch.

'This is my room with a view,' he says.

'Great. Xanthe, can I ask you something?' Jeeves says.

'Is it personal?'

'How do you speak such fluent English? You've hardly any accent.'

'Oh, that. I was sent to an English girls' boarding school for a couple of years. My dad reckoned that was the way to learn English – and to keep his rebel daughter out of the way.' She giggles.

'Oh. Well it did your English good,' Jeeves replies.

'But not my soul,' Xanthe says. 'I was the only lesbian there.'

'There were others, surely?' Jake asks.

'I knew there were but they wouldn't come out. Very English, you know, keep things to yourself, all that,' Xanthe says.

'So, Trish, tell me more about your scholarship thing,' Jake says.

'Let me in on this – what scholarship?' Jeeves asks. 'I seem to miss all the news.'

'I've been offered a schol. to stay on as a researcher, that's all,' says Trish.

'That's all? That's mega.'

'It is a big deal, either way,' she says, looking at Xanthe.

'Sorry, was I interfering?' Jake says.

'Not really,' Trish says, 'but it's a hard decision.'

'I want it for her,' Xanthe says. 'But I've no reason to stay in Italy long term. I have other plans.'

'Mm. Complex, then,' Jake says. 'But is anything straightforward? Try falling for an unattainable girl – straight or gay.'

'Has she fallen for you, too?' Xanthe asks.

'*110% yes*, as they say on TV,' Jake replies. 'But that doesn't help.'

'Were her parents friendly?' Trish asks.

'They were like Jeeves said. Formal, certainly, but her mum had no say in the big issue. That was left with her dad. He had the newspaper articles about us at the football and then asked about *our* relationship.'

'Yours and mine, d'you mean?' Trish asks.

'Yep,' Jake says. 'He followed me out as I left, and spouted some stuff about making the wrong choices, family reputation, all that.'

'Just as I thought he would do,' says Jeeves.

'Has Zany contacted you since?' Xanthe asks.

'No. Not at all.'

'I bet she won't go against her parents,' Trish comments.

'Well they did give her permission to come to Gianni's.'

'Nice one,' Jeeves says. 'But watch it, Jake. She'll be on her best behaviour.'

'Mm.'

'Great. Xanthe's coming too,' Trish says. 'Gianni said the more people his mum has to feed, the happier she is.'

'Reminds me of my grandma,' Jake says. 'Hey, this food is good. I love the aubergines in tomato.'

'And the courgettes – well, zucchini – sliced lengthways, like this. I think they were grilled and soaked in olive oil.'

'But I detect basil – hate the stuff,' Jake says, wiping his chin where the tomato sauce has dripped. 'Still, it's a good feast for the money. So, where are you up to on the Italian scholarship?'

'I have to check it all out carefully. It depends on finance, too: how much I'd get, how much accommodation costs, all that. And getting permission from Manchester Uni to delay my course,' Trish says, looking at Xanthe.

'They should be delighted,' says Xanthe, 'one of their students getting this honour.'

'And how would it impact on you?' Jake asks her.

'Hugely. I need to get back to Greece. Things have been so bad there in the recession, I think my parents expect me to help by graduating there and, hopefully, getting a job afterwards,' Xanthe replies.

Trish puts her arm round her. 'We have time to decide, OK? Anyway, look, it's starting to get dark. Let's go.' She turns to Jake. 'Come back to my place for coffee.'

'No thanks, I think I'll head back. Yours is in the opposite direction.'

'Fair enough. Are you OK, though?' Trish asks.

'I've got to be,' Jake replies. 'I can't expect someone to hold my hand 24/7.'

'There's been a lot of trauma,' Trish says, waving her plastered wrist.

'What about you?' Jake asks.

'Plaster's off this week. Then I have firm support and bandage. Not so terrible.'

'She really looks on the bright side, our friend, doesn't she?' Xanthe says. 'That's why I love her.'

'Can't blame you,' Jake says, as they part. 'See you both on Wednesday. Ciao.'

Monday and Tuesday pass with only brief messages from Zany. One seemed hopeful when she said she loved his new haircut; he tried a chatty one in reply, saying how much like her mum she looked. She didn't respond to that and Jake hasn't spoken properly to her since he was at her house – and even then, they couldn't chat. Still, if he can keep his head down, he has plenty to do.

He goes to an appointment with the doctor, who chats over Jake's anxieties, helping him to deal with them on his own. Jake is glad he doesn't suggest any pills. He also attends an art history lecture, where he had thought he might see Zany; an 'admin-social', where he and Tom are voted on to the hostel committee; and more language sessions. One of these introduces the students to Italian writing – not Dante and the classics, but modern novels. They start by looking at excerpts of Umberto Eco's *The Name of the Rose* in its original, and Primo Levi's *The Periodic Table*. Jake finds the session absorbing, led by a good guy.

Wednesday arrives with no fanfare but with Jake knowing he's survived till then – without Zany and without any further panics. He and his pals have decided they'll each take a small gift for Gianni's parents, so Jake finishes a small pen-and-wash sketch of Todi's cathedral and puts it in a simple clip frame for them. He has yet to find a source of better frames for his other paintings. He starts to get ready and takes out his afro comb, the only comb he has, to tidy his hair. He smiles into the mirror realising his new look hardly needs his attention. As he makes to leave, a text arrives.

'SEE U @ G'S. SOZ NOT IN TOUCH. GRANDPARENTS HERE IN 2 DAYS. IT'S MAD HERE. C U Z XX'

What a relief! He replies just saying 'OK'.

He meets the 'gang' at noon at the bus stop. As they wait for the bus, Trish sidles up to him and whispers, 'Where's Zany? Meeting us there?'

Jake nods. 'She texted. Been busy with her grandparents' visit.'

'Oh. D'you believe her?'

'Yeah… but it can't be the whole story.'

Trish grabs and squeezes Jake's hand. 'Make the most of today, though, OK?' she says.

Jake nods as the bus arrives and they all climb aboard. He takes note of the route to Gianni's house, to see whether he will be able to cycle there for lessons. It is not too far but it's very hilly, of course; he will discuss it with Gianni. He's missing the teaching – the money it brings, the stimulus and the routine.

In contrast to Zany's parents' house, Gianni's is an older country house, slightly faded but by no means dilapidated, and with a lot of land. As they approach the front door they pass a profusion of Mediterranean plants and flowers, with lemon, lime and orange trees amongst them. Jake waits anxiously for Zany to come, still concerned about her. As they start through the trees, she arrives.

'Hi, everyone. Sorry I'm late.'

They all say 'hi' and Jake goes up to her. 'You had me worried. I thought you might not come,' he says.

'Well, I did,' Zany says, smiling.

As they walk between the trees, the sweet perfume of the citrus blossom reminds Jake of Israel, of the orange blossom scent as one steps off the plane at the airport.

'It's wonderful how citrus trees have blossom and fruit at the same time,' he says, to no one in particular.

'They smell gorgeous,' Zany agrees.

'Si. Benissimo, no?' a voice says. Gianni's mum puts her nose up to the waxy white blossom on one of the trees. She clearly understands some English. She and Gianni have come round to the front from their back garden.

'Si, benissimo. Buongiorno, Signora Travesi,' Jake says, air-kissing her hand. 'E Gianni, come stà? Still using crutches, hm.'

'Welcome to our 'ouse. Please. Come to the giardino,' Gianni says, pointing the way, with one crutch.

'This is our friend Zany,' Jake says.

'Welcome,' Gianni says, half offering his hand but with-drawing it when Zany doesn't take hold.

'Buongiorno, Zany,' Mrs Travesi says, kissing her on both cheeks. 'Come!'

They go round the house to a wild garden where the two little dogs are scampering between olive trees till they see the group arrive.

'Carlo! Carlotta!' Trish says, fussing over them. Against their yapping, Jake takes it upon himself to introduce his friends to Signor Travesi. He and his wife welcome them with an overwhelming warmth.

'Benvenuto. Per favore, s'accommodi,' Gianni's mum says,

gesturing to the chairs on the patio. The long, scrubbed wooden dining table stands in the shelter of a vine, loaded with bunches of tiny grapes, that trails in and out of a neglected trellis. It all reminds Jake of an advert for tomato sauce where a jovial Italian family gathers to eat pasta, al fresco – which, presumably, is what they will soon be doing.

'Il giardino è bellissimo,' Jeeves says, taking a photo of the view.

Zany hasn't said much as she's busy trying to avoid the little dogs.

'I hate dogs,' she whispers to Jake.

'Ignore them,' he replies.

'Is all very old,' Gianni says.

'Yeah. The olive trees look ancient,' Suzanna says.

'We work at Agriturismo Da Maria,' Tom explains to the Travesis. 'There are old olive trees there, too.'

'Da Maria? Mia famiglia!' Signor Travesi says, as he pours the wine with a flourish any wine waiter would be proud of.

'Your family?' asks Jake.

'Si. Maria è mia cugina,' Signor Travesi replies.

'Maria is your cousin?' says Tom, surprised.

'Si, si.'

'You have a big family,' comments Jake.

'Everybody is famiglia in Umbria,' Gianni smiles.

His mum offers the wine around to everyone from the tray, which also holds bowls of olives and *grissini* breadsticks. She offers Trish, Zany and Jeeves fresh limonata when they say no to the wine and gradually, glasses in hand, each of them takes a seat at the table.

'Mm, this is lovely,' Zany says, sipping the limonata. 'There's mint in it – I never thought of mint with lemon.'

'Limone, menta, tutto nel giardino,' Gianni's dad says, waving his arm expansively towards the garden.

Jake soaks in the atmosphere and the red wine, contented

now Zany's here. She is a little distant, somehow, but he knows she's shy in new settings. He takes in the view and the welcome, forgetting his worries. Everything contrasts so vividly with the formality at the Chaudrys'. The number of people eating here today clearly offers no challenge to Gianni's mother, who is gradually filling up the table. She brings out breads and glazed pottery bowls containing salads. Then a giant platter of antipasti: glistening grilled aubergines; red, green and yellow peppers and zucchini, arranged in rows with herbs scattered over them.

'Meraviglioso,' Tom says. 'Grazie molto, Signora.'

'Prego. Eat, please.'

'Take – Mamma like you to eat,' Gianni says. 'All. You must finish.'

Jeeves and Tom look as though they would wolf it all down, between them.

'Watch it, there's more to come,' Jake says, seeing more cutlery on the table and sniffing the aroma drifting out from the house. He breathes in dramatically, saying, 'Mm, gorgeous smell, Signora.' He recalls the comfort of home-cooking smells when he was young; he liked guessing what was for dinner as he came home from school.

'More wine?' Gianni asks. The drinkers put their hands over their wine glasses in unison.

'We don't often drink at lunch time,' Suzanna explains.

'Va bene,' Gianni says, offering his empty glass for his father to pour him some more. 'When I play football again, I no 'ave wine.'

'How long will you be off football, Gianni?' Zany asks.

'Not sure. They tell me soon.'

'I hope it's not too long,' Zany replies. She is good at compassion, Jake thinks.

The massive dish embraced by Signora Travesi, as she comes out of her kitchen once more, looks heavy. Her husband carries a second one, holding it out proudly in front of him. There is a pasta dish which, he explains, is made with mushrooms, garlic, cream and mozzarella; and a risotto with spinach, peas and avocado.

'Tutto vegetariano,' the Signora says, as it is passed between them all. That must be difficult for someone so used to cooking with meat, Jake thinks. She's been very creative and it's all delicious. The salad, served on their side plates, includes wonderful home-grown tomatoes with a dressing of local olive oil and fresh basil leaves.

'Da Maria!' Tom reads the label on the bottle of olive oil. 'You use their oil.'

'Of course. Is the best,' Signor Travesi says.

'This is all magnifico,' Jeeves says, savouring the food.

'Prego,' Signora Travesi replies. 'More – eat more.' She gets up and passes round the bowls again. Zany says no and they all gesture that they are full. She looks disappointed, reminding Jake of his late grandmother, who always complained that her guests didn't eat enough.

Despite protests from his hosts, Jake gets up to clear the plates and cutlery. He helps bring out platters of cheese and fruit: figs, melon, peaches and apricots; he's grateful that there are no doughy puddings. However, Signora Travesi does produce a dish containing opened figs topped with toasted goat's cheese. Zany looks at Jake adoringly as he brings these out. He sees, then, that she still likes him.

The figs are irresistible; they all take one and enjoy the juiciness of the other fresh fruits. The aroma of coffee announces its readiness and Gianni's father goes to bring it out. Jeeves stands up and bangs on the table with a spoon.

'Silenzio per favore, Famiglia Travesi,' he begins. Everyone giggles. He then proceeds to deliver a vote of thanks for the exquisite meal and all that went with it. His Italian is excellent. It makes Jake realise he has a long way to go with his own fluency. Everyone claps Jeeves, then Gianni half stands, leaning on a crutch and the table, saying, 'We thank all of you. I 'ope this make us forget the football day. Now we all amici, si? E grazie, Jake, per questo.' He holds up Jake's sketch. 'Is very good,' he says.

'You do draw well,' Suzanna says.

'I didn't know you were bringing that,' Zany says.

'Well, we haven't spoken much, have we?' Jake says.

'True... life's complicated at home.'

They all begin to make a move, despite Signor Travesi's insistence that they stay a while. It is well into the afternoon but they do agree to a stroll round the orchard-cum-garden. This is Jake's first chance since the visit to her parents' to talk to Zany alone.

'Well, Zany, how're things? Why the silence?' he asks.

'You know,' she says.

'Know what?'

'Dad was so... unbending. And he was so rude to you. We've had such rows since you came,' she says, looking down.

'I didn't think him rude, actually. A bit personal, maybe.'

'He tried to stop me coming today.'

'Oh. But you did.'

'Only cos Mum intervened, as usual. She said it'd be rude to let Gianni down.'

'And that's why he let you come?' Jake asks.

'Yeah.'

'Not so as to keep your promise to me, then?'

Zany does not answer that. She takes his hand and strokes his fingers. 'You know how it is, Jake.' The electricity in her touch is still the same.

'I don't. But let's look round the garden, that's easier.'

After the tour, they leave with bags of anything home-grown that is given to them. Jake and Gianni have a little chat about their next lesson, arranged for the following Monday, and

Jake says he'll use the bus to get there. Gianni hands him his completed homework and, with that, they thank his parents profusely and leave.

'Phew. Wasn't that just perfect?' Trish says.

'Fantastic,' Suzanna replies. 'What a treat.'

'Look, I've got to get back now,' Zany says. 'It's walkable from here. Seeya.' She starts off without so much as a separate goodbye for Jake.

He runs after her. 'What's up? At least say when we'll see each other!'

'I'll text you.' He sees she's crying.

'Promise?' he asks.

'Yep,' she says, and runs off, wiping her eyes with her sleeves.

Jake is shocked and, away from that convivial lunch, he's doubly sad.

On the short bus ride, they all doze, the wine and big meal being as soporific as Beatrix Potter's lettuces, Jake thinks. But he also recalls that wonderful minibus ride with Zany on their way to the agriturismo. It was only a few weeks ago. Things were at their best then.

TWENTY-THREE

Until he hears from Zany again, Jake has to get on with his life here. He sends a couple of emails to his parents about his concern. He peppers them with a graphic description of the Travesi lunch, though, so they don't only read of doom and gloom. He opens the envelope that Gianni gave him, which he expects to contain the completed homework. It does, but it also contains some money and a note: 'I pay you for your work. See you next week. Thank you, Gianni.'

Jake's surprise is matched by his delight at having some pocket money at last. He's now determined to do some good preparation for their next lesson and that takes up the rest of the day. He plans to use the Travesis' garden and terrace as a springboard for conversation; that and talking about the meal will build up Gianni's vocabulary.

He then goes to an art history lecture and a literature session. Strangely, he hasn't seen Adriana and now finds himself wondering where *she* is. But what is more troubling is that it is two days since the last message from Zany.

It's coming up to another weekend and he cannot believe that the absence of contact from her is intentional. He toys with the idea of going to the house to investigate but doesn't want to become a stalker, especially as her grandparents will surely be there by now.

So, on the Friday afternoon, moping and pining, he meanders over to the small lecture campus in the hope of... he knows not what. He looks at the list of sessions on offer and takes the first one he fancies; he can't bear to be doing nothing. Just as he approaches the door to the hall, he is tapped on the shoulder by Adriana.

'Ah, so you are interested in the geology of the Apennines? I did not know,' she says, in a far more jovial tone than he is ready for.

'What? I... er... geology, did you say? Oh God, I must have read it wrong,' Jake say, temporarily shaken out of his depression.

'So why go to a lecture? Come and practise your Italian with me, over a coffee,' she says.

'Look, I can't really afford any more coffees at the moment. Hope you don't mind. And I'm not exactly in the mood.'

'I see this,' Adriana says. 'So we 'ave water. 'Ere, sit down.' As Adriana goes to the campus bar for a jug of water, Jake's mobile pings and he jumps.

'SORRY NO CONTACT. WILL EXPLAIN. Z.'

Jake notices there are no kisses. He texts: 'WHY? WHAT'S UP? J XX'

No message comes back. He feels panic rising and though he has a paper bag in his pocket, he can't just take it out and breathe into it, in front of Adriana.

'Adriana, momento per favore,' he says, as he runs to the gents, where he breathes into the bag as instructed. It works, so at least he isn't only conscious of his pulse. Back at the table, he has to try not only to be sociable but to speak Italian. They do manage a conversation, since they can share the discovery of her family connections.

'Is good, my family save the Jew family, non? And the madia. The story make me 'appy.'

'It's fantastic, it really is. But, er... actually, we say "Jewish" family – Jewish is the adjective, you see.'

'Ah, grazie. Jake the language teacher, si?'

'Well, I am, for Gianni, kind of,' he says, smiling. 'And Trish is so clever at searching for things.'

'Oh. You smiling. But why before you look sad?' Adriana asks.

This is hard for Jake to put into words – even English ones would be hard to find. She is astute, for someone only a little older than him, knowing immediately that the problem is about a girl.

'È difficile,' he begins.

'Of course is difficult. Girls and boys – love – is never easy,' she says, sounding like his mother.

At that point he realises that Adriana's English, though good, is still not perfect, so he begins to worry less about the minutiae of Italian grammar when he speaks.

'What is the big problema?' she asks.

This is too intimate, surely, Jake thinks. Yet he tries to explain, not even knowing the Italian for Muslim, but drawn to Adriana's compassionate manner.

'You want to say me what will 'appen?' she says.

'*Tell* you, not *say* you. I don't know,' Jake says.

'It not make you 'appy. So is no good.' Now, Adriana's brusqueness shocks him.

'How can you say that? You don't know me – or her,' he protests.

'I like you. I know you a leetel. I see on your face.'

'It's because she's not called lately,' Jake says, tapping his mobile.

'And if she call, it make you better?'

'I can't say,' Jake says. 'And I can't keep talking to you like this, really.'

'Capito. Understood. OK, so we go a walk, look at the Apennines, OK?'

Jake has never been taken over by someone of the opposite sex like this; he likes it but feels strange, unbalanced somehow.

However, as they walk through alleys that are new even to him – and he knows the place so well through his sketching – he relaxes in Adriana's company. She finds a bench he has not seen on his many forays in Todi and it has yet another magnificent view.

'Ecco la bell' Italia!' she says, making a sweeping gesture with one arm while putting her other hand on his. He turns to her, hardly believing he can be here with her while waiting painfully for Zany's next call. Yet he takes hold of her hand quite intentionally and they intertwine their fingers. She squeezes his hand.

'I like you Jake,' she says. 'I don't know why.'

'You just feel sorry for me. Maybe you want to mother me,' Jake says.

'Non. I did not know you when you came first to my lecture.'

'Hm,' Jake says, flattered, yet ill at ease. 'Look, Adriana, I'm no good for you right now, but you're very kind. I'd better get back now, OK?'

'OK.'

As Jake leaves, he sees her disappointment. It makes him smile, momentarily. 'See you at a lecture,' he says.

'Ciao.' Adriana blows him a kiss.

Jake walks back and is round the corner from the hostel when another text arrives. He is glad that he's alone.

'LEFT ITALY. AM BACK IN LEEDS. LET MY PARENTS DOWN. I'D WRECK YOUR FAMILY TOO. WOULDN'T HAVE WORKED. SOZ JAKE. HAPPY MEMORIES. Z'

This time, his panic is real. He reads it again, his pulse racing. *Shit, shit, shit – fucking hell… Leeds? Oh God…* He feels for his paper bag but it's not there. He must have left it in the gents. He slumps into a doorway but it's very hot, there's no air and, checking on his watch, his pulse is far too fast.

He replies to Zany's text: 'HOW COULD YOU? I LOVE YOU!' But it doesn't send. Maybe this passageway blocks the connection – or maybe it's Fate. He staggers along till he reaches a junction but the message still doesn't send. Somehow, he reaches the hostel.

'Jake, what's up? You look awful!' It's Suzanna, looking worried and putting her hands on his shoulders. Jake leans on her.

'I've got to sit down,' he says, grabbing a chair in the lobby.

Suzanna squats down in front of him. 'Can I get you something? Some water?' He has never seen her caring side before.

'No, not yet. Here. Look at that text, I'm too exhausted to talk.' He gives her his mobile and puts his head in his hands. He tries to feel his own pulse unobtrusively but can't do it in that position.

'Bloody hell, she's done a bunk. God, poor girl,' Suzanna says.

'Poor girl? Poor me!' Jake says. 'How could she?'

'I know, *poor you*. But imagine what she's been put through.'

'She's... she led me on.'

'Did she? I didn't hear any of your conversations. Maybe she actually led herself on.'

'Meaning?'

'Well, she probably knew all along it couldn't lead anywhere. D'you think?'

Jake knows she is talking sense but will not admit it. However, his panic attack is subsiding without recourse to the paper bag, so he agrees to go for a drink. He feels pathetic for his reaction to Zany's text. Most men don't react as he does, do they? It is surely a female trait to be lovelorn. But there were male poets and artists in the past who wrote about lost loves – maybe he is more of an artist than he thought.

'A penny for them?' Suzanna says.

Jake jumps.

'Gosh, are you OK?' she asks.

'Sure. I was just thinking...'

'I know, that's why I offered you a penny,' Suzanna says, laughing. 'I suppose they were worth far more, hey?'

Jake smiles. *What a good friend she is, having the insight to shake me out of my misery.* 'Of course they're worth more,' he says. 'I got to wondering whether I should become a poet.

Y'know, wallowing in self-pity, writing odes to lost loves, all that.'

'You are funny, Jake. You're different, somehow.'

'Soft, d'you mean?' Jake asks.

'Not soft, different in a good way. You feel things, you care. I like that.'

'I need to develop a macho skin, that's what,' Jake says.

Suzanna smiles. 'I think it depends on bravado. What people expose of themselves and what they keep hidden. It's all about stereotypes.' Suzanna has never revealed her analytical side before – at least, not to Jake.

'Gender stereotypes, you mean?'

'Yeah, that mainly,' she says.

'Mm. Who knows. We are what we are.' Jake's pulse begins to race again. For that few minutes he had almost forgotten Zany's text, but now the memory of it floods back over him. He starts sweating, his breathing is shallow and he needs to get out of the cafeteria.

'What now?' Suzanna says. 'Hey look, there's Jeeves. Hi, come on over,' she shouts.

Jake tried to stop her but again realises he has coped with a near panic attack.

'Jake – how goes it, mate?' asks Jeeves.

'She's in Leeds,' Jake mumbles.

'In Leeds? Who?'

'Zany.'

'Oh Christ! Whoops, sorry, Suzanna,' Jeeves says.

'Why apologise to me? Jesus isn't my man.'

'I thought you were C of E,' Jeeves says.

'Nah,' Suzanna says. 'I'm nothing, actually. Just goodness and light, that's me.'

Jake is enjoying the company of the 'new' Suzanna – but it is the first time he has been with her without Tom. Perhaps Tom swamps her.

'So, Jake. Let me guess.' Jeeves gets involved. 'Her parents took her home, right?'

'Yep.'

'And you had no idea.'

'None.'

'But it was on the cards,' Jeeves says.

'It wasn't,' Jake protests.

'Then where was it leading?'

'We hadn't planned anything,' Jake replies. 'We both knew there were problems, yeah, but –'

'Her parents said she'd betrayed them, am I right?' Jeeves asks.

'Right. She "betrayed their trust", apparently,' Jake says, feeling more and more depressed.

'She did, though, didn't she? She knew she shouldn't have a relationship with a boy; she knew her parents wouldn't approve.'

Jake knows Jeeves is right but will not admit it. 'So why did they invite me round?' he says.

'To do the decent thing, to show they respect you, even if they disapprove.'

'I just don't get why she couldn't call me – explain, apologise, something!'

'She couldn't do that and you know that, don't you? She's had a mad fling, her one and only, yeah. And she fell for you, too. But she can't and won't criticise her parents. You won't be able to make her, either.'

'Well, she doesn't even answer any messages,' Jake says.

'Poor Jake, you've had a really tough time,' Suzanna says, joining in again.

Then Jeeves butts in with, 'Yes and what about the footie attack, all that?'

'I'm not the only one,' Jake says, aware that he's crying now. He sniffs, desperately trying to stop. 'For God's sake, I should be able to cope. Look guys, I'm going back to my room. I've got some skyping to do.'

'Don't try to skype Zany, please,' Jeeves says. 'I can tell you she won't answer.'

'Well, I'll go up and think, then,' Jake says.

'Don't think too hard,' Suzanna says.

'No, I'll write a Petrarchan love sonnet, OK?'

Jeeves and Suzanna laugh, though he wonders whether they know much about Petrarch. He goes to his room and lies on the bed, very sorry for himself. He puts his earphones in to listen to music, but all he can hear is Zany's voice. He goes over and over their past conversations and, yes, she did see danger in their relationship, but he never imagined she would just go.

He skypes his dad, who quickly spots Jake's frame of mind.

'Hi, Jake. More panic attacks?' he asks. 'I can't stop thinking about you being attacked. Mum was just on the phone, upset –'

Jake interrupts. 'Dad, it's not that.'

'What, then?'

'It's Zany. She's gone!'

'Bloody hell! Gone where?'

'Back to Leeds. Her parents took her, just as her grandparents were due to arrive. They must have planned it ages ago. I bet they didn't want the grandparents to witness her fall from grace.'

'God, how awful. I'll come over.' His dad looks worried.

'No way. No, I'm an adult, remember? Fighting my own battles, all that,' Jake says, unconvinced.

'But you look so drawn. You're more screwed up than you say.'

'So I'm drawn, that's me, lovesick man that I am.' Jake knows tears might follow and he will not let that happen. 'I just wanted to tell you, that's all.'

'Sure. And I'm glad you did.'

'What would you have done, if Mum had disappeared after you met *her*, Dad?'

'No idea. No idea at all, Jake. But you must feel shitty.'

'How I feel? Don't even go there. I need a new adjective – somewhere between *shitty* and *depressed*,' Jake replies.

'So I *will* come over – there are plenty of flights to Rome, no-frills ones, lots.'

'Dad, no! I'm not a baby, for goodness' sake. I'm OK.'

'Hm… between shitty and depressed isn't OK.'

'Well, y'know I like melodrama. I think I'll try writing poetry. What d'you think?'

'I think you're trying to change the subject,' his dad says.

'Petrarch wrote poems about unrequited love – I could try.'

'Jake, it's not just about love and stuff, there was the attack as well. A bit much, don't you think?'

'I do, yeah. But you can't come running over to mop up my tears. My mates would think we're mad.'

'You're not them and I'm not their dad. I could pretend to have business there: a meeting in Rome or something.'

'Dad, no. Please… I'll cope.'

'Don't be like your great-grandma Freidl.'

'Meaning?'

'Stubborn.'

'Thanks.'

'D'you remember her letters? She refused help, too.'

'And?'

'She needed help with her baby.'

'Yeah yeah, just like me, hey?'

'Shut up a sec, Jake. She was nearly sent to jail.'

'That's nothing to do with me,' Jake says.

'You're right. But are you all right?'

'Yes. And my mates are great. I'm off now. Ciao. Thanks Dad.'

'Love you, ciao,' his dad says.

Jake closes down his Skype.

TWENTY-FOUR

Jake is in a new reality. He must avoid having his dad come out at all costs. His friends would never understand, if he came. There has to be a way to manage without him.

He brings forward his next appointment with the doctor. They are limited by the language barrier but with the doctor's faltering English, Jake's faltering Italian and some miming, they manage. Jake feels confident in the man's kind presence, even when he is asked to measure his anxiety on a scale of one to ten. Jake knows instinctively that this is to find out if he has been feeling suicidal.

'No, I'm not that bad,' he says.

'You can tell me truth, si?'

'It is the truth,' Jake says, reassuring both the doctor and himself.

'You want to go 'ome?'

'No. I do feel low, but I'm happy here.'

'With Italian football?'

'I'm not happy with that and not happy without my girlfriend.'

'You 'ave more friends 'ere?'

'Si. Benissimi,' Jake says. 'Very good friends.'

'Is good. You 'ave parents?'

'Si. In Inghilterra,' Jake replies.

'You skype?'

'Si.'

'Is good. They want to 'elp?'

'Si. But I'm OK.'

'I 'ope. You see me again soon, per favore?'

'Maybe. Grazie molto,' Jake says.

'Prego.'

Jake leaves the clinic much relieved. It's good to talk to a stranger. He doesn't feel suicidal, just very unhappy.

He texts Trish to ask where to find another list of extra lectures. He knows it is best to be busy and he could enjoy more knowledge of Italian classical painters and sculptures. She says she will bring the list round, as she's popping out anyway.

'It's me,' she calls when she knocks on his door. 'How're you doing?'

'Hangin' on in there,' he says.

'You're looking better – and so's my wrist,' she adds pointedly.

'Sorry, forgot.'

'Yep.'

'You've made so little fuss, I've hardly asked you how you are. I'm such a self-centred git…'

'Shut up! It's all gone downhill since your haircut, that's your problem,' Trish says, laughing. 'Anyway, here's that prospectus. I'm off clubbing.'

'Thought you didn't like clubbing.'

'I like it when I'm with someone. Xanthe's following on.'

'Enjoy,' Jake says. 'Let's catch up on research stuff soon?'

'Will do,' Trish says, already partway down the stairs.

Jake marks off the art history lectures and splices them amongst his language lectures, as well as his lessons with Gianni, till his diary looks well filled.

He sits on the second row for Adriana's next session; front row would be a bit too obvious. She smiles and nods. Jake says a lot more this time and realises he is beginning to use Italian phrases without thinking too hard.

He leaves his seat after most people have gone and walks out of the lecture theatre towards the back door. He hears footfall behind him. Only once he's outside does he turn round and see Adriana. He's glad.

'Come stà, Adriana?'

'Bene. Lei? You look good.'

'I'm fine,' Jake says. 'D'you want to meet up later?'

'Is OK? You OK?'

'Si. Yes. Will you come?'

'Yes. Where?'

'No idea,' Jake replies. 'D'you know a fun place? A bar, a nightclub, somewhere with music? I need a bop.'

'*Bop*? What is *bop*?'

Jake jigs around.

'Oh. Dance! Si, I know good place,' she says.

'Come to my hostel at… eight o'clock?' Jake cannot believe how bold he feels.

'Is better, nine,' Adriana says.

'Well, come at eight-thirty and we can have a walk first.'

They part company and Jake spends the afternoon sketching, then finishing off the sketch back in his room. He recreates it in paint and sets up all the messy equipment, just as there's a knock on his door. 'Come in, but not too far,' he shouts.

'It's me.' Trish comes sheepishly into the room.

'I can see that,' Jake says. 'Here: have a bed, I've only got one safe chair.'

She sits down on the edge of the bed, not the usual ebullient girl.

'Are you OK? I mean, you're not, are you?'

'Sorry but there's no one else.' And she starts to cry.

'Blimey, Trish, what's the problem?' He goes to get her a cool bottle of water and offers her a box of Kleenex. 'What's up? Is it you and Xanthe?'

'No, no, nothing like that. It's Dad,' Trish says, eventually.

'Oh, that?'

'Not "that".'

'Out with it.' Jake tries not to sound impatient.

'He's very ill... He's dying,' she sobs.

'Oh God. How d'you know?'

'Mum emailed me. She thought I ought to know.'

'Hm,' Jake says, as he sits on the bed next to her. 'Tough one.'

'What do I do? I haven't seen him in years, he disapproves of me, he's not my birth father...'

'Hold on, let me think,' Jake says. 'Is it different cos he's not your birth father? What's your main beef with him?'

'That he judges me.'

'D'you want to visit him?'

'Dunno.'

'Listen, let's go downstairs. There's a back room where we can sit and chat, OK?'

They go to the sitting room and talk over the unhappy story.

'What is it with parents?' Jake says. 'They give us such stress. Who was the poet who said, "Our parents fuck us up..." Something like that.'

'Larkin. It's a bummer,' Trish adds. 'Maybe I *should* go visit.'

'Has your mum seen him? That matters.'

'Yeah, since she heard – a month ago.'

'Hm. What would it do?'

'You mean, to see him? For him, or for me?'

'Whichever,' Jake says.

'It'd bring back lots of bitterness, that's what.'

'For you, maybe. And for him?'

'No idea. Making peace on the death bed? Not sure. Oh God.' Trish starts crying again.

'Look. He left your mum, and he couldn't handle... y'know, the sexuality bit, but –'

'I was very young when he left.'

'There isn't a right age,' Jake comments. 'It shakes up your image of your parents, whenever. Why not ask your mum if he wants to see you or hear from you. Start with a letter or an email, maybe?'

'Yeah. Will do. I can't go unless he's going to be nice.'

'Or unless he says he wants to see you.'

'Mm. Gotta pave the way,' Trish says. 'I'm off now, OK? Skype me any time.' They hug and come out of the room and then, out of the hostel. Xanthe is there, looking worried.

'There you are. You disappeared.' She pointedly grabs Trish's hand and tugs her away from Jake.

'Xanthe, don't!' Trish says. 'I had to ask Jake something.'

'Why not me? Are you sure you're not... bi?'

'What the – ? How could you? He's my oldest friend. I've told you a million times.'

'Yep,' Jake interjects. 'And I've gotta get changed. Bye.'

Jake goes back to start getting ready for Adriana's arrival. He is glad to have been there for Trish. At least he isn't the only one with shit going on. Still, it's rough for her, now, though he isn't sure what he would do in her shoes. But Xanthe's a jealous girl.

After taking a shower, Jake's usual lack of fashion confidence hits him hard. He knows he can never look like a chill Italian *ragazzo*, so he simply puts on the freshest, newest shirt he has, a multicoloured check one with short sleeves, with cream chinos that he rolls up at the ankles. He wears them with navy deck shoes and no socks. He looks in the mirror, still not knowing how best to handle shorter hair, but works his afro comb through his curls. He notices a sunny glow to his skin now, though his freckles will always show. He turns sideways to the mirror and screws up his face, pushing his nose up with his fingers, wondering what he would look like with a turned-up nose. 'Hm,' he says to himself. 'At least my nose is straight, even if it is a bit too big. Like Dad's, at least.'

He tidies his room a little, straightening his paintings and his model cypress trees and using a T-shirt to dust off his desk and window ledge. He shakes his duvet and bashes the three bright scatter cushions he picked up in the local flea market the day before. He half closes the shutter slats, leaving a window open. And then there's a knock on his door.

Adriana is there, looking shyly at him. He has never found her retiring before.

'I can come in?' she says. They air kiss three times while she slides past him provocatively, making sure she pushes against him as she goes into the room.

She looks beautiful. Her shiny black hair is caught up, but loosely, with strands floating down all round her neck and over her ears. She is wearing big hoop earrings and Jake notices two smaller pairs higher up her earlobes. Beaded straps show underneath her low-necked scarlet top. Her tiny shorts – the sort with tears and fraying threads in them – just about cover her backside, but reveal every centimetre of her long, bronzed legs.

God, she's hot. Jake goes over to her, by the window.

'I love your artwork, Jake. This room looks wonderful,' she says. She peers at one of his family photographs. 'Can I look?'

'Sure,' Jake says. He cannot help but put his arms round her waist, holding her tight as he looks over her shoulder at the photo, whilst explaining who everyone is. Nor can he help nuzzling her neck, kissing it and licking a wisp of hair, but avoiding her ears, which are imprisoned by her many earrings.

She turns round and returns the hug, kissing his neck. Jake pulls her, not too forcefully, towards the bed, where he has piled up the cushions and pillows to make it more like a sofa.

'Come over here and chat. We have to get to know each other,' he says.

'Chat? Is this what English boys do on a bed?' she asks.

Adriana lies back but Jake leans on the cushions and pillows, one leg bent over the edge of the bed, to avoid lying down flat.

Adriana lays her head on his shoulder. She undoes her hairclip and her long, silky hair cascades over Jake's chest. He twiddles a few strands round his fingers, stroking his lips with it – fascinated, after all this time, with female tresses. She pulls his hand down around her waist.

Jake's feelings of arousal shock him. *How can I feel like this when I'm in love with Zany? Is it only because I can feel her skin and stroke her hair?* Yet he leans over Adriana and draws her to him, feeling the shape of her body and the smoothness of her skin. He pushes up the edge of her skimpy top and slides his hand up her back to her bra fastening. Adriana makes no sign of resisting, so he opens the hook – she wriggles in approval and helps him slide one of its straps off her shoulders, together with the sleeve of her top.

As he cups her breast in his hand, she turns and kisses his neck, his ear and finally his lips. There is no awkwardness between them, it feels to Jake as though they've known each other for ages. She slides off the other side of her top and bra, stroking, hugging and kissing him with abandon. Then it is Jake who resists, as she makes to open the fly of his shorts. It has awkward buttons, not a zip, for which he is grateful. He gently takes her hand away but pulls it round his waist.

'Not so fast, signorina,' he says, as he leans over and licks her right nipple.

'Va bene, not so fast, signore,' she says, and pulls her top back up, leaving her bra dangling at her waist.

'What the – ?' Jake says. 'Why did you do that?'

'Why? You stop, I stop.' Adriana looks miffed. 'What you want? What your signals?'

'Signals? I just... I wanted to kiss you. Didn't you enjoy it?'

'Of course. But you take off my clothes, I take off yours, non?'

'See what you mean. Sorry Adriana. Forgive me.'

'Of course. We go to the club, OK? Where is shower? I must

change.' She takes a sponge bag, towel and shiny top out of her bag.

Jake opens his door. 'Across there.'

'Dieci minuti, OK?' Adriana says as she goes into the shower room, blowing him a kiss.

Phew. Now what? He closes the window and shutters and collects his belongings. Adriana comes back in wearing a clinging, shiny top in pink with one shoulder on, one off. The one that's off reveals a jewelled strap and round her neck she has a tight necklace with big chunky stones set in it.

'I like this,' he says, touching it lightly. 'I'm just trying to remember what it's called. It's not a necklace, it's um, a –'

'Una collana, in Italian,' Adriana says.

'Yeah, that's a necklace, but when it's tight, like that... I know my mum has one. Got it! A choker, that's what it is.'

Adriana repeats the word, laughing. 'Why you like women's things, Jake?'

'Suppose it's from living with a sister and my mum for so long,' he replies. 'Come on, let's go – andiamo.'

They set off, hand in hand, chatting in a mix of their two languages quite comfortably as Adriana leads the way through alleys that even Jake has not yet discovered. Eventually she points out a place with dim, multicoloured lighting and crowds of people half in, half out of the door.

'Ecco!' she says and pulls his hand towards it.

The place is packed, steamy and with smoke from the outdoor smokers wafting in and clinging to clothes. There's a good beat from the almost inaudible group who are playing on a rickety little stage. Adriana drags Jake onto the dance floor – or the dance space, such as it is. She starts to dance separately from him, arms up in the air, hips and legs moving as a professional dancer might do. But so sexily. Jake enjoys dancing and gives as good as he can, looking at Adriana and hardly believing that a woman like her would want to be with him – Lovelorn Larry that he is.

He is just about to put out his arms to dance closer with her, when he begins to feel even hotter, smelling not only sweat and escaping cigarette smoke but other substances that waft around nightclubs... and his pulse starts to race. He knows he must get out.

'Adriana, I need some air, I –' He dives for the doorway, realising that he has abandoned his paper bag of late. But then, could he really sit there with a bag over his mouth? He would rather faint than do that.

Adriana finds him outside, crouched against the wall of the club, his head between his knees.

'Jake, you are ill? I get water, OK?'

Jake nods weakly. 'Grazie,' he whispers, thinking, 'What do I do now? She'll think I'm crazy.'

By the time she comes back through the crowds, he's standing up but leaning on the wall. Adriana strokes his cheeks gently, then his arms.

'Ecco càro. Drink. Is cold. Is good.'

'That's wonderful. Thanks Adriana. I'm sorry.'

'Sorry? Why you sorry? Ti sente male – you feel ill. Everybody feel ill sometimes, non?'

Jake looks down, ashamed. She takes his head in her hands and kisses his eyelids.

'You're very kind, Adriana, but I'm no good for you.'

'Why no good? You very good for me.'

'I like you very much, but I'm a bit of a mess right now,' Jake replies. 'It's not the best time.'

'I say is *very* best time. Your amica, she go 'ome. You sad, alone, and Adriana is 'ere. Perfetto!' She slips her arms around his waist and hugs him, not with passion but with warmth.

Jake struggles to loosen her hold, kisses her two hands, saying, 'Honestly, I'm really not ready.'

'You ready for this on your bed, before.' Adriana is angry now. 'We good together. Also we can talk of many thing. Per favore.'

'I just need a break. I don't feel well.' How can he explain a panic attack? He breaks away, kisses her on the neck, saying, 'You're a great person Adriana, but I must go.'

'You no come to my lessons?'

'Sure. I'll see you. Maybe in a week or so, OK? Ciao.'

'I must wait? A week? I don't know… Ciao, Jake.'

He goes off down the alley. When he turns back to wave, she blows him a kiss.

He fancies her big time, but how can he go from one woman to another so quickly? And how can he deal with panic attacks in nightclubs? The relief he feels once he's back in his room and behind his own closed door is like a woolly blanket. He opens his shutter and window wide, then goes to his iPad and checks his emails. There's one from Gianni and one from his mum. Her subject line is 'Sorry about this'. He reads on. 'Jake, hope you don't mind. We've scanned an article we saw by chance in the *North London News*.'

Miraculous escape from coach crash off M1

Forty people travelling in a hired coach from Leeds to a gathering in north London have all escaped unhurt from a collision. As the vehicle approached London, at Exit 1 of the M1, it appears to have skidded.

According to one of the passengers, who asked not to be named, 'The bus hit a taxi, which turned full circle. It ran back into the bus before crashing into the barrier.'

The party was made up of the Leeds family of student Zainab Chaudhry. They were travelling to the Mill Hill home of the parents of her fiancé, Dr Ibrahim Sarwar. Dr Sarwar is an A&E consultant at the Whittington Hospital. He and Ms Chaudry are due to marry in a month's time.

Ms Chaudhry did not wish to be interviewed but a friend said, 'Zainab is relieved that none of her family was injured. She just wanted us all to have a good time, meeting Dr Sarwar and his family. She never thought anything like this would happen.'

Police are investigating.

Shit. Jake tries to think straight. Not only did Zany's parents take her home, but they found her a husband. Bloody quick work! And a surgeon, no less – a fair bit older than Zany. So that's that. He chucks his cushions at the walls, one by one, furious and frustrated. Then he punches his pillows and lies on them, head down, like a toddler having a tantrum. But he starts to sneeze and cough as the feathers fly out.

For God's sake! Grow up, Jake.

He feels guilty that he ignored the possibility that Zany could have been injured. But she wasn't. And why should he care, if she didn't care enough even to call or write to him? He is furious. And it's all up to him now.

He takes out his mobile and makes a call. It goes to voicemail. 'Adriana, you were right,' he says. 'Per favore, let's meet again soon.'

Acknowledgements

Thanks go to:

Almira and members of Womanswrite M/cr for their support and honest critiques.

Dr Barry Hobson for happily sharing his professional expertise in archaeology.

Jack and Tim Levy and Talia Ingleby for details about students abroad.

My Muslim friends for their advice.

My friends with inside knowledge of football, here and abroad.

My late mother who started me on the writing path.

My family for their sustained interest.

My husband for his never-ending supply of loving patience.

Jenks of Jenks Design for the cover.

And Helen Sandler of Tollington Press and Louise Muddle for their good-humoured professionalism.

About the Author

This is Charlotte Gringras's second novel. After the publication of her first, *The Purple Rose* (Tollington, 2012), she started to wonder how Jake, its young fictional character, would turn out as an adult. Together with her curiosity about a *madia* (an ancient breadbox), *Not in Our Hands* began to emerge.

Charlotte is a teacher by profession, with a degree in Italian and French and an MA in Jewish Studies, both from Manchester University. Her knowledge of Italy and Italian, combined with a fascination for Jewish history, helped her create the backdrop for this novel. Her enjoyment of football (the right team!), spurred on by living in Manchester, led her to investigate the mores of the Italian game.

Manchester is both Charlotte's birthplace and that of the suffragette movement, which is at the core of *The Purple Rose*. Many of her two dozen published poems were written for and about her native city, which is also home to the second-largest Jewish community in the UK.